*Volu*

# *Welcome Back Jack*

## *Frank English*

2QT Limited (Publishing)

First Edition published 2017

2QT Limited (Publishing)
Unit 5 Commercial Courtyard
Duke Street
Settle
North Yorkshire
BD24 9RH

Cover design: Charlotte Mouncey
Cover images: main photographs supplied by ©Frank English
Additional images from iStockhoto.com

Printed in Great Britain by IngramSparks UK Ltd

A CIP catalogue record for this book is available
from the British Library
ISBN 978-1-912014-81-1

*For Featherstone Book Club*

To my family.

*with best wishes*

*[signature]*

# Chapter 1

"I still can't believe the bare-faced brass neck of that woman," Jenny said once they'd snecked and locked the back door of their new home, "to turn up in the street without any warning. I can't imagine the shock at seeing your lad like that for the first time in ages."

Jack's impassive face gave no indication of what was churning around in his head as he switched on the kettle. Jenny was right. He could have ripped into her verbally for the agony she had caused him over the time he had been separated from his son, but that would have served no purpose in his world.

"Nothing to say, lovely man?" Jenny cajoled gently, knowing full well he would be thinking about his next moves.

"Nothing to be said, really, Jen," he said, as he poured out his favourite tipple. "It won't go from my head of course, as you well know, but I won't be goaded into taking any action that might prejudice our case. She will get what they are due, but not a penny more. Anyway, enough of that for now."

"Are you happy, Mrs Ingles?" Jack asked after a few moments of silence, luxuriating in their beautiful, big, new house. "I mean, was it all worth waiting for? Could what we have be any better?"

"What do you think, Mr Ingles?" she replied. "I just love everything you've done for us. I never thought in my wildest dreams during the dark months before I met you again that I should be living somewhere so ... posh, and big. There's only one thing I think we need in a house so grand."

"Oh aye?" he said, smiling at what she might come out with. "And what's that?"

"Well," she said, a look of mock seriousness nestling in her eyes, "a pair o' binoculars to si thi wi' in this big room."

Jack burst out laughing at the image she had just conjured. She was funny, was that Jenny. She had always been able to make him laugh. That was the sort of thing his granddad would have said.

"You are funny, Jenny Ingles," he said, still giggling. "Tell you what. I've only a couple of weeks left before I re-engage the great British unwashed. How do you fancy a few days at Filey?"

"Filey?" she puzzled. "I'd love to, but why Filey?"

"I went once or twice as a teenager," he said, "and from what I remember, the sands are fantastic ... for youngsters. I just thought our two might enjoy digging and building sand castles and stuff."

"I can see that gleam in your eyes, Our Jack," Jenny replied, a knowing smile showing she'd sussed out his real reason. "You fancy a dig and paddle yourself, don't you? Come on, admit it."

"Well," he laughed, "how do kids learn the time-honoured skills of castle-building with turrets and a moat, if their old man doesn't show 'em how it's done?"

"Two questions, then, Mr Builder," she said. "One – whereabouts in Filey do we go? And two – how do we afford it?"

"Simple," he replied, an almost imperceptible smile betraying his ridiculously improbable answer. "We camp and take our sleeping-out gear with us – you know, tent, sleeping bags, thick clothing. It'll be great—"

"You know that lump you're going to have at the back of your head?" she harrumphed, a look of indignation accompanying the smile that told him this wasn't such a good idea. "Camping gear costs—"

"The bit about camping wasn't strictly … accurate," he laughed. "The only time I ever wanted – foolishly – to go camping was in Harry Bowles's back garden when I was a nipper, and that lasted only until about ten o'clock. Not my scene, really."

"You bugger!" she guffawed. "I'll get you for that. So, watch out … and you've told me that one before."

"Can't wait," he replied, a wicked glint narrowing his eyes. "Devious native guile against superior strength, I'd take … you to win every time."

"Ha ha!" she exclaimed, fingers clicking menacingly close to his neck. "And don't you forget it."

"I had thought about the White Lodge," he suggested.

"White Lodge?" she answered. "Not heard of that one."

"When was the last time you went to Filey, Jenny?" Jack asked, a mock-puzzled look on his face.

"Er," she said, grinning sheepishly. "Never been."

"Then that's why you've never heard of it," he pointed out in triumph. "And don't even think about it," he warned, instinctively drawing his neck into his shoulders as he noticed her clicking, flicking fingers, and that evil gleam under her eyelids.

She burst out laughing and leaped on to him as he tried valiantly to protect his neck. False alarm. She simply wanted to hug and kiss her man, who always seemed to want to look after, entertain and amuse his family.

"We've enough cash in the bank to allow us a few days of luxury being looked after for a change," he explained, as she wrapped her legs and arms around him. "Don't forget that we've not had a traditional honeymoon, and I just thought this might be fun. On the other hand, if you aren't fussed about a few days at the seaside…"

"Nay!" she hooted. "I've already packed mentally. When shall we go?"

"I've booked for this Friday," he said, "and…"

"You've booked? Already?" she said. "So, all this was…"

"A bit of fun, my lovely," he smiled. "I knew you'd agree. Anyway…"

"And if I said I didn't want to go?" she asked, putting him on the spot.

"Then, I would have cancelled it," he added quite seriously. "So, are you saying you *don't* want to go? It's no trouble to phone Mrs Eves."

He reached for the phone, trying hard to keep that authentic look of seriousness on his face.

"Don't you dare, Buster!" she shouted. "We all want to go to Filey, don't we, Jessie? To dig in the sand and paddle in the sea with Daddy."

"I wantopaddlesea," Jessie said quite seriously. "What's 'paddlesea', Mammy?"

"I remember my first paddle in the sea when I was a bit younger than Our Jess," Jack said, a slight smile flickering across his face. "Only it was Bridlington, and I thought mi father were off to throw me in. I remember the sands … and the donkeys. They didn't half smell. I remember standing on the beach, mi hands and backside caked in wet sand, not knowing what to do."

"*You*, not knowing what to do, and you can remember *that* far back, Our Jack?" Jenny laughed. "I would have thought no human alive had such a good memory."

"Cheeky bugger," he guffawed. "I'll have you know I can remember being in the womb, just before and after birth, and I've vague memories of being wrapped around close to mi mam, on our way home from the hospital. She told me *exactly* how it was – buses, freezing winter weather, getting home to Scarborough Row – but only *after* I had mentioned those vague feelings. Mi granddad said he could remember from *before* he was conceived."

"Yeah! Right!" she laughed, not really knowing whether to believe him. You never knew with Jack. He could be telling the truth – or he might be spinning one of his long yarns.

"It's true," he continued, deadpan. "I even remember mi bedroom window being blown in when I was three months old. We lived on Scarborough Row then – two up, two down – and I shared that room with William."

"Never!" she gasped. "Three months? That's incredible, but rayt believable wi' you. Two up, two down? Does that mean you had neither bathroom nor toilet … inside?"

"Correct," he smiled, almost wearing that fact as a badge of honour, a rite of passage, "and did so until we moved to Garth Avenue when I was six, or thereabouts."

"Well," Jenny said at last, "it's a wonder you've grown up at all. Compared with all that, I've led a sheltered life of luxury. It takes all sorts."

"It's what cards life deals you, I suppose," Jack replied, a wistful look creeping onto his face, "and then how you play em, eh?"

"How did you get to know about the White Lodge? Did you say?" she asked again. "Childhood haunt?"

"I didn't, and no," he replied, playing her along, as he slipped into the kitchen to put on the kettle, smiling secretly as he did so.

"Well, come on then," she insisted, trying to peel away his silence. "Spill."

"Never been. Don't know anything about it. Don't know where it is," he explained. "It'll be a whole new world of experience for all of us. I heard somebody at school talking about it, and thought it might be a good place to go to."

"So, you've booked for somewhere you know nothing about?" she said, finding it hard to understand. "Just because it sounded OK in a passing conversation?"

"Aye," he replied, flashing that self-satisfied smile. "Oh, and … they had a fifty percent reduction for a family of four."

"Ah!" she laughed. "Now we're getting to it."

"Late booking near the end of the season and all that," he said. "Something about needing to keep the place open? Anyhow, too good a deal to pass up. I *know* Filey's good, because I've been there, and the kids *will* enjoy it."

"I'm sold," she laughed. "Are we going now?"

"Just as soon as we're packed," he replied, pulling her towards him.

"Mammy?" Jessie's voice piped up, interrupting their passionate clinch.

"Yes, my lovely?" Jenny said, turning towards her daughter's upturned face.

"Got tummy ache," she replied, a frown overtaking her blue eyes. "Need to…"

"OK," Jenny interrupted quickly. "Don't need details. Upstairs then … sharpish."

"Don't be long," Jack shouted, as mother and daughter reached the top of the stairs. "Tea's mashing."

–o–

"Do you think your mum would like to come?" Jack mumbled through a mouthful of porridge.

"Here? Today?" Jenny puzzled. "But we're in the middle of packing for our Filey hols."

"No," he said more clearly once his spoonful of nectar had slid down his throat. "To Filey. It'll be a bit of a squeeze in the car, but there'll be enough room. Well, *would* she like to come, do you think?"

"No idea," Jenny said, "but I've no doubt you'll find out

if you ask her."

-o-

"OK, then, Mrs M. Speak to you when we get back," Jack said. He put down the phone and sat by its table in the hall for a few minutes in silent thought.

"What time do we pick her up?" Jenny's happy voice drifted down to him from their bedroom.

"We don't," he replied, slowly, as he climbed up to her.

"But I was sure…" Jenny's puzzled voice accosted him as he rounded the door frame.

"She would love to come with us – but some other time," he replied, shrugging his shoulders. "Got some other arrangement, although she didn't say what."

"Oh," Jenny mumbled, still shaking her head at the mystery.

Mum didn't usually have something else on. She was always ready for an outing of some sort, no matter what it was or where it might take her. After all, she rattled round in a house on her own that was designed for a family – a family that came to her, usually, out of need rather than out of genuine desire.

"Just thinking," Jack said, breaking into her thoughts. "You don't think she – dare I say it – has a man she's seeing? I mean…"

"Mum?" Jenny gasped. "Another man? I *don't* think so. She had all on to manage Dad, with all his foibles and idiosyncrasies. I don't think she'd want to break another in, at *her* age."

"Hang on a bit," Jack said, not quite understanding her dismissal of Mum's attraction and needs. "Your mum is still a strikingly good-looking woman, and don't dismiss her needs and desires so out of hand. Think on that she lives a lonely solitary life, where once it was full-on. She must feel lonely sometimes, no matter how much she likes her own company."

"Ark at you!" Jenny laughed. "An expert on women's wants and needs now. Jack Ingles, lovely man that you are, don't try to tell a woman what she *needs*, particularly when *your* wife is psychic and intuitive in the extreme."

"Just saying," he shrugged, "but don't rule it out. I don't want to turn out to have been the intuitive one. You wouldn't be able to bear that, and I know I would suffer from being tickled to death by those whirling, devilishly dervish fingers of yours."

The strident jangling of the telephone shattered the peace that had descended as Jenny and Jack attended to their individual packing needs.

"I'll get it," Jack shouted from the spare room. "Sounds urgent."

"Daft bugger," Jenny shouted back, a guffaw bursting from her lips. "How can a telephone sound urgent?"

She carried on with her packing, catching Jack's mumble and occasional laugh, wondering who it might be. Somebody he knew, obviously. It wouldn't be his brother, because they didn't have that sort of a casual relationship. School? No. He had left one, and wasn't yet into the other. Interregnum, *he* would have said. Could it be David or Irene?

"Who was that?" she asked in passing.

"Nobody, really," he said, suppressing a smile. "It was a wrong number, I think."

"You *think*?" she rounded on him, fingers flicking. "It was an 'interesting' conversation for a wrong number, don't you think?"

"OK, OK," he capitulated, one eye on those dratted fingers. "It was Irene."

"And?" Jenny insisted.

"They're having a day out in Scarborough tomorrow,"

he said, "and wanted to know if we would like to join them."

"Do I have to squeeze every last drop out of you?" she went on with a smile, menace lacing her words.

"I suggested they might like to join *us* in Filey," he answered defensively. "I gave them the White Lodge's number, and she said they'd book."

"So, it looks like they might be coming with us?" she said, excitement building.

"She'll let us know when they've found out," he replied, to be interrupted by the phone's insistent trill, "which would be just about … now, I should think."

The second Jenny put down the phone, it began its insidious, insistent jangle, as if pleading to be picked up again like some needy pet. Jack got on with packing the one or two bits he felt he would need for a few days by the sea, bringing back memories of the first time he had packed his little suitcase for his first stay with his mam, grandma and granddad at Mrs Ridge's in Blackpool. That stopped him in his tracks, and brought a glistening to his eyes and a smile to his lips.

"There," he said, as Jenny joined him in the second bedroom. "Done."

"I bet your mam had a field day when you were a nipper," she laughed, as she peered into his sparsely packed case. "We just going for half a day?"

"Why, what's up in that?" he asked, seriously. "We're not emigrating, are we?"

"May I make one or two serious suggestions, my lovely man?" she said, an indulgent smile raising the corners of her mouth. "One spare pair of underpants? What happens if you have an … accident?"

"Then I'll send for a doctor," he replied, a light smile raising *his* mouth corners.

"No!" she laughed at his perceived naivety. "If you don't

get to the toilet in time, for example."

"Hmm," he huffed. "I suppose I'll…"

"And," she went on, "are you planning on wearing just the *one* shirt all week?"

"All right. All right," he relented, "perhaps I might need to take one or two more things. If you hadn't been so long on the phone, perhaps you might have been able to offer advice? Who was it anyway?"

"The first was … Val," Jenny said, slowly, the smile sinking from her face. "It sounds like her and your William won't be together too much longer."

"Oh?" Jack said, taken aback. "Still not sorted out when to leave his pants on, eh?"

"Something like that," Jenny answered. "It seems like this Samantha was at the High School at the same time as Val, and they knew each other. It also appears that she might be expecting William's bastard."

"Serves him right," Jack harrumphed. "He needs to be less sanctimonious about himself and his precious life. It's Val I feel sorry for. She's a lovely woman and she deserves better."

"She's talking about coming back up here to live," Jenny continued.

"And how's she proposing to do that?" he said, incredulous at the thought. "Is she going to *magic* the money to buy somewhere? Or put the children out to work?"

"Daft bugger," she laughed. "Oh, by the way, Irene and David *have* booked for the White Lodge, and she says they'll see us there."

"Excellent!" Jack shouted, punching the air in triumph. "This is going to be such a good holiday. I can feel it in my water."

–o–

14

"Everybody all right in the back?" Jack shouted as they reached the Filey turn off, just east of Muston.

"Yes, Daddy," Jessie muttered, as her eyes closed sleepily again.

"Takes me back, does this road," Jack said, quietly, as he prepared to turn right towards Filey.

"What?" Jenny asked. "You remember from when you were a nipper? I thought it was Bridlington you went to, on the train?"

"No, not then," he replied. "It's the Caton sign. T'other side o' t'road I remember. The one pointing left."

"I didn't know you'd been to Caton," she said. "You never told me."

"Been twice," he said, slowly, a half-smile creeping up on him. "Once when I was sixteen, with Curfy Wood and his parents and brother, David. But the better time was when I was about fourteen or so."

"Fourteen?" she said, a wicked glint betraying her sharp wit. "I didn't know anyone could remember *that* far back."

"Cheeky mare," Jack laughed. "I had a good mate called Dave. David Hartley. He lived in the house next to the off-licence at the top of Princess Street – Queen Street end. Remember?"

"How could I forget?" she replied. "Passed it every day."

"I can't remember how we got to know each other," Jack went on, "but we became quite close – same interest in rugby and athletics, I think it was. Anyway, his mam had decided to take Dave and his sister, Christine, to Wallis's Cayton Bay Holiday Camp, in a caravan. I liked caravans. Did I tell you—?"

"Jack?" Jenny interrupted his expected digression. "The story? David and Christine? Cayton Bay?"

"Eh? What?" Jack paused. "Oh, yes. Cayton Bay. David thought it might be a good idea to ask me along, I think, probably so he didn't have to spend every day amusing his ten-year-old sister."

"Jack!" Jenny started to remonstrate. "Don't be so unkind."

"I was only joking," he explained, trying to defend himself. "We had a really good week, actually. His mam, sister, and his Aunt Lucy and Uncle Jim were in one caravan, and we had a smaller one next door. We felt really grown up, not being supervised by adults in the same space all the time. We were even allowed to have our meals in the refectory on our own if we wanted to."

"You didn't keep in touch?" Jenny asked. "You know, after the holiday."

"Yeah," he answered slowly. "We *did* stuff together for quite a bit after, but then exams and school intruded, and we kind of lost touch, because we didn't go to the same school. That was always a big regret, because we got on well and *I* didn't have many *real* friends. He was a good mate and an excellent rugby player – better than I ever could have been."

"Surely—?" she butted in.

"No, Jenny," Jack carried on unabashed. "I know quality when I see it, and he was good. Played for some top teams as well, I think – Leeds, Featherstone – all good stuff. All rugby league, of course."

"Still," she said, taking his hand in hers, "life's full of regrets."

"Yes," he replied wistfully, "and some of them stay with you, reminding you of the 'what ifs' and the 'why didn't Is'."

# Chapter 2

"So, you finally got rid of the last vestiges of Jack's former wife?" Irene asked Jenny as they drank their morning tea around a wooden table on the hotel's lawn, overlooking the sands. Jack and David amused the two Jessies, building whole garrisons in the sand, while Imogen Rose and Florence May gurgled happily in their prams, at arm's length from their proud mothers.

"We were delighted to see the back of yon clapped out Mini, certainly," Jenny replied, "and, yes, we thought it was the end of *that* particular chapter – until the other week, when we were heading for a Saturday coffee shop on Street Lane. Jack was looking forward to a cup of tea and a large piece of sponge cake, when who should crawl out of the woodwork, as brazen as anything, but his former wife; just verbally tapped him on the shoulder. If looks could have killed, she would bother us no longer – he was that angry."

"So, what happened? What did you do?" Irene asked eagerly, leaning forward, mouth open and eyes wide.

"Jack turned, asked her what the hell she was doing there," Jenny went on in triumph, "and told her to bugger off, because she had made her bed, and was no longer welcome."

"Wow!" Irene gasped. "And his son?"

"He was there," Jenny said quietly, "but he didn't recognise his father. That was the hardest and most upsetting part. You know Jack. He didn't show any emotion, but I knew he was hurting."

"Poor dear," Irene clucked, understanding how this might have affected him. "I can't begin to know how he must have felt. Auntie Flo always said he kept his feelings tight, never letting on that he might be upset inside, until much later when he had control over them. Only then would he rationalise – even as a six year old."

"You two enjoying the bracingly beautiful air of sunny Filey?" Jack shouted, as he approached their woman's lair, having sniffed out their fresh pot of tea. "Is that 'Yorkshire' tea I smell there?"

"Tea from Yorkshire," Jenny laughed, happy at the beaming smile of contentedness on her husband's face. That was the world's exterior. You never got to see what was underneath the surface, but she, of all people, knew him. She *knew* him well, but even she didn't know all that was simmering, or for how long it had been there.

"I think our fortification will be proof against the sand creatures," he said taking a mouthful of tea to slake his thirst, "but not against Old Poseidon out there, I fear."

"And what's on today?" Irene said, eager to know if she was to be prised out of her comfortable deckchair in the sun, a pot of fresh coffee now to hand, and nibbles to take off the taste of the coffee.

"Well," Jack answered, a grin widening, "I thought we might go for a paddle in the North Sea. It's bound to be warm, and…"

"Just had a message from reception," Jenny blurted out, interrupting his bit of fun. "They said Mum rang earlier asking us to phone her back, which I did."

"Your mum?" Jack asked, the grin evaporating in double-quick time. "How did she know we'd be here?"

"Bit of a rhetorical question, don't you think?" she said.

"You asked her if she'd like to come to Filey with us, and I felt she needed to know exactly where we were in case of an emergency. And now I was proved right."

"What's the emergency, then?" he asked. "Val and William?"

"Bingo," she said, clapping his perception sarcastically. "He won't stop seeing his floozy, and so she says she might as well come back up north, forcing him to sell up."

"She does know we're happy to accommodate her, doesn't she?" Jack offered, genuinely. "For as long as she needs it."

"That might be an offer closer than you think," Jenny said, kissing him briefly, in acknowledgement of his goodness. "But I think there was some other reason Mum wasn't letting on."

"Because she's 'seeing' someone?" he replied, his face non-committal.

"Seeing someone?" she laughed. "How do you make that one out? She'd never do that. She's too set in her ways, and comfortable in her own company."

"Don't you believe it," Jack insisted. "Don't forget that I still have good contacts in Normanton, and *they* tell me she's been seen out with a man, who I think you'll know."

"You're a secretive bugger," she harrumphed, a frown of concern licking her face. "How come you didn't share that nugget with *me*? Aren't I your *wife*?"

"Didn't know for sure until recently," he said, "and I didn't want to jump to what might have been catastrophic conclusions. Besides, she's a right to a bit of excitement in her life without some Jack-the-lad poking his nose in. I think a lot about your mother, as you well know."

"And I love you for it, Our Jack," she replied, giving him a reassuring hug, "but I wish you'd said."

"Why, what are you going to do about it?" he asked, not sure what her next move might be. "Besides, we're here to enjoy our holiday with our friends. Aren't we?"

"Come on, Jackieboy!" David shouted from the edge of the sands. "What about that paddle?"

"Later, my lad," Jenny warned, pointing at her husband with an arm outstretched, as he minced towards the water, blowing her a kiss on the way, as he hoisted Jessie on his shoulders to her whoops of joy. David followed suit, causing great screams of glee from both children.

"We are very lucky, you know, Jenny," Irene said, as they sat down at the table, a fresh pot of coffee, this time, in front of them.

"And why do you say that, Cousin?" Jenny asked, as she refilled their cups.

"Just look out there, at those two men," she replied, "giving those girls a wonderful time, splashing about and making them feel special. They'll do whatever it takes to make us all happy."

"Good point," Jenny said, a smile creeping up on her, "and all we have to do is ... let them."

–o–

"And this man whom you reckon I should know is…?" Jenny asked, as Jack drew into their driveway.

"Jim Arkwright," he said quietly. "I believe he was your Dad's under-manager."

"Jim Arkwright?" she repeated, not really understanding the importance. "Are you sure? I thought Dad's deputy was Harry Smailes."

"He was," Jack explained, "up to your Dad's collapse. Jim was with him before Harry took over, because he became manager of another pit. At Glasshoughton, I think."

"She never told *me*," Jenny replied, trying to work out the whys and wherefores of this affair.

"Well, she wouldn't, would she?" Jack said, smiling at her

puzzled face. "I've a feeling she might be almost old enough to make her own decisions. Perhaps she hasn't let on because she's not sure yet – just trying Jim on for size."

"Jack!" Jenny gasped at the perceived crudeness of his remark.

"Not like that, thou brazen hussy," he laughed. "Bit like a new coat, really, I suppose. I don't know. Sex, sex, sex; all you can think about."

"Yes, please," she said, grabbing him with a smile of anticipation.

"Cup of tea first," he grinned, "and…"

"I know," she said. "I *think* I have some … somewhere."

They both laughed at the joy of shared memories and experiences, as they hugged each other enthusiastically. There had never been such a happy couple that belonged together; always had, always would. Nobody else could possibly understand their relationship, developed from years of needing each other, of being the perfect fit. When people talk about being childhood sweethearts, they don't know the half. The one wasn't complete without the other.

True love, actually.

A gentle knock at the front door interrupted their tea and the remaining time they had before Jack was dragooned into the new school. Merton Grange had stepped over their threshold, and wouldn't take its toe out of their door until October half term – eight weeks away.

"Val?" Jenny said, as she ushered her sister inside. "Come and sit with us. William and the kids?"

"Cup of tea, Val?" Jack's voice echoed from the kitchen, to the click of the automatic kettle and the rattle of the tea caddy.

"Please!" Val shouted back, a vaguely wan smile trying to destabilise her pale lips. "Just wanted to let you know that, since I gave William my ultimatum, we've begun to work things out."

"Ultimatum?" Jack asked, as he poured them all a fresh cup of tea.

"Der-er," Jenny muttered, pushing her bottom lip forward with her tongue in good-humoured derision. "Keep up, dear heart."

"That he had to ditch his whore," Val explained, a look of disappointment and betrayal haunting her eyes still, "and devote *all* his spare energies to his family. Fortunately, he's agreed, though I had to threaten him with divorce and selling up."

"Rightly so," Jenny said, detecting a harder edge to her sister than she had seen before. This saddened her, because she had always looked up to her big sister as a strong and steadfast woman, and here she was now … different.

"He's finally agreed, after all his shilly-shallying," Val went on, "but things won't be the same. I want him back with us for the sake of our children. If they weren't here, neither would I be. This is his one and only chance to redeem himself. If he relapses, or changes his mind…"

"Is there any chance of that happening?" Jack asked, concerned about his sister-in-law, and to some extent about the dilemma facing his older, but by no means wiser brother.

"I don't know him anymore, Jack," she said, a forced smile of resignation crossing her tired face. "I think I used to be the light of his existence, but those memories have been crushed under the weight of this secret life that doesn't include me … and our children. He's still deciding whether to recognise his bastard."

"I'm so sorry, Val," Jack said, putting his arms around her and drawing her to him. She responded by laying her head on his chest and holding on tightly. "He's a daft bugger, but he's still part of all of us – just. You know there's always a place here for you and the kids – if the worst came to the worst."

"It means a lot," she replied. "Both of you. Now, any chance of staying the night?"

"Daft beggar," Jack replied. "Your bed's already made up. Just one thing though. It does have a small bathroom of its own, so you don't need to leave your room to use the family one."

"En suite," Jenny prompted, authoritatively.

"Bless you," he replied, laughing as he did so. "Tea'll have to be a take-away though."

"No, it won't," Jenny butted in. "You, my dear, are a lovely man, and you know all sorts of … stuff. The one thing you know nothing about is home management and … cooking. You'll have to leave that to me. We will be having omelette and chips and peas. That OK?"

"Too right it is!" he exclaimed, clapping his hands. "My favourite."

"But," Jenny replied, "everything I *do* is your favourite."

"Sounds just fine to me," Val said enthusiastically. "I've not eaten since yesterday."

"Then, you must be … dead," he said, gobsmacked that she was still there and functioning.

"My Jack is an organism that couldn't function without regular – and I mean regular – chunks of sustenance," Jenny said, laughing at the grimace on his face. "The only time he's quiet, usually, is when his belly is empty and draining away his life force."

–o–

"Things *have* to be worked out for the children's sake," Val insisted, as she finished her omelette. "Joey's close to secondary school and, although I suppose he could go to the grammar school if we went back to Normanton, I need him to have stability in the first years of secondary schooling.

23

Mary would go anywhere because she's smart and very gregarious."

"There are good schools around here as well, you know," Jack pointed out. "My new middle school's only spitting distance from us. If the worst came to the worst, I could take Joey and his brother with me, and Mary could go to one of the local primaries with our Jessie."

"But I thought Jessie…" Val said, unsure.

"Is four," Jenny interrupted, "and ready soon to move on to the big school from her nursery. Do you remember moving up to the Big School at Woodhouse, eh, Our Jack, from Miss Cordle's little school?"

"Like it was yesterday," he answered, eyes half-closing to draw back his memories. "You weren't at Woodhouse, were you, Val?"

"No," she replied, the first genuine smile for some time creasing her face. "We'd not long moved into the area and, as we lived closer, I went to Queen Street. Served me well. I made lots of friends and enjoyed the experience. That's what made me want to become a teacher."

"I don't remember much about you in nursery, Jack," Jenny recalled, "except for that spiky hair – straight as a yard o' pump watter."

"You jumped into the Big School same time as me," he said, "into Mrs Gunn's class, followed by Miss Jollif. I didn't think I'd be able to go."

"Why on earth not?" Jenny asked. "You were one of the cleverest in the school."

"Reading and stuff weren't the problem," Jack explained. "I thought we might have to pay extra, and as such mi father wouldn't have forked out. I *did* have to have a reading test, though. Didn't have any reading books at 'ome, you see. Father wouldn't waste his drinking money on 'em."

The evening slipped by, steeped in reminiscence and

counter-reminiscence, as they sat comfortably cocooned by the lounge's softened lights. Though saddened considerably by her husband's infidelity, Val knew she could rely on her sister and her brother-in-law to provide the support she craved, without question or demur. They were what family was all about, and she knew that Jack would do whatever was necessary to make sure she and her brood had a roof over their heads and were as comfortable as they needed to be. This was the man *her* husband didn't want to spend any more time with than necessary, but *she* knew in whose hands she could place her life.

"Mammy," a soft little voice stole into the room from the hall doorway.

"Yes, my sweet girl," Jenny said, turning towards the door. "What is it? Come on. Come and sit on Daddy's lap."

Jessie rushed into the room and, sliding onto Jack's lap, she snuggled into his waiting arms contentedly.

"What is it, my little floozy?" Jack cooed. "Something frightening thee?"

"Nooo, not reeeally," she drawled. "Just feeling a little bit … hungry."

"Oh no!" Jack said, throwing up his hands in mock horror. "We can't have you hungry. If you don't have something to eat now, you'll be too thin and weedy to eat your breakfast in the morning."

Jessie started to giggle, happy to be playing the hunger game with Daddy – a game they'd played many a time before.

"And what must we give you to frighten away that nasty hunger monster?" Jack asked, a mock-serious and fearful look crossing his wide eyes.

"Let me think," she started, tapping her temple with the soft point of her little forefinger.

"Banana? Bunch of grapes? Turkey dinner? Pound of plums?" he asked slowly, to the look of joy on her face.

"No, silly," she said finally, in triumph. "I know – a slice of jam and bread."

"Oh, my goodness me!" Jack gasped. "I don't think we can afford that."

"'Course we can," she giggled, her face shining with joy at their game. "Lemon cheese – and a glass of milk."

"Lemon cheese?" he said, lifting her into his arms as he got up from the settee and carried her to the kitchen. "But that's not jam. It's…"

"Lemon cheese!" they called out together, to excited giggles.

"He's wonderful with her," Val said. "Treats her like his own."

"But, she *is* his own," Jenny corrected her, "and he loves her as such. He *did* adopt her, if you recall, and the fact that he had nothing to do with her birth is irrelevant. He is responsible for turning her into the lovely, happy child she is. Jessie Ingles is *our* daughter in every respect."

"I tell you what," Jack said as they made their slow way back into the lounge. "I'll carry the tray with all the cups, tea pot and things and, because I can't carry everything, you bring that empty plate of yours. Deal?"

"Of course, Daddy," Jessie replied seriously. "We wouldn't want you to have a accident – would we?"

Jenny suppressed a snigger at Jessie's response. My, she *was* growing up.

# Chapter 3

The building was cold, inhospitable and unwelcoming like no other school Jack had been in, even for early September. A dodo waiting for the touch of extinction, Merton Grange stood, glaring at passers-by out of dozens of unblinking eyes, daring them to approach. It had two redeeming features – an exciting opportunity for Jack to develop and grow as a professional, and just over two thousand pounds of annual salary with which to keep his family. Yet he still wasn't sure whether he had made the right move. Only time would tell. If nothing but pragmatic, calculating and forward-looking, this could be the turning point in his career, for good or for ill.

The school, as an organisational entity, was taking its first breaths in two stages. On this momentous day, the first cohort of nine-year olds was to be stitched into its new outfit as part one of the whole fashion shebang, with the rest of the school testing its place on the catwalk the next day, seamlessly. Make-up and sequins for the whole show would, hopefully, be stuck on later. It had to be faultless because this was to be the show case, the flagship of the education authority's master plan for this phase of education in the city for the foreseeable future. The largest organism of its kind in the country, it had to be beautiful. Didn't it? Jack wasn't so sure.

The first outriders, the vanguard of this new year group, were due to gather at the school's outer defences at ten o'clock sharp, which was an hour and a half away. Yet a few lone, pathetic-looking bodies had begun to gather – children whose parents worked and wouldn't allow their children's daunting new schooling to stand in the way of *their* life. *They* had been dropped off at the 'usual' time for school, with no regard either to the new arrangements, or to their child's personal and emotional needs.

This would never change.

Jack had always found it astounding that some children were so resilient and stoically accepting of their situation, that he felt it was his duty to offer as much support to them as he was able. This had probably sprung out of his own experiences as a nipper growing up in Normanton, where the privations were slightly different but no less effective.

He was looking forward to taking his own assemblies, delivering a proper message to his two hundred and forty eager minds. This day's assembly, however, would be led by the triumvirate of head, deputy head and senior mistress, to underline the gravity of this day. If this were to be anything like his previous experiences of senior staff assemblies, they would all be back in class very soon.

The thoughts of a triumvirate shot his mind back to that first time he met his cousin Irene. How that had enriched his life. She was now the only link he had with real family. Although he was blood and all that, Jack never considered William as 'real' family, because *he* hadn't moved towards him as he considered a real brother should. He was much closer to Irene, and to Val for that matter.

The poky staff room was relatively full, both with teachers and with the inevitable blue haze of cigarette smoke, greedily sneaking into as many unsuspecting nostrils as it could. Although confident in himself, Jack had never been big on aimless chit-chat with strangers. He wove his way through knots of people towards the steaming tea urn, dodging deftly to avoid the endless 'morning' greetings from falsely jovial people trying equally hard to thrust themselves upon him.

"You're Jack, aren't you?" a big man with a giant of a ginger beard said, his dancing eyes betraying his good humour.

"I am," Jack replied, "and, if I'm not very much mistaken, you're Brian."

"Good memory," Brian said. "I like that."

"Actually, no," Jack added, with a cheeky grin. "I heard you introducing yourself to that tall, severe-looking woman over there by the notice board."

"Ha ha!" Jack's companion guffawed. "I can see you and I are going to get along."

The tea he allowed to gurgle into a city council standard issue white mug was hot and tasted of urn infused with hot water. He sipped it unenthusiastically, noting mentally the two items he needed to bring with him the following day – a non-standard, Jenny-issue mug and a bag or two of tea from Yorkshire.

"Ladies and gentlemen," a gruff voice boomed from the doorway, "may I have your attention, please?"

The chit-chat in the room trickled to a deafening silence as the new king of this fledgling country began to impose himself upon the courtiers of his newly presented court.

"We will be starting our indoctrination process within the next fifteen minutes," he announced, a self-satisfied smirk crossing his bulbous face, "when our new children will be ushered in for a gathering in the hall. As you know, we have only the nine year olds with us today, and then only until lunchtime. They, of course, will have the whole morning – after assembly – with their class teachers in our mobile classrooms, the other side of the dining area, where they will – we all will – be having lunch; but not today. They will escape at midday precisely, when those parents who are able will collect them."

"And what will happen to those children whose parents either don't, can't, or just won't collect them?" Jack asked unexpectedly, and annoyingly pointedly.

All eyes turned towards this young man who had the brass neck to ask *that* pointedly pertinent yet impertinent question that *had* occurred to them all silently.

"Only," Jack went on unabashed, "I've noticed that a number of parents dropped off their youngsters very early, despite our later opening time."

"They'll no doubt find their way home – eventually," the head said lamely, after a few moments' deliberation. "Parents' responsibility."

"Will they be fed before they are ushered out?" Jack insisted. "I'm quite sure, in my limited experience, that some won't be fed until tea time."

"Nail on head, then," the head replied, putting down this upstart's interruption with a dismissive flick of the hand. "Your 'limited' experience might get you involved where you ought to distance yourself."

"Can't really," Jack insisted, his compassion for those less-fortunate children growing. "You see … Bob … I know what they feel like, and I don't see how we can let them go hungry, in all conscience. They are *our* children when all said and done."

Although virtually the whole staff agreed with his sentiment, and admired how he expressed his feelings, not *one* articulated that support. They didn't want to incur the wrath of *this* particular head teacher because of his high-up connections throughout this city. They might need a reference at some stage, and it looked like *he* would be here for some considerable time.

Jack was astounded and mortified that no one else backed his stance, and that they, no doubt, would fill *their* bellies, with scant regard to those who were to be cast out onto the streets to fend for themselves. He now knew where he stood on *this* staff.

"You're a brave one," Beardy Brian said quietly as he walked out to the Crush Hall with Jack, "but you have just alienated one of the most powerful men in this God-forsaken education authority with your forthrightness, I fear. We all agree with your sentiment, but not with how you express it. My advice to you, Young Jack, is to bite your tongue a bit more."

"So, becoming teachers in a leviathan like this," Jack butted in, "we are supposed to leave our honesty and integrity at the door, are we, Brian? Can't do it, I'm afraid, old chap. You see, I was always brought up to deal with other folks with honesty and compassion. I will neither prejudice nor dilute my principles for any tin-pot little dictator."

"Don't get me wrong, Jack," Brian said defensively. "I agree with you, and I like your mettle, but we have to live with these 'tin-pot dictators', and I for one am not going to make a rod for my own back just so I can luxuriate in my principles. That's not going to get *me* very far."

"OK, Brian," Jack smiled. "'Nuff said. Now, about that assembly."

–o–

"Wrong move, I think, Our Jenny," Jack said, once he'd splashed out of the shower, after school.

"What is, my lovely?" she asked, as he dried himself.

She loved to sit and watch how he de-glistened his body, and how he meticulously dried every nook and cranny. He often said that if he didn't dry everything, some of his bits might shrink, and that just wouldn't do. The finale of his walking away from clouds of Johnson's baby powder brought tears of mirth to her eyes. Wherever the towel wouldn't reach, the powder would.

She had arranged a larger, dry towel on the settee by the window so he could sit next to her. She still couldn't believe that their bedroom was big enough for a settee and easy chair, as well as a huge bed. This gorgeous man not only loved her unconditionally, but also he had provided a beautiful house for her and her children where she had always wanted to be.

"This 'ere new-fangled school," he said, as he relaxed to cool down on the settee next to her, "is not what I had hoped it would be."

"How's that?" she asked, a quizzical look marauding in her eyes. "Does that mean…?"

"No, my lovely lady," he smiled, pulling her towards him, "*this* house isn't negotiable. All it means is that, like my last school, I'll have to give it my best shot until the *right* job taps me on the shoulder. I'm beginning to wonder if it's really out there and I'm being too picky."

"Too clever, compassionate, and too principled, more like," she said, kissing his limp spikes with a smile. "All *we* need is for you to be happy in what you are doing. Perhaps I need to go out to work to make things easier for you?"

"No fear!" he exclaimed, emphatically. "You will only do that if *you* decide it's what you feel you would like to do. I'm fine doing what I'm doing. When did you ever know me to shy away from a challenge?"

"You know what's best," she said, smiling indulgently.

"I'm sure there are some lovely people on the staff," he went on, "with whom I *should* be able to get on, but it's just the man at the top who has all the say. Unfortunately, a lot of what he says I don't agree with. 'Bite' and 'tongue' seem to slip into mind all too readily, I'm afraid. If I don't heed those words, I'm in for a rocky road to a battle I can't hope to win, and I might as well look for a job elsewhere."

"You'll work it out, Our Jack," she said, with a knowing smile, as she drew him closer. "Now, tea'll be a while yet, so, if you're up to it, I thought…"

"And if I said I didn't know what you were on about?" he replied, a huge grin overtaking his face.

"Then, I'd phone the police," she said, laughing, "and tell them my Jack had been kidnapped and an imposter smuggled in his place."

-o-

"A class of thirty-two twelve year olds?" Chris Woodhead, a young French teacher, said with a look of horror on his face. "For French? Don't you find that, well, terrifying?"

"Not really," Jack replied, as he sipped his break-time tea and nibbled half a digestive from his snap tin. "Don't forget, I taught in a down-town sec mod for a year or two, and there I took the full secondary age range."

"My goodness!" Chris gasped. "This man's a god. I'd be scared witless."

"In fact, I've got them next, in G7," Jack said. "You know, the classroom opposite the dining hall. Not an ideal room, but why don't you pop in for ten minutes if you're free, and if you fancy?"

"I'll just double check the substitution list on the staff notice board," Chris replied, a cross between fear and awe invading his face, "and if I've not been caught, I'll drop in for a bit, if that's all right."

"Course it is," Jack said, making for the door. "I'm just off there now. See you in a bit then."

Bell for the end of break hadn't sounded yet, and still what seemed like the entire child population of North Leeds was hurtling around the airfield of a playground. The Indian summer they had enjoyed for the last few weeks since shortly after starting back at the beginning of September seemed to have no intention of deserting them yet as they let off steam in what Jack called the 'boiler house'.

Because of the overwhelming numbers of children of all sizes on this area, the smaller ones from his classes kept well out of the way of the charging bull elephants of the older boys. The little ones played on the spit of grass in front of and under the hedge between the school wall on Talbot Avenue and the upper tarmac edge of the playground, or on any of the many small green patches around.

Jack had expressed his concerns on a few occasions about the tinies versus the grandies, pointing out the accidents waiting to happen. He had been promised that playtime for the youngsters would be switched to the fenced tarmac tennis courts next to their classrooms in the near future. The 'near future', however, was fast approaching, with no action as yet raising its head above the horizon.

"Sandra?" Jack said to a willowy young girl sitting at the back of the room.

"Yes, Mr Ingles?" she started her slow answer, surprised to be jolted out of her late morning reverie, a look of embarrassment growing on her face. "Me, Mr Ingles?"

"Yes, Sandra Jordan, you," Jack replied, a look of resignation invading his face. "Have you brought your books and stuff today?"

"Yes, Mr Ingles," she replied, flushing crimson as she shuffled in her chair and watching him under half-closed lids, to titters from her female peers.

"In fact, Sandra Jordan," he asked again, his eyes twinkling as he looked steadfastly into her embarrassed face, "I can see you are here in body, but have you brought your mind with it, too? Or have you left it at home in bed?"

The boys guffawed loudly and the girls sniggered as Sandra shrank further into her blazer.

"I don't know what you mean, sir," she stammered, mortified that she had been picked out at all. "I always bring…"

"Don't worry about it, Sandra," Jack went on, flashing one of his winning smiles, ready to relieve her confusion and obvious embarrassment. He never intended to upset, just to bring her usually wandering mind back to the lesson in hand. He was quite sure he didn't wish to traipse the worlds she inhabited in her head, wherever they took her.

"Homework for this week will then be…" he said, as the cracked end-of-lesson bell burst into their thoughts, like a swarm of angry wasps.

"How did you do that, Jack?" Chris Woodhead asked, in awe of what he had just witnessed. "I mean, I wouldn't know what to say."

"I've been in this game a year or two longer than you, Chris," he replied, "so, nothing fazes me. It's a matter of self-confidence, I suppose, stitched together with the unshakable belief that what I am doing and how I'm doing it is right. You'll get there one day. Practice really does make perfect."

"I'll never be as good as you," Chris replied quietly. "I know that."

"Yes, you will," Jack assured him. "But just remember that the mutual respect between you and your youngsters has to be earned. It's a two-way street. Once you both understand that, and act on it seriously, you'll never have any problems with them."

"And that girl you spoke to towards the end?" Chris asked.

"Sandra?" Jack said. "She's a good student. Bright, but does tend to wander off into her own world at times, and needs to be brought back to the lesson from her mental travels elsewhere in *her* universe. Trick is not to intrude *too* much – just to remind. She'll take no harm from it, and she'll probably remind and thank me when she's fifty, if we're both still around."

# Chapter 4

"May I offer you a bit of advice, Jack," Tom, the deputy, said quietly to him as he passed by his office, "between you and me?"

"I probably know what you're going to say," Jack acknowledged, equally quietly.

"Then you're more astute than I gave you credit for," the deputy replied. "I certainly appreciate your very relevant opinions and views on the issues that matter in a school such as this. They are sound and well-articulated, but open forum is not necessarily where they should be aired, particularly in *this* environment. Do you understand what I'm trying to say?"

"I do indeed," Jack replied. "Then, may I—?"

"Come to me with any of your views?" Tom suggested sensibly. "That would be best, I think, for you. The head has a high regard for your intellectual and organisational strengths, but what he won't tolerate is public challenge. Your ideas and views are admirable, but you need to articulate them privately."

"OK," Jack agreed. "I understand."

"Just watching your back, Jack," Tom said, finally. "That's all."

"Thanks, Tom," Jack said with a smile. "Much appreciated."

Tom was a good, hard-working deputy whose background and experiences were rooted in primary-school education. Probably the best man for the job with *this* head, he maintained that elusive balance between the man at the top and the minions beneath. Unfortunately, however, the views he articulated were usually those of his head teacher rather than his own.

Jack was a pragmatic, straightforward, Yorkshire lad, who believed in calling a spade a spade, unlike his head teacher who called a spade an instrument for turning over sods. Yet Jack did know when to hold his counsel when someone in higher office made a statement that was counter to his own solid views. He would, however, store away those erroneous statements, and he wouldn't be afraid to recall them should they be contradicted at a later time.

As far as being a member of a team was concerned, there was nobody more supportive of the group ethos than Jack. Yet his dearly held and guarded views and values on honesty, integrity and individuality he would never prostitute.

"Been a bad lad, Jack?" Beardy Brian quipped with a grin, over coffee that morning break time.

"Actually, Brian," Jack replied, "Tom and I were just mulling over what you and I had been discussing earlier. He offered sensible advice, which I took pragmatically. He obviously knows *this* head better than any of us."

"Couldn't agree more," Brian said quietly, wiping the coffee froth out of his facial hair. "I have a good friend who worked for him, and he said that he wasn't a man you would want to cross."

"Tom reckoned it might be a good idea to take any concerns to him as opposed to the head," Jack went on, "and, I must say, although I have known Tom all of five minutes, I tend to trust his judgement … I think."

"I've known Tom for many years – same RC church

you see," Brian said, "and his one fault? He works too hard. He needs to slow down, or he'll come a cropper. Mark my words."

"You're a doom monger and no mistake," Jack laughed. "Remind me not to get to know you *too* well."

"Break time soon over, Jack, mi owd son," Brian sighed, running his fingers through his knotty beard. He had a volatile face with dancing eyes and a ready smile to brighten any murky day. "I do love these free lessons."

"Oh, you mean the *two* I get are worth it, eh?" Jack replied, a grimace of displeasure creeping in. "Most folk get at least four a week. Why I get only two, the Lord only knows."

"Because you are *so* good, my boy, you don't need any more," Brian said, a loud guffaw drawing Jack into his good humour.

"Do you know, Brian," Jack went on, "I think every world should have a Brian Undercliff. You make everyone want to smile."

"I'd be glad if you'd tell that to my wife sometimes," Brian sighed, a mischievous grin growing.

Their bonhomie was interrupted by the rattle of the aging change-of-lesson bell. Jack had often wondered on the chaos that might ensue should the warning system finally collapse and become permanently defunct. He wasn't allowed to dwell on that premise for long, as an uproar urged him to hurry past the open cloakroom bays on his way to the heavy outside double doors that children had been warned not to use as toys or weapons.

Unfortunately, some mean-spirited youngster had used them against a fellow nine year old, swinging one of them against him to catapult the child into a set of four unforgiving concrete steps. These steps allowed a level shift from the narrow gully between the building and the yard, around which a four-feet retaining wall stopped children from crashing into the school's glass façade.

Robert Arrowsmith had tripped and head-butted the top step, cutting his forehead just below the hairline, enough to expose three inches of skull. He was sitting inside the doors, his head swathed in a bloody towel from Miss Chambers' Home Economics room, looking – and no doubt feeling – as if the makers of all doors in the world were against him.

The bell and blue light of an ambulance reversing towards the bloody scene caused enough consternation and excitement to slow the entry of most children to adjacent classrooms. The last vision for dozens of craning necks and goggling eyes was of the ambulance carting the unfortunate lad off to Leeds Infirmary, lights flashing and bells warning all traffic to make way.

Alan 'Jonny' Johnson, a thoughtless but neither calculating nor wicked lump of a lad, was by now standing outside the deputy's office, awaiting retribution.

"Another one bites the dust, eh, Marjorie?" Jack said, as he neared the Home Economics room

"Aye," she replied, a slight north-eastern lilt edging her words, betraying her roots. "Poor little mite."

"I was thinking more of your towel," he replied, a wicked grin growing.

"Oo, you are a wicked man," she laughed, as his broad back receded down the corridor, "but I *like* you."

The bottom corridor that linked the two sets of cloakrooms and the children's entrance and exit points, suffered the permanent artificial daylight of fluorescent strip lighting, because the twenty-yard block of boys' and girls' toilets to the outside of the building at this point stole all the natural daylight. At change of lessons, this dark and oppressively threatening tunnel of concrete and empty, dilapidated display boarding was filled with purposefully aimless and quietly noisy children.

Because Jack's base was at the end of this dungeon stretch and round into its last-gasp corner, he had to endure the torturously tortuous journey umpteen times a day as he made the trip from class to staff room. The teachers' rest room couldn't have been further from his work area. His terrapin mobile class bases were half glass, thin-walled boxes that obliged their occupants to freeze in the winter and to fry in the summer. Shipped in several years before middle schools were foisted upon an unsuspecting educational clientele, they provided a respite for students during the comprehensive school's high alumina concrete scare. Once the problem had been solved, these temporary classrooms had claimed this spot as their permanent home.

"It could have been worse," Jack said, usually. "We might have been housed in the main building."

The bottom corridor by the dining hall was a sea of miniature human bodies, like lemmings unknowingly, blindly following a recently resurfaced buried instinct leading to one implanted goal. Six larger bodies valiantly surfed the breakers, carried to the same goal, unable to swim away from this urgent surge, until it dwindled and faded.

"Mr Ingles?" a piping, tremulously panicking little voice by his side tugged at Jack's senses. "May I hold your hand, please? Only, I don't think I can manage all this pushing and shoving on my own."

"Of course you may, Alyson," Jack urged, looking down at a struggling elfin body to his right. Relief invaded her face as she grabbed his hand and arm, a huge sigh escaping her lungs.

Once through the double glass doors by the canteen and out onto the uneven concrete slab of an inadequate pathway leading to the outside classrooms, the crowd thinned, spilling on to the small stretches of grass that marshalled the path.

"Steady on now," Jack's voice boomed at the surging

41

throng. "We'll all get there eventually. Continue pushing and shoving if you'd like to spend the rest of your break times this week with me."

Desired effect.

They knew he was always fair, but they also knew he *would* carry out his threat. Much as they liked Jack Ingles, nobody wanted to spend break times in his company.

"I don't like crowds, and all that not being in control," Alyson said finally, as they reached their classroom door. "It feels like I'm being washed away."

"I understand what you mean," Jack said, as they reached the throng of bodies pushing to get inside.

"Now then, riff-raff," he boomed at his class, "will you never learn? I *will* let you in, but only ... James?"

"If we line up properly, sir," a bespectacled, ginger-haired little boy in short trousers piped up.

Jack didn't have to utter one more word, as they formed two lines – girls and boys – ready for entry to their castle. They understood, too, that because their coat area was tiny, they had to be well organised so they didn't have to queue outside to hang up clothing. Without intervention from Jack, they stood behind their group tables, ready to take their turn in the cloakroom. Well taught, well organised, well ... easy. Very simple.

Quiet descended, as reading books plopped on to tables, ready for his lesson's attendance register. The inside door hinges creaked their oil-less protest as a latecomer tried to creep in under Jack's radar. No chance. Although his head and his eyes didn't leave the register, he knew who had just entered. She managed to reach her place quietly, as Jack started to speak.

"Good afternoon, Gabrielle Sarah," he started. "Nice of you to join us. I was just about to send out a search party, thinking you had been abducted by the Lateness Gang."

A quiet snigger raced around the room, bouncing from table to table, gathering momentum and sound as it went.

Gabrielle sat down, a slight suffusion of pink beginning to decorate her cheeks. She had been late at the start of each half-day session before, but never at the beginning of a mid-morning lesson. Her older brother, Damien, further up the school, was a budding artist of no mean talent but Jack knew him by association only.

The children had come to understand that Jack could be wittily sharp on occasion, but where he had cause; it was always with a cheery smile, and he *never* reminded them of misdemeanours nor bore any grudge. They felt it was safe to say that they all got on particularly well.

"Mr Ingles?" an ingratiating little voice piped up midway through maths problems.

"Yes, Gabrielle Sarah," he replied cheerfully. "What can I do you for now?"

"Well," she went on, "would it be all right if I left school at the end of the day...?"

"Of course it would," he interrupted with a laugh. "If you didn't, you'd be pretty tired and hungry and bored by the next school day, as tomorrow's Saturday."

She laughed along with the rest of the youngsters, but frowned at having her question cut short.

"Mr Ingles?" – same voice, same tone after a few moments' pause

"Yes, Gabrielle Sarah?" he said again, lifting his head this time. "The sixty-four-thousand-dollar question now is...?"

"Well," she continued from her last broken request, "would it be all right if I left school ten minutes before everyone else? You see, I have to call at the post office, and..."

"Honest answer, Gabrielle Sarah?" Jack said, straight faced.

"Please," she replied, her elfin face pointing up towards

43

him, a look of keen anticipation etching her brow.

"No," he said with a smile, "unless you happen to have a magic piece of paper in your bag."

"Magic…?" she said, an uncomprehending frown covering her little face.

"A note from your mum, written in golden ink on light blue paper, dated two years next Saturday," he smiled, admiring her flamboyant furry footwear. "I like the boots, by the way. But, aren't they a bit warm at this time of year? Fur-lined?"

"Haven't got any others, really," she said quietly.

"Not to worry," he said, not wanting to labour the point, "but I would remind you that we do have quite a way to go to the end of school, and your release. Maths, please. You know how you love it."

–o–

"Your class is very lucky, you know," Jenny said, her head resting on Jack's chest and arms wrapped around his neck, as he squeezed through the front door.

"How come?" he said, divesting himself of his wife, his coat and all thoughts of school.

"Well," she replied, "they get to spend all day with you … and we don't."

"Needs must, I'm afraid," he returned with a laugh, "if you want to continue living in this palatial dwelling, enjoying the luxuries you have today."

They both laughed as she flung her arms around him again and kissed him once more before leading him to the kitchen for his tea and biscuit.

"Any word from your Val?" he asked through a mouthful of chocolate digestive.

"Funny you should ask," she said, as she squeezed his hand. "She phoned earlier this afternoon. Says she's cut down her hours in school to two days, and wants to know if it's all right to come stay for a few days over Christmas."

"What? The whole tribe?" Jack asked, surprised that his brother might want to become part of their family at last.

"As it stands," she answered, "but that's not cast in stone, by any manner. It means, as well, that if they don't have enough money, *he'll* have to do extra to make up her shortfall."

"Clever, your Val," Jack said, a knowing smile growing. "And what if he doesn't?"

"She'll leave him, and bring the kids up here to live," Jenny said, shrugging nonchalantly. "She's testing his resolve to do whatever is right to put his family first."

"She may not appear so, but she's 'ard," he laughed. "Just like her sister. I suppose we'll just have to watch this space."

"My concern is where she would live," Jenny puzzled. "I know William would have to provide for his children, but still…"

"As an expedient," Jack replied, reaching for another biscuit, "she's two choices. One's in Normanton, and the other's here. Would she make him sell up, do you think?"

"I suppose anything's possible," she replied, "but I really have no idea. I hope it doesn't come to that."

"William's a daft bugger to let matters get to this state," Jack muttered, losing a few crumbs as he chomped his digestive. "Never was too bright, nor ower-endowed wi' common sense."

# Chapter 5

"Are you glad you came, then, William?" Jack asked, as they sat quietly in the dining room, a glass of Tetley's to hand. "Who'd have thought we'd be sitting here together, you and me, a few days before Christmas?"

"I've got to be honest, Brother," William started, as he wiped away the froth from his newly-grown beard and tash, "that I didn't want to come at all, but…"

"Thanks for sharing that with me," Jack replied, sharply.

"No … but listen," his brother butted in. "*Now,* I'm glad I did. Things haven't been great for me over the last few months, finally being shown by my wife and children what a selfish and thoughtless twat I've been."

"I can't disagree with that one," Jack said, a wry smile jumping into his face, "but these things sometimes happen. What was it Granddad used to say? What doesn't kill you will make you stronger?"

"Aye," William sighed, "but I'm not so sure in this case. I just don't know what I can do to make things right. It turned out that Sandra wasn't pregnant after all, but that doesn't take away the fact that I was unfaithful, and…"

"You've got to show Val that you understand all that, Bro," Jack urged, "and are willing to try to make amends."

"Not heard that for a while," William smiled as he sipped his beer.

"What? About making amends?" Jack puzzled, scratching his spikes.

"No," William said, an uncharacteristic smile of enjoyment playing round his eyes, "you calling me 'Bro'."

"That's because *this* is the first time you've been here," Jack remonstrated gently, "and the first time we've been together since Granddad's funeral. We've never spent much time in each other's company, Bro. What with you being such a lot older than me."

"Steady," William said, laughing at his brother's gentle wit. It was true. The age difference had never allowed them to share quality time together, but the only difference since Jack had started his working life had been distance. "Perhaps we might start seeing more of each other. You've not been to ours at all, I don't think?"

"Birmingham?" Jack asked in mock seriousness. "Where's that?"

They both laughed easily, drinking their beer as they tried to find enough common ground to lay foundations for their new relationship.

"Daddy?" Mary and Jessie echoed in unison. "Will you come and play games with us?"

"Joey *refuses* to play," Mary piped up. "Says he won't play with *girls* because we don't play fair."

"Fair?" Jack asked. "How…?"

"Mary *always* wins," William explained with a smile, "and Joey always says she cheats, which she doesn't, of course. She just happens to be…"

"I get the picture," Jack interrupted, a huge grin showing his approval. "Of course we'll come and play, M and J."

"M and J?" Jessie asked. "Who are they, Daddy?"

"It's our initials, Jess," Mary explained, as they trooped into the front room. "Uncle Jack's done that before. Joey didn't understand it then, either, and he's a lot older."

47

The two brothers looked at each other as they finished their beer, then stirred themselves, ready for a hard-fought game of Ludo, Tiddlywinks, Monopoly, or whatever. Mary, so competitive for one so young, would be no pushover, so they would have to be on their mettle.

"Let the Games begin," Jack said, sucking air deeply into *his* competitive lungs. Quarter neither sought nor given.

"How are things?" Jenny asked her sister, as *they* now relaxed in the warm seats vacated by their husbands a few moments before. They felt they needed a little space from the whoops of joy and the hoorays of battle being waged in the front room. Val's sons had now decided they too needed to be in the competition, largely because they had nothing much to do to amuse their teenage intellect – and they didn't want to be left out.

"He's trying, the poor mite," Val replied, "although it's neither natural nor easy for him. He's nothing like his brother, I can see. Jack finds rationalisation and decision making easy. Comes of being able to see things through to a logical conclusion in his head, I suppose."

"True," Jenny said, "but don't get the idea that everything's a bed of roses, with his 'pragmatism', Val. It's not. I love him dearly, and I couldn't imagine life without him, but…"

"But?" Val said, a look of disbelief beginning its journey to her eyes. "How could there be a *but* with a dependable man like your Jack?"

"Annoying on occasion," Jenny laughed. "Believe me, because he tends to *over*-think things in his quest for the perfect answer, and that can be mildly irritating for someone like me who thrives on spontaneity."

"You don't know you're born!" Val harrumphed. "I wish *I* had a man like your Jack. You know where you are with him. No corners. No skeletons in cupboards. Easy. Heaven."

"There's progress, then?" Jenny said, changing the subject.

"I get the impression he's finding it tough," Val replied, "because he's not a natural thinker-through of consequences. He follows his nose without dwelling on what might happen ultimately."

"And Jack is totally the opposite," Jenny smiled. "He over-thinks things, and will give you five different scenarios from which to choose. Then the whole process starts again to find the most advantageous outcome. Nightmare occasionally, but I love him and wouldn't change him."

"William's whore wasn't pregnant at all," Val said, after a moment or two sipping coffee and choosing the right accompanying chocolate. "What do they call them these days – phantom pregnancies?"

"And how did *her* husband take that one?" Jenny asked, drawing closer to her sister.

"She didn't tell him," Val replied, dropping to a low whisper. "He knows nothing about the whole sordid affair. Poor sap."

"Poor sap?" Jenny asked, more intrigued than ever.

"It turns out," Val continued, checking all around her that she wasn't being overheard, like some old-film Dick Barton, "that it's happened before. Trust *my* husband to get suckered in."

"And?" Jenny went on.

"I haven't forgiven him, and don't know if ever I will," Val said, "but I'm working on it."

"That's not fair!" Mary's irate little voice rattled round the room, as she stomped in and slumped into one of the chairs.

"What's the matter, my pretty?" Jenny asked, turning to the noisy whirlwind that had just blown into their zone. "People not playing fairly?"

"Daddy's just won," she harrumphed.

"And what's wrong with that?" Val said. "You can't expect

to win *every* time, Mary."

"He *never* wins," she complained, bottom lip curled in annoyance. "He *must* have cheated. He doesn't even know how to *play* properly."

Val's face split into a huge grin as her daughter shuffled across to her lap.

"Out of the mouths of babes, eh, Jenny," Val said, finding it hard not to laugh out loud at this scrap's assessment of her husband's practical abilities.

"What's happening with Mum over the festive days?" Val asked, after a few moments of quiet. "And Jack's gran?"

"We asked," Jenny said, "but Marion's spending the time with close relatives. Mum is coming to stay for a day or two over Christmas, and Jack's going to pick her up early Christmas Eve."

"Hang on," Val said, a note of uncertainty in her voice. "If Mum's coming to stay, where's she going to sleep? Four bedrooms means two couples and two sets of children, doesn't it? You need another room, surely?"

"We've made another bed up in yon integral garage for you and our William," Jack said cheerily, as he popped his head round the door, "and we thought your mum could have the room you were going to have."

"Just ignore him, Val," Jenny said, throwing a cushion at his head, "and he'll go away. The settee in the lounge is a sofa bed, which *we'll* have, allowing Mum to have ours."

"How long did you say she was staying?" Val went on.

"Christmas Eve and Day," Jenny replied. "Jack's taking her back on Boxing Day."

"Strange time to go back," her sister puzzled.

"She's got something else planned for later that day," Jenny said slowly, a puzzled frown pulling down her brows. "I think Jack was right."

"Jack? Right?" Val laughed. "When is he ever anything

else? What do you mean 'right'? Something you're not telling me?"

"We think she's 'seeing' someone," Jenny replied quietly, mouthing the last two words, once she'd checked again that they were alone in the room.

"Mum? Another man?" Val gasped through a hoarse whisper. "Since when … and who could it possibly be? Do I know him?"

"I should think you do," Jenny said, her air of finality shocking her sister.

"Well, come on then," Val insisted, ushering out the descended silence. "Don't keep me in suspense."

"Jim Arkwright ring any bells?" Jenny said, bending closer to her sister to create a secrecy bubble between them.

"Wasn't he something to do with Dad's pit?" Val said, her answer coming slowly, as if she were dredging a deep but scant memory.

"He was," Jenny agreed. "But what? Can't remember much else, other than thinking he was a bit tall and broad for a miner. Good looking too, I seem to remember."

"He was the under manager for a while before Dad died," Jenny added.

"Well, if my memory serves," Val said with a smile, "she could have done worse."

"Val!" Jenny gasped, surprised to hear her sister's unexpected answer.

"She's a grown woman, Jen," Val said, "and if she wants male company, then who are we to deny or speak against?"

"But, she's—" Jenny replied, almost uncomprehending her sister's view.

"Our mum," Val replied quickly, "is no fool. If he's not right for her, she'll know – and so will we. She has to be allowed to live and be much more than a babysitting service at times."

"…And a good man by all accounts," Jack added. They hadn't noticed his entry, as he slid stealthily into a corner seat.

"Jack," Jenny gasped, jumping in surprise at his voice. "I didn't hear *you* come in."

"It's my SAS commando training," he laughed.

"And how do *you* know about Jim Arkwright?" Val scoffed. "He lives in Normanton, umpteen miles from you, here, in Leeds."

"Actually," Jack replied, a superior look springing into his face, "he has a lovely, big detached bungalow on Pinfold Lane, Methley, not that far from where I used to play rugby."

"Oh yeah!" Jenny scoffed, with an unconfident smile, "and how do you know that? Become friends with him, have you…? And now you're going to make me regret I doubted you, aren't you?"

"As I told you some time ago," he replied, "I still have very good contacts in t'owd town, from where I am reliably informed that, a qualified engineer by trade, he left the pit some time ago to start his own engineering business. Quite successful, I'm given to understand, hence the detached bungalow. She could do a lot worse, your mam, you know, Jenny. He's a good man. There aren't many of us left."

"I think I'll have to have a word with her when I see her," Jenny said.

"I wouldn't," Val advised firmly. "She'll only please herself, and you might cause resentment. That's the last thing we want, particularly at this stage. It's a good idea to keep an eye, but don't interfere. How many times did you tell her not to butt into your life? Mmm?"

–o–

"You know, don't you?" Jenny's mother said to Jack, as he turned into Pinfold Lane on their way from Normanton.

"Know what, Mrs M?" Jack replied, feigning ignorance, but knowing full well what she meant.

"How long have we known each other, Jack?" she said, seeming to move off subject.

"Seems like forever, Mrs M," he replied.

"Then, don't you think it's about time you stopped being so formal?" she said, a slightly mischievous smile playing around her eyes.

Jack's slight frown of uncertainty made her smile even more, because he had obviously no idea what line she was following.

"And about time you called me Flo?" she went on.

"Why would I want to call you Flo?" he puzzled, shaking his head slightly, perplexed.

"Because that's my name," she said. "Flora Mae McDermot."

"You're kidding me!" he exclaimed. "No way! Mi mam's name was Florence May. How crazy is that?"

"Well?" she added. "Is it to be Flo or not?"

"Thank you … Flo," he said. "I'd be honoured."

"You *are* a strange young man," she said, smiling at the formal way he embraced informality. "Strange but rather charming, in a wonderful sort of a way."

"To go back to your original question when we turned into Pinfold Lane," he said, after a moment or two of quiet. "Yes, I *do* know."

"I'm going to tell you something now, Jack, that I would like you to keep to yourself – for the time being," she said, quite deliberately. "I'll give you the nod when it's all right to tell Jenny. Can you do that, Jack?"

"Mmm," he hummed in a moment's indecision.

"Jack?" she insisted. "If you can't then I don't want to put you in a difficult position with our Jenny, but I need to tell someone. My daughters wouldn't understand – yet."

"OK, Mrs … Flo," Jack agreed. "I will be your confidant, but hopefully not for too long. I promise I will keep the secret I think you are about to share."

"I should imagine you do," she laughed, "because, unlike most men, you understand us."

"Us?" he smiled, playing along.

"Women," she said, nodding, "and their needs. You are an honourable man, Jack Ingles, and you've made our Jenny the happiest I've ever seen her."

"OK," he agreed. "I'll go with that. Your 'secret' that only you and I … and Jim … know?"

"Even *he* doesn't know yet," she laughed, clapping her hands in glee.

"Oo, I do like a juicy bit of intrigue," he said, a throaty chuckle joining them as they passed on to Methley Lane. "So, whom do I have to assassinate?"

"I like Jim Arkwright," she started, "a lot. We've been seeing each other for some considerable time, you understand. I've been lonely since Jenny's dad went, and Jim's very considerate and extremely good company. You and he have many traits in common, actually, like honesty, compassion and an innate desire to take care of folk close to you. Since his wife passed away, he has thrown himself into his work to try to fill his time."

"Any children?" Jack asked, in passing.

"Just one," she replied. "A son, living in New Zealand, whom he hasn't seen since the funeral. He's not too happy about that, but there's not a lot he can do to change it."

"I know *that* feeling well," Jack sighed, as his memories bubbled to the surface.

"The upshot is that we've been seeing each other, as I said," she went on, "and although he has asked me to spend time with him in his lovely bungalow, I haven't yet given him an answer."

"By 'spend time' you mean…?" Jack asked, trying to put it delicately.

"Living together, Jack," she said bluntly, "you know, as man and wife, but not yet married."

"You say *not yet married*?" he queried. "Does that mean you *might*?"

"It's an option, Jack," she smiled, as she touched his arm gently. "I simply want to try him for size before I decide."

"Good thinking, Flo," Jack said, a smile of recognition flicking across his face. "You can't find out what a person is really like until you—"

"Live with them," she interrupted, finishing his sentence. "I knew I was right to talk to you, Jack. *You* understand, whereas my daughters wouldn't have. They would think he was taking advantage of a poor defenceless woman."

"You? Defenceless?" he scoffed. "You're anything but. If Jim Arkwright scores with you, he'll be the second luckiest man on the planet."

"In fact, if anything, I think I'm taking advantage of him," she said. "Second luckiest man?"

"I'm the first, Flo," he laughed, "because I've got Jenny as my beautiful wife, and you as my lovely mother-in-law."

She smiled, satisfied that Jack understood, was on her side, would be true to his word and would be there if she needed him. She felt her life was about to take off in a way that excited every nerve, and brought joy to her stagnating existence.

"And if the fit is right, Flo?" he asked, as they hit the traffic on Crown Point Road, heading for Regent Street, Sheepscar, and the A61 beyond. "What then?"

"Then, life begins again in earnest," she said, a soft smile gracing her eyes. "Certain things in life you have to take on trust, don't you think, Jack?"

"Agreed," he replied, "but there needs to be a degree of

caution, Flo – a Plan B, perhaps?"

"Ha ha!" she laughed. "You are a good friend to have, Our Jack,"

"That was one of the endearments mi mam used a lot," he said, quietly. "Our Jack. You go for it, Our Flo. I'm sure Jim won't let you down. And when the time comes, you leave your daughters to me."

The road to North Leeds was quiet for a change at this time of year, perhaps because it was still relatively early in the day. Black slushy piles of melting snow, from the day before's minor fall, lined the streets, hoping to be gone by the following day. Although not as cold as the previous few weeks, folk were still rushing about their business, huddled against the chill, trying for last minute necessities before the big day only a few hours away.

As Jack turned into their long drive, he could see the welcoming party crowding the large front room window, the youngsters waving wildly, to greet their grandma's arrival.

# Chapter 6

Christmas with the Ingles was a scary saunter into the unknown, as they had never celebrated together under the same roof at the same time. Christmas Day was a boisterous, noisy affair from very early morning, with five children ranging from early nursery to early secondary whizzing around this new untried and untested combat ground. Unfortunately, the almost constant curtain of heavy drizzle that had been drawn across North Leeds persisted throughout the morning, corralling excited youngsters indoors – much to the relief of the adults, but frustration for the children.

Once the debris from present opening had been cleared, the washing up from breakfast had been done and the children had been settled to putting their favourite presents through their paces, the adults could settle to a drink and a nibble or two in peace and comfort.

"Christmases ever like this, Flo, when your two were little?" Jack asked, as he nibbled on his first festive, chocolate biscuit.

"Flo?" Jenny mouthed to her sister. "Who's Flo?"

"I am, my dear," her mother said, quite deliberately. "As it's my name, I asked Jack yesterday if he'd mind using it."

"But, you're called Flora," Val said, puzzled why suddenly she needed to be called something different, "and Dad always called you that."

"At least when we were about," Jenny added.

"Your aunts, Joan and Barbara, always called me Flo," their mum insisted, "and so did your dad, whenever you weren't about. I much preferred it, because Flora always seemed so – I don't know – so … old fashioned. You perhaps didn't know either that my middle name is Mae – after Mae West, the Hollywood film star."

"I remember her vaguely," Jenny said, a smile flickering. "Didn't she have a rather large—"

"Bosom?" her mother broke in, puffing out her ample chest. "My father was prone to theatricality, but he wasn't to know how close he would be."

They all burst out laughing at Mrs McDermot's exaggeratedly prophetic gesture; that is all but William, who smiled uncomfortably at their obvious shared enjoyment.

"Anybody notice the similarity in Christian names?" Jenny said. "Flora Mae – Florence May?"

"Jack noticed straight away, in the car yesterday," her mum replied. "Quicker than you, my dear. He's a very intuitive young man, and *you*, young lady, are very fortunate to have him."

The room fell silent for a few moments, punctuated only by the mutterings and whoops of joy and fun from the whole of the ground floor.

Jenny followed Jack as he ambled into the kitchen to prepare another round of coffee, Christmas cake and mince pies. This was the time of year when he felt no guilt at indulging his favourite foods, as often as his belly called and would allow.

"What's with the 'Flo'?" Jenny asked her husband as he filled the kettle and the large cafetière, ready for another dose of caffeine for his guests. Jenny's mother and Jack were the only tea addicts.

"We spent a lot of time in the car together yesterday, talking about inconsequential this and that, and she said it was about time I used her Christian name instead of Mrs M all the time," Jack explained. "It was then I drew the comparison with mi mam's name. No big deal. No need to create a fuss where none is needed, really. Don't you think so, Our Jen?"

"I suppose," she replied. "It just seems a bit … strange, I think."

"Just what *I* said," he went on, as he finished making the drinks, readying himself to carry the stuff in to the front room on a poky little tray, "but she insisted, very sensibly as it turns out."

"Your William's not overly keen on this informality lark, I noticed," Jenny observed.

"Snap," he answered, with a grin. "He looks decidedly uncomfortable, I think. Soft bugger. She's cool, your mam, you know. I like her a lot."

"And I'm not about to be told what I can and can't do with my own children," William insisted sharply, as he followed Val into the kitchen.

"But you don't do anything with them," she said, her hole-in-one ricocheting off the flagpole. "You never have."

"That was low," he complained.

"That was the truth," she insisted, very pointedly. "You wouldn't know *what* to do with Mary, for a prize example. Part of the deal for you to try to ingratiate yourself back into almost full membership of *this* family."

"Am I going to suffer *this* all the time, then?" he replied.

"By this, I assume you mean the hurt and humiliation you heaped on me, the wife you promised to love forever?" Val threw back at him. "Until *I* consider otherwise, yes. Now, enough."

William wore a sulky look as Val stood by the sink,

looking out on to a soggy back garden. Jenny prepared to carry the second tray of tea and coffee into the lounge as her brother-in-law sucked his bottom lip petulantly.

"Shall I give you a hand with those, Our Jen?" Val offered, turning round at last.

"Please, Val," she replied, quietly.

"Bit of advice, William?" Jack offered once the girls had gone. "Take it all on the chin and do the time. Don't cause any waves and she'll come round eventually."

"It's all right for you to say," William replied, sulkily, "but you never—"

"Don't say it, William," Jack warned, sternly, with a painful smile. "I had all of this in my first marriage, and I'd been married a lot less time than you, don't forget."

The house had fallen still and quiet, except for the vaguest low murmur from the three most important women in Jack's life. He couldn't imagine the hurt William had caused to the mother of his lovely children, and for what? Lies, deceit and more aggravation than he knew how to handle. Val *would* forgive him – eventually – because she loved him, but he would have to make it easier for her by playing *his* part

Small price to pay.

He always was a daft bugger, even his mam accepted that. Apple of his father's eye early on, but certainly not the shiniest one in the fruit bowl. If he didn't get to grips with *this* mid-life crisis, he would certainly be working through it on his own.

His main trouble was that he didn't know how to deal with intelligent women – or with *any* women, for that matter.

–o–

"Well," Jenny's mum said over breakfast on Boxing Day, "that was the best Christmas I have spent for many a year – even since before your dad died, dare I say it?"

"There's always space for you in my home, Flo," Jack said earnestly, as his empty spoon slid around his empty porridge dish. "You know that."

"Indeed, I do," she replied, a smile of satisfaction and happiness underlining her sincerity, "and it's very much appreciated and comforting to know, Our Jack, but now I must pack my stuff and be off, if you wouldn't mind."

"Can't we prevail on you to stay a little while longer?" he replied. "We've thoroughly enjoyed your company."

"Nothing I'd like better – but some other time, maybe," she smiled. "I have a long-standing arrangement I need to attend to."

"Going anywhere nice?" William ventured, lamely.

"Just lunch with friends, which has been organised for quite a while," she said, "which I am looking forward to very much."

Jenny knew instinctively that this 'lunch with friends' was more than just that, and Jack's silence reinforced it. Normally, he would have engaged with her about where she was going, what she was going to eat, and to urge her to bring back a recommendation, but – nothing. She was convinced he knew something, which she would get out of him later.

"Let's go, then, Flo," Jack started, one of his interminably dodgy rhymes bubbling up ready to flow. "We don't want to be slow, otherwise you won't know where to go, then—"

"Enough!" Jenny shouted, her fingers in her ears in fun. "I don't think you'll make Poet Laureate any time soon – thank goodness."

Flo laughed at their good-humoured banter, taking comfort in their obvious joy in each other's company. She couldn't help but draw a marked contrast with her elder daughter's relationship. Theirs seemed to be a going-nowhere union. William paid little attention to his mate, making neither physical nor intellectual contact throughout the time she was there. She was happy and deeply gratified that Jenny had found the man who loved her unconditionally, would never hurt her and who brought her to life. She had worried about both of her daughters, but now Val was the one needing concern.

"You are a good man, Jack Ingles," Flo said in the car as they approached Three Lane Ends. "My Jenny's happier and more content than I've seen her since she was in junior school, and that's down to you."

"All *I've* done, Flo, is give her the love and stability she needs and deserves," Jack replied. "We were meant to be together, right from being nippers. Destiny, really, I suppose."

"Shall you come in for a cuppa when we get back?" she asked.

"Not really, but thank you for asking," he replied. "I ought to get back. Is Jim taking you somewhere nice?"

"So, you worked it out then?" Flo said, a smile of satisfaction showing her happiness.

"Not too hard, bearing in mind our conversation of the other day," he laughed. "You'll have to be careful, Flo, because if I can work it out, Jenny will too. She's smart and often much quicker than me. Even though she won't hear it from my lips, she'll work things out according to how *I* behave and react. I shall have to be very much on my mettle to give nothing away, otherwise, with the slightest whiff, she'll badger and bait."

"Anyway, Jack," Flo went on unabashed, as they passed the Black Swan and headed towards Dr Twist's corner surgery, "I've a feeling that tonight might be the night."

"Don't you think that might be a bit *too* much information, Flo?" Jack responded delicately. "I mean—"

"No, daft beggar," she laughed. "Not *that*. I think he might ask me."

"What?" he puzzled, feeling he was getting into this

conversation just a bit deeper than his comfort zone. He appreciated her confidence but this was a bit ... too personal. "Asking you to move in?"

"No," she said quite deliberately. "I think he might be asking me to marry him."

-o-

From Advent to Epiphany, Christmas gave all those who celebrated its magic, excitement, wonder, and ... hard work. The aftermath was very different from its build-up in many households – flat, anti-climactic, disappointing. Although the Ingles family felt a little deflated when the period had reached its nadir, the celebration was one of the best they had ever had.

"Anything to report?" Jenny asked of her husband as soon as he rejoined his family after his travels.

"By that you mean?" Jack said, his frown warning them he was puzzled by her question.

"That puzzled look cuts no ice with me," she said, a condescending smile warning him she was about to lay bare his subterfuge. "Don't forget, I'm—"

"I know 'intuitive and psychic'," he interrupted, "but there's nothing for you to intuit or psych about."

"You spent umpteen hours in the car with Mum over the last couple of days or so," she pointed out, "and you can't tell me you only talked about the weather."

"Amongst other things – yes," he added, a non-committal smug look inflaming her desire for him to tell all. "We talked about this and ... that."

"And ... the other?" she prompted. "You know, a certain ... other?"

"Well," he said, the slightly uncomfortable wrestling with the downright wicked in his mind, "we talked about her grandchildren, her husband, her friends, and ... you three. If

I were to tell you what she said about that, I should have to kill you."

Val laughed out loud, watching the clever way he was evading all her sister's attempts at squeezing out of him the information she wanted to hear. He was more than a match for her, and if there *were* any secrets Jenny would like him to share, he was more than able not to. She couldn't imagine there would be anything Mum might want to share with him, and not tell them, though. After all, they *were* her daughters. Yet, if she had anything she *had* to share with anyone, Jack would be the logical one to do it with. Now *Val* was intrigued. Should she…?

William was deep in thought, taking no notice of anything going on around him, no doubt considering his position still. Allowing himself to be taken in so gullibly rankled much more than his acts of unfaithfulness themselves, risking everything he had always wanted for a brief fling with a woman he hardly knew.

The vaguely naff and embarrassing warble of the telephone in the hallway reminded Jack that he had to change the machine as soon as he was able.

"I'll get it," Jenny said, leaping out of her chair by the fire, "but don't think for one minute, buster, that you're off the hook."

Val raised her eyebrows towards Jack, who responded with a non-committal downturned purse of his mouth, a slight shake of the head, and an "I've no idea what you mean" shrug of the shoulders.

"It's for you, husband," Jenny said slowly, as she returned to her seat, a seriously puzzled look playing with her features. "It's Mum."

"What on earth does Mum want with Jack?" Val whispered, nonplussed in the extreme.

"We'll soon find out," Jenny replied, equally puzzled.

"Here he comes now."

"Cup of tea, anyone?" Jack asked cheerfully. "And a piece of spice cake?"

Jenny and Val turned slowly to face Jack, eyebrows raised and heads slightly inclined sideways, waiting for his explanation.

"What?" he said, a sardonic smile chasing a look of innocence, as he made to hide in the kitchen.

"What … did … she … want?" Jenny asked, flicking her fingers at him threateningly.

"Who? Your mum?" he grinned, drawing out the agony to its edge, and realising it couldn't be stretched any further. "Seeing as Will and Val are on their way home the day after tomorrow, she's asked if she might come over before they go. She's something she wants to say to us all. So, I've said I'll fetch her tomorrow for lunch. Is that all right, Jen?"

"Course it is," she replied, impatiently, "but did she tell you why?"

"Well," he went on, looking around and over both shoulders in his exaggerated way of checking to see that nobody else could overhear, "in a word … no."

"She must have said…" Jenny sighed.

"You now know as much as I do," he insisted. "We'll just have to wait until tomorrow. Tea anybody?"

–o–

"You've certainly set the cat among the pigeons, Flo," Jack said, as they approached the end of Princess Street. Normanton's streets had suffered a pounding from rain and gale-force winds as usual for this time of year. When he was a nipper, they almost always seemed to have snow or soil-lifting deep frosts, but these days all they seemed to enjoy was wet and wind.

"Thought I might," she smiled, "and were you in the

middle of it, Jack?"

"I was that," he laughed, "but they never got anything out of me, despite the women's tortures and William's death by silence. The call to worship really had them hung out to dry. I had a whale of a laugh at their expense, I can tell you."

"The reason you have picked me up today is—" she started.

"No! Please, Flo," he insisted, "don't tell me. I need to be able to react in a normal surprised way, otherwise these intuitive women will know there's something fishy. I'd rather know when they get to know, if you don't mind?"

"You're far too clever, Jack Ingles," Flo said, a knowing and understanding smile signalling her agreement.

"Not really," he said. "It's simply self-preservation, that's all. They can't accuse me of something I genuinely know nothing about."

Flo gazed out of the window as countryside, punctuated by the towns and villages en route, drifted lazily by. She thought about her family and her home, but most of all she remembered the good and not-so-good times she had shared with her husband. This was almost an expiation of all the things she hadn't handled as well as she might, but mostly saying her goodbyes to past life and, in particular, to her husband. Time now to move on.

The rest of the journey, for the most part, was spent in silence, apart from the odd snippet of polite conversation of little consequence.

"Here we are," Jack said, drawing in to his driveway. "Let the inquisition begin. Nervous?"

"No," she said, quite deliberately. "On the contrary, I feel quite excited and elated about what I'm about to spring on you all."

"Mother," Jenny and Val choroused, as she took off her coat and settled in the easy chair in the corner, facing the television, "it's lovely to see you again."

"Cup of tea, Flo?" Jack asked, poking his head around the door. "Anybody else?"

The chorus of 'yes please' gave him an excuse to break out the dark-chocolate digestives he had been saving for a special occasion while the tea was mashing.

"You set us all quite a conundrum when you told Jack you had something to tell us," Jenny waded in. "He wouldn't tell us what it was about, though."

She turned to him and threw him a playful glower, which, although it was supposed to warn him of things to come, had no effect on his serenely smiling face at all, as he put the tray of goodies on the coffee table. The children were all occupying themselves with their Christmas gifts, somewhere in the house, as the adults settled to Flo's mysterious business.

"He wouldn't tell you," Flo started, to Jenny's triumphant frown, "because I didn't tell him anything."

This pile-driving side swipe knocked her daughter completely off her stride, throwing a huge dollop of confusion in her face.

"Well, Mother," Val said, "what *was* it you wanted to tell us, then? This stuff that Jack knew nothing about? To do with money?"

"In a way, I suppose it is," Flo answered slowly, after a moment's hesitation.

"I knew it!" Val butted in. "If you're having troubles, why didn't you come to us? We could surely have helped."

"It's only about money," her mother replied slowly, "in so far as I am moving house—"

"Moving?" her daughters gasped. "But you can't. That's our house – the house we were brought up in; the house we shared with Dad. You can't."

"Why?" Jenny asked, once the hysteria had settled. "Why

now?"

"I want to move now because of several things," Flo started, once she had gathered her thoughts and had polished off her second cup of tea. "You all know very well that I have maintained the house for two main reasons close to my heart. Firstly, it's been my home that I shared with those dearest to me for close on twenty or so years. I have lots of lovely memories there, and never a day goes by that I don't spend time in each room, reminiscing about those happy times."

She paused for a few moments, as if struggling to draw herself back from those days. Jenny gripped Jack's hand to give herself strength not to become upset at the thoughts *she* had crowding *her* mind, too. Val sat in silence, tight-lipped, fighting not to betray her emotions. William's eyes were closed, taking no part in the proceedings. *His* thoughts were elsewhere.

"It's always been a delight, of course," Flo went on, "to have you come visit, so I can hear the house ringing with excited children's voices again, filling that otherworldly silence that crowds in on me a lot of the time. Now ... it's become *too* big. The memories have filled those spaces, and I should like to leave them there, and have them inhabit my mind only. I should like somewhere where I can make new memories, where the old ones won't follow me about when I move from room to room."

"Have you had the house valued, Flo?" Jack asked, his ever-practical mind taking them all away from too much emotion.

"One of the reasons why you, Jack, are so important to us all," Flo said, a huge smile underlining her words, "is that you always bring us back to the practical here and now."

Jenny linked her arm through his, a smile telling him how she felt.

"Yes, it's been valued," her mum continued, "and in fact, I

already have someone interested in buying it, complete with furniture and furnishings."

"Furniture…?" Val puzzled.

"And furnishings?" Jenny added. "But won't you need those for your new home?"

"No," she said, slowly, "and this is the part you are going to have to listen to carefully, and try to understand. I won't need them because—"

Jenny and Val sat bolt upright, hardly daring to breathe, though Jack sat back with a relaxed smile on his face, feeling that he knew what was coming next.

"Jim Arkwright has asked me to marry him," she continued, deliberately, "and I have accepted. I will be moving in to his – our – big new bungalow on Pinfold Lane, Methley, in the near future."

# Chapter 7

"That's a cough drop and no mistake," Jenny said, as she slid into bed once the family had all gone home. The gathering had been an unqualified success, with four children interacting and integrating with consummate ease, and with each of the adults, unsurprisingly, enjoying each other's company – except for William. He felt uncomfortable and out of his depth, as usual.

"A cough drop?" Jack said, not quite sure where his wife was going with that metaphor.

"Mum's announcement?" she said, mildly sarcastically. "Remember?"

"Why should it be any more unusual or outlandish than ours, when we announced we were to be spliced?" he replied, pragmatic to the last.

"She's *my* mother, and—" she harrumphed.

"She deserves happiness where she can find it," he insisted, "and I for one will support them both in this. After all, she's no longer sixteen, and consequently needs no one's permission."

"Sarky beggar," she muttered. "You know what I mean."

"I certainly do, my lovely," Jack smiled, "and we all want her to be happy without fear of her being used. Jim Arkwright is an honourable man, I believe, who will not take advantage. She's no pushover, your mum, you know, and is

70

tough enough to stand up for herself. She'll do what she feels is right and enjoy the experience into the bargain. She's going to try him for size, and—"

"Jack!" Jenny gasped. "This is my mum we're talking about."

"Her words, my beauty," he smiled, "and we both know what she means."

"Mmm," Jenny mumbled.

"Did you hear the one about the old Yorkshire chap and his wife, who were being interviewed about their sixteen children?" Jack said, after a moment or two's quiet.

"No," she began to smile, knowing how pathetic his jokes could be, "but I bet you're about to tell me."

"The interviewer asked him what he put their large family down to," Jack went on.

"'Well,' the old chap said, 'I put it down to deafness.'"

"'Deafness?' the interviewer puzzled."

"'Aye,' t'owd chap replied. 'Ivry night as we start to climb yon wooden hill to bed, I says to 'er "Are we goin' to go to sleep or what?" And being a bit hard of hearing like, she allus says 'What?'"

Jenny burst out laughing at his funny.

"Well?" he asked. "Are we?"

"What?" she replied, a hugely demure grin splitting her face as she finally twigged the point of the tale.

–o–

"Mmm, cold," Jenny murmured in her sleep, almost inaudibly, as she drew the bedclothes slowly around her neck.

Seven o'clock, and the steely cold light of early morning was beginning to creep through the curtains, nipping at the ears and uncovered toes, as the new-fangled central heating tried to chase out the shrinking pockets of another chill, late-December day from their room.

71

Even her unconscious body hated the cold, shrinking from its ever-present threat to freeze as it slunk around unsuspecting bare skin, nipping here and scratching there.

Jack was awake, his half-covered naked body trying to shed the heat that always built up during sleep. He'd been awake for over an hour but would never move for fear of waking his wife and youngsters. *They* didn't need to be up yet. It was still too dark and cold for them. Another half an hour should do it, and then breakfast, a brisk walk and the rest of the day enjoying the company of his family.

Sleep was often elusive for Jack. His father had always said that an hour before midnight was better than two after, but this didn't hold for him. In bed by eleven and no sleep between five and seven, he always found. During the time he was awake, many issues in his life usually vied for his attention, although the lack of sleep never seemed to affect him, or concern him, or stop him doing the things any normal person needed to do.

He turned over quietly so as not to disturb his wife, to be met, full gaze, by two small, unblinking eyes, looking at him over the edge of the bed nearest the door. Jessie had decided it was time to rise. Jack looked back at her, crossed his eyes and pulled a face which made her laugh as she squeezed between the sheets and, climbing over him, nestled between him and her mother.

"Don't speak or move," he whispered close to her ear, "or you'll wake Mummy."

"It's all right," a muffled mutter joined them. "I'm awake. Is this central-heating thingy working? It still feels cold."

"On and belting it out, lovely," he said, poking his foot and half a leg from under the bedclothes to test the radiator, two feet from his side of the bed. "Go back to sleep and I'll get up in half an hour. Oh, you have."

Jenny's rhythmical buzz told him she was back among the

mystically strange characters that inhabited her subconscious worlds of mystery and myth, fighting wars or meeting that knight in shining armour that reminded her of the window cleaner down the next street, where the occasional catch in her breathing heralded a change in action, or a reaction to its outcome.

Jack waited patiently until he was sure Jessie had drifted off and was comfortably safe before he decided he had had enough of this inertia and was of a mind to rise to prepare breakfast. A week's holiday gone but still the best part of a second one left. He loved this time of year – no gardening, no collecting leaves, watering plants and making sure the soil was well-hoed and cultivated. He was in his element when the only exercise on the agenda was a gentle walk and the rise and fall of his knife and fork at the table.

He was about to put a light to the stove when he was disturbed by the insistently annoying warble of the telephone. His initial instinct was to ignore it, feeling that it would go away, but … no.

The call was short, terse and annoying, fortunately imposing only a short interruption to the culinary adventure of him preparing breakfast.

"Anyone exciting or important?" Jenny asked, as she kissed the back of his neck.

"Hello, my beautiful girls," he said, with a huge smile, as he kissed Jessie and his wife. "Where have you been all my life?"

"Been in bed, Daddy," Jessie insisted, a little puzzled frown tickling her brow. "Silly Daddy."

He laughed as he picked her up and threw her into the air, much to her enormous delight and squeals of joy.

"Again!" she gushed. "Again, please?"

"You've got soldiers waiting," he said, quietly, nodding towards the dining table. "They'll need to be brought under orders in two minutes, my poppet."

She rushed round to her place, to whoops of excitement, shuffled onto her chair and stared open-mouthed at the bread soldiers standing to attention around her plate, all looking intently in towards the empty egg cup, which awaited their commanding officer – the usual soft-boiled egg.

"Going to eat you all today," she said seriously, winking slyly at Jack. He turned away, finding it hard not to burst into huge guffaws.

"And how did you get them all to stand up?" Jenny asked her husband. "Whenever I do it, they always flop."

"It's called 'Taking Orders'," he replied, tapping the side of his nose to try to distract her from the difficulty he was having in keeping a straight face.

"Don't forget the consequences of telling porkies, my man," she warned, her fingers flicking by her sides.

"The other trick," he went on, mentally drawing his neck into his defensive shoulders, "is to cut them into strips, and then…" He looked around surreptitiously to see no one was near to hear, and then he whispered, "Toast them just a bit to make them rigid enough to … stand to attention," he replied quietly, sharing his secret finally, raising his eyebrows and nodding gently.

"Clever Daddy," Jessie said, clapping her hands in anticipation of the breakfast she could almost taste.

"Egg's done!" he shouted, looking at his watch. "Ready, young lady?"

"Yes!" Jessie shouted back. "Now … please!"

"Can you manage, Jess?" Jenny asked, as she removed the sharp end of the egg enough to take as many soldiers as she could eat.

"Is my other young lady sitting down, ready?" Jack continued. "Porridge … is … in … the … building."

"Yum," Jenny said.

"Yuk," Jessie replied. "Don't like porridge."

"Ever thought about having soldiers in porridge?" Jack said, as he dug into his dish of sliced and diced fruit with a grin.

"How do you decide which bits of your fruit to eat first?" Jenny asked, after watching him from across the table. She *knew* there would inevitably be some sort of a system, because she had seen him making some sort of an assessment as he ate. "Are you counting them?"

"Partly," he replied, matter of fact, "but once I've done that, making sure I have an equal number of all the pieces of fruit I've cut, I eat them—"

"In alphabetical order," she said, twigging his method. "Got it."

"Banana, kiwi, pineapple, plum," he went on, "followed by porridge and … tea. Perfect. A simple system which makes sure all my fruits get equal stomach space and digestion time. There is a continuum there called—"

"Obsession," she said quickly. "I know it well. Never knew it existed until I got to know you, Our Jack."

"I'm not that bad, am I?" he said, sliding his cutlery into his now bare dish, perfectly straight and in order, fork before spoon. "I onny like stuff to be rayt."

"You'll do for us, Our Jack," she smiled, blowing him a kiss. "We love you … even if we don't understand you … occasionally. Like, how do you finish your food *so* quickly?"

"I think I've told you before," he explained, as she shook her head slowly. "No? Well, I once nearly 'ad mi full plate o' dinner knocked ower. So, I've been rapid-like, ever since. Don't like to waste. Never 'ave, never will."

"You still haven't answered my question," Jenny reminded him.

"Question?" he puzzled, not really sure what she was on about. "Which question?"

"The one you ignored shortly after you put the phone down," she went on, a false smile creasing her face as her slightly inclined head accentuated her raised, questioning eyebrow. "Remember?"

"Oh yes," he said, "I do."

"Well?" she repeated, impatiently. "Who was it?"

"The head of my school, giving me forewarning that the school might be without heating at the beginning of next term," he replied dispassionately.

"No heating?" she said incredulously. "Does that mean you will be staying at home then?"

"Unfortunately not," he grimaced. "The boiler has collapsed and it may not be working in time, but we have to report to school as normal."

"How are you going to keep warm, for goodness' sake?" she gasped, not really believing what she was hearing. "What about the children?"

"The staff has to be prepared to wear appropriate clothing," he said, "but the children might be told not to come in, or might even be sent home if they do."

"Ridiculous!" she exclaimed. "You should—"

"I know what I *should* do," he explained, "but as usual I would be a lone voice, bleating against power I can do nothing to budge. I *will* have my say, but that's all it will amount to, I'm afraid. My original view, I feel, is coming home to roost."

"Original view?" she said, not understanding.

"That it was a mistake leaving Broughton," he said, bluntly. "Had I stayed, I would probably have been a deputy by now. Delusions of grandeur and all that, I suppose. The glitz of being a bigger fish in an even bigger pond."

"You were only trying to provide for a better life for your family, my man," Jenny replied, sliding her arm through his.

"Mi granddad would have said 'Sometimes tha's got to

meck best on a bad job, cos if'n tha dun't, it'll onny come back to bite thee on t'arse," he said, a sigh accompanying his words. "There's a lot of sense in that."

"What's on t'agenda today, then, Our Jen?" Jack asked, once the washing up was out of the way. "Canaries? Somewhere even hotter?"

"I wish," she replied, a wistful smile creeping up on her. "No, I feel I need to go to see Mum."

"Me too," he agreed. "I need to go see *my* mam. Well, sort out and tidy her room, really. Not been for a while, and can't leave it to brother because he wouldn't, even if he lived next door to yon cemetery."

Jenny laughed. One of the things she loved Jack for. He could make you laugh in some of the most serious situations – mostly when his funnies were unintentional.

"Probably best phone first, though?" she ventured. "You never know."

"Nay," he replied emphatically, "she's always in."

"New man and all?" she added, tentatively.

"Be rayt," he replied, sure she would be there. "Let's get ready then. Mi mam's grave first stop?"

–o–

Although the last Saturday of the year, the roads both on the way to and in and around Normanton were reasonably slack. Jenny had insisted they drive into town and turn left by Womack's fish and flower shop into Church Lane, so they didn't have to drive past her old house on Queen Street.

Church Lane, Dalefield Avenue and Neville Street were quiet, as was the Grammar School. Its new hall thrust itself into what used to be a big playground when he had started there in the late fifties, standing proudly like a beacon of the new order.

"I think we've come on a wild goose chase, Jenny," Jack

said, as they pulled into the cemetery. "It looks like mi mam's and granddad's graves have been seen to."

"I wonder who might have done that, then," she answered, puzzled in the extreme.

"Well, it won't have been William," he harrumphed sarcastically. "That's for sure. It wouldn't be mi grandma because she's not well enough, and she doesn't like such places."

As the car slid to a halt a couple of yards from the two plots, they got out to examine them and to search for clues, like some latter-day Sherlock Holmes.

"It might have been granddad's sister, Lizzy, as what did *his*," Jack ventured. "But ... mi mam's?"

"Could it be your dad, do you think?" Jenny said, at a loss what else to suggest.

"I shouldn't think so," Jack started to reply. "Anyway—"

"I think I recognise that face," a gruff voice accosted Jack from by the rubbish heap and water tap, near the outer fence. "That *has* to be Cary Grant."

"Which daft bugger needs a stronger pair of glasses?" Jack guffawed, recognising the voice straight away.

"Or could it be Boris Karloff?" the disembodied voice went on.

"How are things, Alan?" Jack laughed, as he spun round. "Farm still running, despite your best efforts?"

Jenny stood by the grave, virgin witness to this well-rehearsed repartee of jovial insults, a half-smile of regret on her face, that she wasn't party to the past life now unfolding before her.

"My good friend, Alan Myles," Jack began, "I should like you to meet my beautiful wife, Jenny."

"Wow!" Alan said, as he kissed her hand. "Frank Einstein done good. Lucky man. Does *she* need glasses?"

They all laughed at the funny scene of two grown men,

who had not seen each other for at least ten years, talking like two late teenagers used to trading good-humoured insults.

"Did I hear," Jack continued, "that you had married a lady with a white stick and a guide dog?"

"My Josie has *all* her faculties," Alan returned quick as a flash, "I can assure you."

"Josie?" Jack said. "Not Josie Gales?"

"The very same," Alan replied, a self-satisfied grin betraying his joy. "And we have two tiddlers," he went on after a pause," James and Annie. Tell you what, are you in a rush? Only I'm meeting her in Normy, on our way for a coffee and a bun at the Majestic Café. Fancy a chin wag?"

"That would be wonderful," Jenny agreed. "I love to meet Jack's close friends from his school days."

"I wouldn't go so far as to say 'close'," Jack guffawed.

"Or even 'friend'," Alan replied, a wicked grin overtaking his weathered face. "In fact, I barely know him."

"Meet you there in half an hour?" Jack said, as he turned the engine over. "You sure that's OK with you, Jenny?"

"Course it is," she replied with a smile. "It'll be fun. Let's drop the kids off at Mum's, and then we can take our time."

–o–

"This is so much easier than trying to find somewhere to park in Normy," Jack said, as they strolled down Cambridge Street towards Church Lane. "We'll have half an hour with Alan and his wife before spending time with Flo."

"Did she seem a bit … distant to you, Jack?" Jenny asked. "Only, she didn't have much to say."

"Lot on her mind, really, I suppose," he replied, holding her arm closely linked with his. "She might be married to Jim Arkwright by now. You never know."

"I think I'd know if she was," Jenny assured him. "She's not *that* difficult to read."

"It seems an eternity since we lived here," he said, pulling her closer, as they passed the end of their old street. "Any regrets?"

"About leaving this dead-alive hole for my palace in fairy land, you mean?" she laughed. "No fear. I couldn't be happier. I have everything I have ever wanted. Oh, and you, of course, Jack."

He let out a hearty laugh. She was a caution was that Jenny, and no mistake. She always had been able to make him laugh.

"I love you, my little pixie," he said, as they approached the Majestic Café.

"Alan," he quipped, as they neared a nice little table for four in the window, looking out on to the grand edifice that had been the Majestic Cinema before it had been closed in 1964. "And this beautiful young lady has to be either your daughter or your carer?"

"Jack," Alan Myles replied, a huge grin lighting his face. "You look almost human in the cold light of day."

They all burst out laughing while taking off their coats and sitting down to tea and cakes.

"This place brings back a few sad memories for me, I'm afraid," Jack said, settling to his tea and slice of Victoria sponge. "Mi mam and granddad's send offs, but that was a long time ago – and this is now."

"A lot's happened since we last saw each other, when we were eighteen," Alan said, eyeing his cake hungrily.

"You wouldn't believe he had breakfast only a short while ago," Josie said, sipping her tea from a real china cup. "*I* think he's got worms."

"My Jack's exactly the same," Jenny agreed. "Never knows when he's had enough."

"You shouldn't be such wonderful cooks, then," Alan accused.

"Give that man a pat on the back," Jack agreed. "I love mi vittels, but only because Jenny's such a lovely cook, which is more than could be said for mi first wife. Mi granddad allus said that you should eat whatever you could whenever it was offered, because you never knew when you might fall on short commons."

"He always was one for his grub was your Jack," Alan said, "and his beer. Do you remember our Saturday nights—?"

"After rugby at Methley?" Jenny butted in with a smile, much to the amusement of Josie Myles.

"So, you've heard about the legendary sessions with Newky Brown, then?" Alan replied.

"Do you remember that time we were a bit late and missed yon Warmfield bus," Jack went on, "and you picked me up on your 50cc moped?"

"My God, do I!" Alan guffawed. "How much did you weigh then?"

"Sixteen stone," Jack replied. "All muscle."

"Yeah! Right!" Alan scoffed, laughing at his "slight" exaggeration. "You were big though, and strong. Coming from your house on Garth Avenue with you on the pillion was no problem, but climbing Dodsworth Hill and – even worse – the hill up Wakefield Road towards Boundary Lane, the turn off to Warmfield and the Plough beyond, was laughable."

They both chuckled at their shared memory.

"If I remember right," Jack continued, barely able to contain his mirth, "we only managed those hills with the front wheel in the air, and with my little feet and legs paddling us along on the road in a slow run, like two fat blokes on a motorised unicycle. I wouldn't have cared, but it wasn't even a proper pillion seat – more like a tight metal grille that you strapped parcels to."

They all laughed at this conjured image.

"And was the evening worth it?" Josie said, wiping the tears from her cheeks.

"Too right it was!" they both chorused. "All the lads drank the landlord out of goodness knows how many crates of that glorious amber nectar."

"Never felt the same about Newcastle Brown after that session," Alan said, feigning a look of intoxicated nausea.

"So, how did you get into the farming game then, Alan?" Jack asked, once the cake had been polished off. "I mean, you always insisted you would do anything rather than drop in to the family business. Did your dad make you an offer you couldn't refuse?"

"Aye, lad. He did that. He died," Alan replied quietly, acknowledging Jack's look of sympathy. "I did my degree in farm engineering at Leeds, and dropped back home to run the farm. I was just in the graveyard to put some flowers on his grave."

"And?" Jack went on.

"Best thing I ever did," Alan said, a satisfied grin taking hold of his mouth. "Otherwise, I wouldn't have met Josie, and my life would have taken an entirely different path. You?"

"Well," Jack started, his explanation tailing off into the general hubbub of a busy café and commercial thoroughfare, that touched the shop's front step, reminding them all that theirs weren't the only dramas to be unfurling in this little corner of the West Riding.

–o–

"I enjoyed that little interlude, my Jack," Jenny said, linking arms as they climbed Cambridge Street again, "and by the looks of it, everything's all right at Mum's."

"And how do you make that out?" he queried.

"No ambulances or police cars outside the house," she laughed, "but—"

"One Rover 95 that wasn't there before?" he said, casting a puzzled look at his wife.

"Two cars I always hankered after as a teenager," Jack sighed, as he drooled over the sleek, shiny, dark-green lines of the beautiful machine before him. "One was a Mark 10 Jaguar, and the other was a Rover 95 – the poor man's Rolls Royce."

"Be nice if you drooled over me like that," Jenny laughed, poking him in the ribs.

"As you well know, Jenny Ingles," he harrumphed, pulling her closer, "I drool over you every second of every day."

"You say the nicest things," she replied, a grin still stitched to her face. "Now, come on. Business to see to."

"Who on earth can afford a Rover 95, Flo?" Jack laughed, as he hugged Jenny's mother. "I've always…"

His words remained unfinished, as a tall smartly dressed man came into the lounge, bearing a tray laden with cafetière, mugs, and … scones – the quickest way to Jack's heart.

"Something you baked earlier, eh – Mr Arkwright, isn't it?" Jack jumped in quickly.

"And you *have* to be Jack," the older man replied, setting the tray on to the glass coffee table. "Nobody else could possibly fit the description."

"Description?" Jack puzzled.

"Flo's description," Jim explained quietly. "Nobody could be higher in her estimation. So, I'm looking forward to getting to know you, if that's all right with you."

"My pleasure, Mr Arkwright, my pleasure," Jack replied.

"Please," he replied, "it has to be Jim."

"And these little ones have been so good," Flo said, as she led Jessie and little Flo into the room, "I didn't know they were here. Such dear, lovely little poppets."

"I hope they weren't too much trouble for you, Mum," Jenny said, gratefully.

"None at all," her mum replied. "Jim has been amusing them for most of the time. So, he's the one you need to thank."

"Just played a few little games with Jessie, while Florence May sat in the playpen with her teddy and watched," he said. "No trouble at all."

"So, the size is right, eh, Flo?" Jack said quietly, a satisfied smile creasing his mouth corners.

"Too right, Our Jack," she replied, hugging him tightly, "and I *know* it will be right, just like you said it would."

"Jack?" Jenny said, puzzling over the conversations she knew nothing about. "And you said you knew as much as the rest of us?"

"A gentleman *never* breaks a promise, dear," her mother interrupted, "and this one is a gentleman of the highest order."

Jim sat back, a smile of happiness on his face, and took no part in this family discussion but he couldn't wait to make Flo Mae his wife.

"Since we last spoke," Flo went on, "we've had an offer on the house, which we have accepted. Signing day is in two weeks, and then we move. I shall be taking *some* sentimental knick-knacks, so if there's anything you'd like, now's the time."

A hissing silence enclosed the gathering in its unexpected bubble, forcing each into her or his own world of supposition and uncertainty.

"I love your mother dearly," Jim Arkwright's voice burst the bubble finally, "and I mean to make her happy. Neither of us is getting any younger, and we have decided there is still much in this life we would like to do together. I don't want us to leave a scattering of 'what ifs' on the floor when we have gone."

"And your wedding day?" Jenny asked, half-expecting a

non-committal answer.

"Don't know yet," Flo said, confirming her daughter's thoughts. "We may just nip out and do it. It all depends on what's on, where we are, or if there's nothing better to do. I'll let you know."

"What, when you've done it?" Jenny asked, not sure of the response.

"Probably," Flo replied. "To be honest, the event's not important. Our being together is."

"Good on you, Flo," Jack said, a supporting arm round her shoulders. "I'm sure this man will make you happy. Right size, right time. If you need a hand moving, just let me know – as long as it's a Saturday."

"We might just take you up on that, Our Jack," Flo replied, a smile of satisfaction growing.

–o–

"Right size, right time?" Jenny queried as they swooped down Castleford Road, on their way home.

"Something your mum said on the way to ours at Christmas," Jack explained. "She said she would try Jim for size – but not in the way you thought or are thinking now. I was sure I'd explained before?"

"They've really thought it through, haven't they?" she went on, still unsure what she had heard this day. "Do you think she's being a bit previous? I mean…"

"The important thing, as you say, is they have thought seriously about it all," Jack replied. "I've a feeling she knows what she's doing. She is nobody's fool, and will be certain that Jim Arkwright is the man she wants, and *is* sure about."

"Ah, but—" Jenny continued.

"I know," he said. "You're bound to be worried, but just think about the number of times she was concerned about you, and you've not done *too* badly, despite all her qualms."

"Taking up with you was different, though," she protested.

"*How* was it different?" he continued. "As far as I can see, it's no different at all. Unknown and untried male stealing away a beloved female family member. Lots of similarities I can see."

"Mmm," Jenny mumbled, accepting his sense reluctantly.

"Besides," he said, "it's a done deal. They'll be married before long, you mark my words. Just like us they want to be together, and then you will be able to stop worrying about her, once and for all."

# Chapter 8

"Do you realise it's Florence May's first birthday in just over a week," Jenny said, Saturday morning, mid-February, "and we—?"

"Haven't had her baptised yet?" Jack interrupted. "I know. I have no idea where this year's gone, and what we have achieved in the last six months."

"What?" she replied. "Apart from my sister and your brother almost splitting up, our moving house to my fabulous palace, my mum remarrying and not telling us until they had done the deed, her selling her house, and, oh yes, not … having … Flo … christened."

"Very full six months, I would say," Jack agreed. "Two things I should like to do in the next six months, if it's all right with you."

"Oh, yes?" she asked, not sure which way this conversation was leading. "And what, pray, had you in mind?"

"Christening and birthday party for Florence May," he began, a triumphant smile underlining his ideas, "and a week's holiday touring Scotland in the summer."

She was quiet for a few minutes, hinting to Jack she didn't share his enthusiasm, until she leaped at him, a huge grin covering her face. Because he was convinced she was about to tickle him, he drew his neck into the protective barrier formed by his shoulders and clenched his eyes tight shut. When the anticipated incapacitation didn't arrive, he opened an eye to see her standing before him, hands on hips, laughing quietly at the fear lurking in that one eye.

"Don't forget," she went on, "that our two won't be able to car travel *too* far, and Yorkshire's east coast might be far enough. We need, perhaps, to wait until Flo is Jessie's age now, and just stick to holidays at Filey or Brid, or even Scarborough, for now."

"Tell you what," Jack said, an idea pinging into his thoughts, "how about if we see if she can be done at All Saints Church in Normanton, where *we* were both christened? Tradition? And your dad and mi mam could be guests, watching over them?"

Jenny was quiet for a moment or two as a tear gathered at her eye corner, welled and threatened to roll down her cheek, urging several others to follow.

"I think that … that's a wonderful idea," she said quietly, preventing in time the one tear from becoming a cascade. "We've got the whole of your half-term break next week, so Monday might be a good time to visit the church, don't you think?"

"Sounds like the start of a plan," he grinned, "and I think Flo's birthday is on the Sunday. Perfect timing. Christening and party all on one day."

"Then what do you think to paying our Val a visit after that Monday?" Jenny suggested, tentatively. "They always seem to be here, so I thought it was about time we returned the compliment."

"Never thought of that," he grinned. "But will they have enough room to put us all up?"

"We've accommodated them at ours," she continued, "and Mum, don't forget."

"Very true," he said, nodding his agreement. "Shall I phone, or will you?"

"Better leave it to me, I think, my big-footed husband," Jenny laughed. "There *are* ways and means, but yours are neither of those."

–o–

"Not keen on these motorway things," Jenny said, huddling in the seat next to Jack, in the front of the car. "I'll be glad when we get to Val's. Fortunately Flo and Jessie are asleep, but then why wouldn't they be at this daft o'clock? Did we have to set off *so* early?"

"If you're going anywhere of any distance," Jack insisted, "it's always a good idea to set off in reasonable time, I always say."

"But, there's *reasonable* time," she added, with a snigger, "and then there's … *Jack* time. We'll probably be there for breakfast."

"We've had…" he protested, puzzled at her forgetfulness.

"Joke, Jack. Joke," she laughed. "I hope you know the way, because I'll probably be asleep in the next…"

Jack smiled. She was probably right. He had planned the route and set it indelibly in his subconscious and conscious minds – once travelled, never to be forgotten. So, used to his own company and concentration, he rather hoped she would nod off – sooner rather than later.

"Daddy?" Jessie's little voice piped up after almost three hours on the road.

"Yes, my little sweet pea?" he replied, noticing in his rear mirror that she had only just woken up.

"Are we there yet? Only…" she said slowly, jiggling her legs as she indicated her obvious discomfort.

"Yes, Jessie," he said. "Could you hold on for another few minutes? Two more corners, and we're there."

He pulled into the long curving driveway of a large, old detached house, just as Jenny's eyes opened.

"Be long, love?" she asked, gazing out onto a stationary tarmac road. "Only, I could do with… That's our Val in that doorway. We can't be here already. I've only been napping for ten minutes or so."

"Add three hours or so to that," Jack laughed. "We need to move because I think Jess wants the loo. Flo's still asleep."

"She would be," Jenny replied, laughing at his exaggerated show of stretching exercises once his feet hit firm ground. "It's only just breaking light, for goodness' sake."

"Jenny! Jack!" Val shouted, as she strode across the driveway to hug them both. "It's so good to see you all."

"On your own?" Jenny said, yawning and stretching to get some air into her stiff and aching body.

"Joey's out at rugby training, Ed's inside watching cartoons, and Mary," she bustled, "is … reading."

"Reading?" Jack gasped. "But she was never a reader out of choice."

"Just hit her – boom!" Val laughed, pleased at the change. "Can't get her face out of a book now."

"Excellent," Jack said, a smile of understanding spreading over his face. "Her dad was never much of a reader, and I never had the opportunity as a nipper at home, because mi father wouldn't buy me any books."

"William around?" Jenny puzzled, as they settled to a pot of tea and… "Fruit scones. Val, I'm impressed."

"William doesn't teach anymore," Val replied, a look of consternation clouding her face.

"How does that work, then?" Jack said, a little crossly. "Isn't he supposed to provide for his wife and family?"

"Jack," Jenny warned sharply. "She'll tell us in her own time, I'm sure."

"*He* decided he wasn't teaching anymore," Val went on, an edge of sarcasm and annoyance to her words, "and now he works as a 'fitness consultant', in a semi self-employed sort of a way."

"Typical William," Jack sneered. "Never thinks things through as to how his actions might affect other folk."

"So," Jenny asked quietly, not wishing to add to her sister's upset, "is he … at work today?"

"Unfortunately, yes," Val replied, welling up. "So, I'm sorry your brother isn't here to greet you, Jack."

"It's no worry to me, my lovely," Jack said, a huge supportive grin spreading across his face. "At least he's still working, and it's you and the kids we came to see, anyway. I have to say … these scones are wonderful. May I—?"

"Of course you may, Unca Jack," a little but authoritative voice assailed them from the sitting-room doorway, an open book hanging from its hand. "We don't stand on ceremony here, you know."

It was all Jack could do to stop a huge guffaw erupting from his scone-filled mouth.

"Mary," he said, a muffled conversation impossible to sustain through scone and dried fruit. "Wovewy to fee you."

"It's all right, Unca Jack," her level of perceived linguistic understanding and expression several years ahead of *her* eight. "You don't have to talk until you've finished Mum's scone. I'll just have a sit and read until you've finished and are ready."

"If William's working," Jenny asked, readjusting her mental plans, "would it be all right to stay a couple of nights? Only…"

"*Please* stay until the weekend," Val pleaded, desperate to have friendly conversation that was longer than two words. "That'll give us three nights together. I imagine Jack's in school next Monday?"

"Unfortunately, yes," he answered. "Could do without, but bills have to be paid, high-maintenance wives have to be kept, and urchins need to be fed, watered and washed."

"If you're sure?" Jenny asked. "Three nights would be lovely. We've brought a few 'things' to help with the catering and my husband's excessive tastes. They're in the boot, which we'll need to unload pretty soon."

"Is that a 'Mary' I see in the corner," Jack started again, mouth now empty, "with her face in a … book? I thought you weren't so keen on reading stories?"

"I think I must have been," Mary replied, loath to peel her eyes from the page, "but I just hadn't got round to it."

"I think you must be very clever, Mary," Jack said, a mischievous glint in his eye.

"How's that, Unca Jack?" she replied, turning the page.

"Well," he went on, slowing to a drawl, "you can multitask."

"Mull – tee – task," she tried to repeat slowly, frowning at her own attempt, her face still attached to the page. "What's that?"

"It means you can do at least two different things at the same time, young lady," Val interrupted. "It's Uncle Jack's very polite way of saying you are not paying attention to the conversation you are involved with."

"But I *can* do two things at the same time," she insisted, quite put out by the suggestion she was doing something wrong.

"It is extremely rude not to look at the person you are talking to," Val said, becoming cross at Mary's insistence. "Now, put your book down and speak when you are being spoken to. I hope you don't try to treat your teacher like that in school."

"But…" Mary tried to protest.

"No 'buts', young lady," her mother insisted firmly. "It's either take part in our family gathering, or go to your room – *without* your books. Which is it to be?"

"Hello Uncle Jack, Auntie Jenny and Jess," Edward

butted in, as if invisibly emphasising what had been said and cocking a snook at his sister, a huge grin on his face. "I hope you are all well. Long time no see."

Then he was gone, off to finish the homework for the following week his mother had been nagging him about since breaking up. The interaction had lasted all of five seconds.

"How *is* William, then?" Jack asked, half way into his second scone.

"Not the man I married," Val replied quietly. "He was even talking about joining the army as a regular."

"Army?" Jenny gasped, incredulously. "What would he hope to get out of that sort of a move? I should think he'd be too old, anyway."

"I told him he wouldn't have *this* family following him around all over the place," Val harrumphed, eyes flashing at the thought. "There's no way I would either give up our home, or traipse after *him* in barrack-style housing. We belong here. If he did that, we would sell up and move back to the West Riding."

"He's not … you know…?" Jack asked, not really knowing what to say.

"No," she replied. "He gave up that fad when he realised how serious I was. He's like a directionless adolescent at the moment – moves whichever way the wind blows. I dread adverts on the telly searching for this recruit or that trainee – not that he sits with us in the lounge much, anyway."

"I'm so sorry, Val," Jenny said. "You don't deserve any of this."

"Enough of this boring stuff, anyway," Val replied, cheering up. "We've got a few precious days together, thank goodness."

"Now, don't you be doing anything special, or going to any trouble, Val," Jack said, a mischievous glint heralding his humour. "Just three square meals a day, and lots of … tea, will be enough."

They all laughed as Mary shuffled back in to the room, without her book.

"Why so miserable, Mary?" Jack asked, ever ready with his wit and repartee. "Lost a bob and found a tanner?"

"What's a 'bob' and a 'tanner', Unca Jack?" she said, having a little trouble with the pronunciation. "Never heard of that before."

"Your mum and dad never taught you?" he replied, looking at Val, surprised at Mary's ignorance.

"No, Jack," Val butted in. "We don't use such expressions here. Anyway, those coins and terms were ushered out by decimal currency in 1971. So, she has no idea what you mean."

"OK. Sorry," Jack apologised, with a grimace and a shrug.

"Have you seen Mum lately?" Val asked.

"We visited a little while ago, as you know," Jenny started. "We were told a couple of weeks later that they had moved in together and tied the knot, as you also know. Then – nothing. I don't want to keep on badgering, so we'll have to wait for the next instalment."

"I think we should leave them be," Jack butted in, careful – for him – what he said with the two-blood-sisters surrounding him. "She's old enough to please herself and, whatever you may say, she *will* do as she wants. Antagonism is not an easy thing to take back."

"You do phone her regularly, don't you?" Val asked.

"Don't you?" Jenny replied sharply, detecting a slightly admonitory tone. "Of course I do but the question never arises. She always sounds happy and upbeat, telling me where they've been and what they've been doing. I'm beginning to think Jack is right."

"Is he ever not?" Val laughed, more than a little envy edging her words. "I wish I had someone who took the trouble to *care*."

"Val," Jenny sighed quietly, "I wish things were better."

"So do I," she replied, "but it is as it is, unfortunately."

A piercing scream and the pounding of running feet jolted Val back to the here and now as Ed burst through the living room door, as if the hounds of hell were snapping at his flapping coat.

"Mum, quick," he blurted out. "I think Mary's broke something."

"Brok*en*, dear," Val replied, matter of fact. "What do we need to mend now?"

"No," he gabbled on, "I mean broke – broken – something important."

He was interrupted by a sorry little girl dragging herself into the room slowly, baleful eyes telling her all was not right with the limp, misshapen right elbow she carried reluctantly by her side, as if she wished it belonged to somebody else.

"Mary!" she gasped, leaping to her feet. "What on earth have you done?"

"Tripped in an 'ole in the lawn," she whimpered. "It hurts, Mammy."

"How many times have I told your father about that blessed piece of grass," she hissed. "It's all—"

"Not helping, Val," Jenny soothed, touching her sister's arm.

"It's broken," Jack said, dropping to his knees to cast his eyes around the deformed joint. "I did *exactly* the same thing, in exactly the same place, when I was Mary's age. She'll have to have a pot on that. I suppose I should say 'snap', Our Mary."

Always quick on the uptake, Mary's face tried to respond with a faint smile, which quickly returned to a grimace. "It hurts, Unca Jack," she winced, as she turned around slowly.

"Damn," Val said. "No car. William has it for his stupid

job."

"*We* have," Jack said, "but I think you ought to call an ambulance. If they're busy, I'll run her over. Put her out of her misery."

Their laugh at Jack's funny brought the beginnings of a slight smile to Mary's face again, although it evaporated quickly with the next wave of pain.

"The ambulance will be here in five minutes," Val said, as she dropped the large black Bakelite receiver on to its enormous cradle. "So, we need to be ready. Shoes and coat then, young lady."

"Coat needs to be around her shoulders, Val," Jack advised. "She won't be able to thread *that* arm through its armhole. I think she'll have to go barefoot as well."

"Not funny, Unca Jack," Mary said, admonishing him with her big green eyes. "You don't know what it's like."

"Ah, but I do, my little one-armed poppet," he replied quickly. "I did exactly the same thing – TWICE – when I was your age, within eighteen months of each other. So, I *do* know. I can feel it now. I can feel your pain."

"You'll no doubt be in the ambulance with her, Val," Jenny observed, "so we'll see to the boys, and William – if you're not back. When Mary is released, phone and Jack will come pick you up."

"In the meantime," Jack said, with a mischievous twinkle, "we'll be having lunch, so no worries."

"What about me?" Mary whined, a look of horror invading her face at the thought of going without. "I'm hungry, too. What am I going to have?"

"Nothing for you, young lady," Jack warned. "There's no knowing how bad the break is. They may have to anaesthetise you, which means you can't have anything to eat or drink until the bones have been set and potted up."

"Nothing to eat?" she complained. "At all?"

"'Fraid not," he replied, a sympathetic smile coating his face. "If you did, it would make you sick, and the nurses wouldn't allow or like that."

An urgent banging at the front door marked the arrival of the ambulance, much to Mary's consternation.

"Come on then, my girl," Val said, heading for an exciting ride through town to the infirmary. "Sooner we're off, sooner we'll be back."

"Don't let them keep you in!" Jack shouted from the hall, his sense of humour skipping out to the ambulance after his niece.

# Chapter 9

"Well," Jack clucked, as Val and Mary got back with William in tow, "look at you – pot arm and all. You'll find it hard to scratch your nose now."

"No, I won't," Mary replied, a little happier than when she had set off four hours before. "I can use my left hand. See?"

"Never thought of that," Jack laughed. "You are *so* clever, Mary Ingles."

Jack's laugh was infectious, drawing in his niece, too. She loved the silly repartee with her uncle because he made her laugh, now that her age had brought her to an understanding of his humour. They were very similar, Jack and Mary – almost *too* similar to be just uncle and niece. Even *he* recognised the traits in her that he had had when he was her age. It was almost an instinct that allowed him to draw her response to his conversations. Now, breaking her arm in similar fashion – 'tripping in an 'ole' as he had said, too, was too much of a coincidence.

Val recognised this, of course, as did Jenny. She could see similar traits developing between him and *his* daughter, although *she* was a lot younger. He could say and do things that drew both children into his world, because of the shared chemistry, and it fascinated her no end. She enjoyed watching him interacting with children – a bit like a Pied Piper, really.

He was clever, was her Jack, in ways that other people would never know or understand.

"Was your Daddy in the hospital?" Jack asked his niece. "Broken his arm too?"

"Not unless he has a *invisible* pot on *his* arm," she replied quickly, a broader grin crossing from ear to ear. "I saw his car in the par cark."

"*C*ar *p*ark, dear," Val corrected, in passing. "On business. Give him his due, as soon as he knew about Mary's little accident, he stopped what he was doing, and brought us back home."

"And so he should," Jack said, his quick response betraying his disdain for his brother.

"Can I have the pot taken off day after tomorrow, Unca Jack?" Mary asked, her pleading eyes seeking a resounding 'yes' from him.

"I'm afraid not, my little one-armed bandit," Jack replied with a shrug. "Six weeks I should imagine – at least. It *was* with mine, and then you have to have bending exercises to make it completely better – another six weeks. And then—"

"Unca Jack!" Mary exclaimed, throwing up her one good arm in mock shock and surprise, as she had seen him do many times. "My goodness. Six weeks? No."

–o–

"So, what's the new job, William?" Jack asked, as they sat down to a belated sandwich and crisps and coffee.

"You wouldn't understand if I told you," William replied, not even taking the trouble to look up from his lunch. "I can't stay long. I've got calls to make."

"Try me," Jack said, undaunted and unabashed. "What's so difficult to understand about driving about in a car all day? Consultant something or other, *Val* said."

"Sports consultant," William said, as he pushed the

remnants of his snack away from him and made a move to leave.

"Going already?" Jack asked.

"What is it with you people?" William snapped, a rush of anger washing over his face. "Questions, questions, questions. I'm off back to work. Someone has to." With that, he was out of the front door and revving his engine before the others had time to swallow, let alone move.

"Jack," Val said, "I'm *so* sorry for that uncalled-for outburst. I really don't know what's come over him. Now you can see what *we* have to put up with."

"Don't worry on my account, Our Val," Jack replied, a reassuring smile supporting his words. "It's you I feel sorry for. He was quite distant when I was a nipper, but also quite affable at times. I always put it down to the age difference. So, it doesn't affect me."

"Perhaps a bit less … direct next time, eh, Our Jack?" Jenny offered, raising her eyebrows in support of her advice.

"Nay, lass," Val butted in. "Why should Jack change the way he is because William can't be civil? Jack's worth ten of his brother right now."

"Front door?" Jack said, hearing the ominous squeal of protesting hinges crying out for oil.

"It'll be Joey, back from rugby practice," Val smiled, "ravenous as usual, no doubt."

After a few minutes of patient waiting, with no glimpse of number one son, Val wandered to the foot of the stairs, to see the back of her offspring trying to creep quietly to his room.

"Joey?" she said, puzzled why he hadn't joined them. "Not coming in to say hello?"

At the sound of her voice, he froze mid-step, neither turning around nor saying anything. He gripped the handrail, as if to steady himself against falling.

"Joey?" his mother insisted. "Why are you standing there? Is there something the matter? Turn to look at me, please."

"Joey!" she gasped, as she noticed his swollen left eye and cheek bone. "What on earth…?"

At this, Jack had wandered quietly into the hall to see what was causing the delay. Seeing his nephew on the stairs, and the look of alarm and shock on Val's face, he recognised the cause straight away.

"Hard match, eh, Joe?" Jack interrupted, trying to ease a potentially fraught situation. "I should hate to see the other chap. I bet he's in a state."

Joey smiled, appreciating his uncle's attempt at taking the sting out of the confrontation with his mother.

"But, my little boy's injured," she yelled. "We should take him to the hospital to…"

"Val," Jack soothed, "your 'little boy' is now a man, playing the toughest contact game in the world. If he wants to continue and to get better, he has to learn to take all the knocks and injuries in his stride."

"But—" she began to complain again.

"Give him a break, Val," Jack urged. "You can't keep him wrapped in cotton wool forever. He'll be fine. High tackle, eh, Joey? And you…?"

Jack fell quiet and, raising his eyebrows, he nodded and inclined his head slightly in silent recognition of the retaliation Joey had visited on his attacker.

The boy smiled and nodded almost imperceptibly so his mother wouldn't know, appreciating his Uncle Jack's understanding. Shouldn't this have been his dad's role? Shouldn't he have been the one to be watching his back?

"Anyway," Val said, recognising Jack's wisdom with her son, "washed and down quickly. We are all ready for something to eat that Auntie Jenny has prepared. Chop-chop."

"Home-made soup," Jack whooped, as they all sat down

to eat. "My favourite. Followed by bacon sandwiches. Divine."

Jenny and Val laughed at this replay of each time Jack sat down to satisfy his hunger.

"And two injured soldiers to be mindful of," he went on. "If either of you two can't manage – you know – my dish and plate are always big enough to—"

"I think we'll be able to manage, Uncle Jack," Joey replied, the hint of a grotesque smile on his swollen face. "Thank you for the offer, though."

"Not having mine," Mary harrumphed, placing a guarding, potted, shielding arm around her dish to ward off intruders. "Not sure about the bacon, though. I think I might be becoming vegetarian." She drawled the word comically, not too sure of its pronunciation. "Not sure," she added, watching suspiciously her uncle's look of joy. "Might start *that* next week."

She found extreme difficulty wielding her spoon left-handedly, spilling more than reached her lips, but she got there in the end. Although not injured, Ed was still the last to finish, as he always was an inordinately slow eater. Having soup, which should have been a cinch to polish off, made not a scrap of difference.

"Well," Val announced, once they had all settled to various activities, "it looks like we'll be staying here for today. Your father's not home, and your Uncle Jack's car isn't big enough to carry us all, not with two seriously injured bodies in our party, anyway. Any objections to that, anybody?"

–o–

Determined to make his newly chosen job work, William put in all the hours he could spare. Self-employed, and with none of the benefits being a teacher provided – high salary, thirteen weeks holiday, free weekends – life in general was a lot more demanding. He missed a lot of the perks most other normally working people took for granted – weekend lie-ins, time spent with the family, the luxury of chatting with his wife over a cup of coffee. He hadn't done much of *that* in recent history, that was for sure. Had he really missed that aspect of his life?

Then, there had been Samantha. He hadn't seen *that* coming – either the affair or that she had taken him for a patsy. Naïve about relationships in the extreme throughout his life, he had no idea how to put right the hurt he had visited on the one woman who should have been uppermost in his mind all the time. It seemed to him that he was within a whisker of losing her, but what could he do to make things right? He had nobody to turn to for advice. Except for one obvious person, who would give it to him straight. Pragmatic, straight-talking, honest to the point of being brutal.

Would he feel right? Would he be able to ask his brother's advice?

Why not?

Jack was family and had a track record of doing the right things, almost to the point of nausea. *He* was the obvious person to offer solutions to his failing family and social life.

"Jack?" William said, late afternoon, before tea, when he had finally dragged himself away from his work.

"William," Jack replied, knowing there was a simple but searching question to follow. William's simple questions of old had always contained a problem that was too difficult for him to follow to a conclusion. Whatever the question, Jack always gave an honest answer without layering it with too much gloss.

"Fancy a stroll around the garden?" William asked quietly. "Something I need to run by you."

"Of course, Bro," Jack replied, reminding his brother what he had lost sight of during the last year or two, "but why not run it by Val?"

"She's a woman and wouldn't understand," William said, not realising how derogatory *that* sounded. "Besides, I know I can trust you will give an answer no one else would have thought of."

"I'll just get my Indian cloakroom attendant, then," Jack smiled, realising his brother wouldn't understand his funny.

"Your Indian—?" William puzzled.

"Mahatma Coat," Jack replied, deadpan. His funny scraped the top of his brother's head, as it whizzed past with nothing to stop it.

"Going out, lovely?" Jenny asked, as he slid his jersey on before his top coat.

"Just for a stroll with our William," Jack said, winking as he did up his buttons. "I think he wants a bit of advice on his garden."

Jenny smiled, knowing there was more to it than he was letting on by the history they shared and by his wicked glint.

"I'm in a quandary," William started, as they headed slowly for the pavement. A chill breeze threatened to dent William's enthusiasm for walking as they turned the corner into its full force. "I seem to be drawing further and further away from Val and the kids, and I've no idea how to stop the drift."

"Precisely why you should run your concerns past your wife, old chap," Jack advised, pragmatic as ever. "She's a woman and would always understand, the main reason being, of course, that she's your wife of more than fifteen years."

"Do you think?" William asked quietly, not sure where their conversation was heading. When *had* he ever understood his little brother's means of reasoning, even from when he was a nipper? He was a caution, was yon Jack, and a deep one at that.

"*I've* not been in my present job long, but I've been unsettled since day one," Jack began. "It's all been to do with the man in charge – and other stuff. Should I get another job? Should I get out? Dichotomy as to which way to jump. Usual man stuff about wanting the best for family and self, I suppose. So, I talked it through with Jenny, as I always do, and she settled my mind. Val *will* support you, despite your blip with Samantha, because she wants you all to be happy, with a roof over your heads and food in your bellies."

"Sensible and wise as ever, eh, Our Jack," William said, smiling. He *was* glad he had him as a brother but he couldn't ever tell him so, even though he might want to. Whereas Jack was open and not afraid to express his feelings and opinions, William was closed, introverted, finding difficulty saying what was in his mind. Chalk and cheese. Garlic and lavender.

"Talk to her, man," Jack urged. "She *is* your wife, and still wants to be. Trust me on this. If she didn't love you, we wouldn't be having this conversation. You have a longish, difficult road to traipse to prove that you still love *her* – you do still love her, don't you?"

"Course I do," William insisted, "but—"

"Then, show her," Jack butted in, "if you really mean it. I shall always be around if you want to talk and take advice from a much, much younger person."

"Steady," William laughed. "You may be my wise younger brother, but you're not too old to get a clip."

Jack joined in the laughter, realising it hadn't happened between them for a long time and was the first step on his road to redemption.

"It won't be easy, Our William," Jack warned. "It never is when you have to try to persuade a woman you've been a twat, and don't want to be one anymore. A lot of very hard, in-depth persuading ahead, I'm afraid. All the sort of stuff you've always taken for granted. You'll have to bring out your A game to work on. The rest of your life is all about *her*.

Unconditional."

"I don't know whether I can…" William said, doubts creasing his face.

"Then," Jack emphasised deliberately, "you have to call it a day, because if you don't, *she* will."

"And how do you know that…?" William asked, puzzled as to how his brother seemed to know *his* wife better than *he* did.

"She's said so," Jack advised, bluntly, "in very clear and honest words."

The air and atmosphere about them became cooler, as they turned the corner back towards home and physical warmth. A straightforward but entirely naïve sort of a chap, William's mind was now completely confused about the direction he should take, or what he should do to retrieve the marriage and his life that were slipping inexorably from his grasp.

# Chapter 10

Early Sunday morning – the day after they had returned from Val's – late February cold seemed to have seeped into the very fabric of the house. The central heating hadn't yet got into its stride, even though Jack had set it for auto turn on. This new programming still tickled Jenny because, seemingly, without interference, the rooms could be transformed from clap-cold to passably and livably warm in no time, consigning coal-fired inefficiency to prehistoric memory.

Jack was up, performing his ablutions ready for porridge time, giving Jenny a much-enjoyed lie-in under her warm eiderdown and blanket, when the jarringly strident jangle of the telephone disturbed her peace. Realising her husband was in the middle of shaving, she grabbed the bedroom's extension receiver under the covers, and closed out the cold again. Jenny's mumbled conversations, and occasional muffled chuckle, were all he could catch.

"Who on earth was that at this time of day?" Jack asked, annoyance furrowing his brow. "I trust you told them to bugger off."

"It was our Val," she replied, ignoring his Jackness, "thanking us for being with her and telling me how much she enjoyed our company, despite the two injuries."

"And she couldn't have waited until later to tell you that?"

Jack replied quickly.

"That wasn't the only thing she said," Jenny continued, undeterred. "She said, and I quote 'I can only guess what Jack said to William on their walk together, but, thankfully, it worked'."

"And what's that supposed to mean?" he said, pulling his clothes on. "I onny told him the truth, as I saw it."

"She said they had had a long heart-to-heart after we'd gone, early yesterday," Jenny went on, a smile on her face, knowing that *this* was all Jack's doing, "and not only does he want to get back to where they were pre-fling, he wants to get back into teaching."

"Well, now," Jack said, "sense at last. It always did take a boot to his backside to galvanise Our William into some sort of forward movement. Hopefully, this'll herald the swing back to normality in our sort of universe. Pigs might fly."

"You don't believe in your brother's ability to deliver, then, Our Jack?" Jenny said, with a smile.

"The only belief I have in William, my lovely woman," he added, cynically, "is what's brought to me by my own two eyes."

"Last day of your holiday today, Our Jack," Jenny pointed out. "Anything you'd like to do?"

"It's early and sunny enough," he said, pointing out the clear blue sky, "to do either Roundhay Park or ... Malham Tarn?"

"Funny you should say that," she laughed, "but I just happen to have a nice batch of corned beef sandwiches in yon new-fangled fridge that I med last night."

"Our psychic Jenny wins the day again!" Jack yahooed in delight. "Malham it is then. Just need—"

"To make a flask," she added quickly, "and summat for Our Jessie and Flo. Then we're about ready. Well, come on then cowboy, finish your porridge, and let's away. We need to make the best of the day's unusual February sunshine."

"Just one minute," Jack replied, chasing the last spoonful of porridge around his dish. The pieces of fruit had already gone down his throat in the appropriate order, and all that remained was alphabetical porridge and tea. "Nearly there."

"Jessie," Jenny uttered in mock shock, as she turned to her daughter, "where are all those soldiers and that goggy egg?"

"They've marched down to my tummy, Mummy," she replied, a broad grin crossing her face, "and taken my egg with them. Off to battle to make me big and strong. Look."

She jumped up from her chair, flexing her arm muscles several times to prove her point, making Jenny and Jack laugh at the intensely serious look on her face at every flex.

"Mammy," Flo gurgled, trying to imitate her sister, flexing her chubby arms in a parody of Jessie's action, making them all laugh again as they cleared the table and made ready for their outing.

"Just nipping to the bathroom before I get changed," Jack shouted, as he reached the top of the stairs.

As he clicked the bathroom door shut, the telephone spat into life once again, urging them not to ignore its insistence.

"Ingles' residence," Jenny chirruped, as she engaged the receiver. "Lady of the house speaking."

Jack adored his family time, begrudging anything that might interrupt or disrupt its path. All he needed to make his life perfect was his family and his home. Jenny and Jessie and Flo provided the necessary ingredients to make his existence as near to perfect as it could be.

"Somebody else wanting a piece of the Ingles family?" Jack said, grinning broadly.

"You'll never guess who's invited us out for the day," Jenny teased.

"Mmm," Jack began to think, "let me see. It can't be Val

and co because they are too far away. It wouldn't be your mam, because … it wouldn't. Queen of Sheba? Your ex-husband? My ex…? Not even going there. Not David and Irene and Jessie and Imogen Rose, by any vague chance?"

"Nope," Jenny said, giggling.

"Then who, for goodness' sake?" he replied. "I don't know anybody else."

"Irene," Jenny said, unable to stop giggling.

"But I said…" he protested.

"Irene needs us to go over for the day," Jenny urged, quietly persuasive. "David's away for the week, and doesn't come back until early evening. She's not seen him all week, and needs some company."

"No Malham, then," he said, disappointment wrapping up his words. "And, what about mi corned beef sandwiches?"

"You'll just have to take them for your snap tomorrow, that's all," she replied with a patiently understanding smile.

"So, why's David away?" Jack puzzled. "It's holiday, for goodness' sake."

"I suppose we'll find out – if we ever get there," Jenny said, sarcastically. "Time to go, Our Jack?"

"Course it is, SB," Jack replied. "We're ready, aren't we, Jessie."

"Yes, Daddy," she said seriously. "Course we are. Are we going to Malham, then?"

"Uncle David and Auntie Irene have asked us to go to their house instead," Jack said, taking hold of her proffered hand. "You'll be able to play with their daughter. Do you remember her?"

"Of course I do," she replied, an indulgent smile on her lips. "I like Jessie. She makes me laugh, and lets me play with her dolls. She has more dolls than me."

"OK," Jack said, raising his hands in submission, "point taken."

"SB?" Jenny asked, as she settled in the car next to him.

"Silly—" he started.

"Bugger," she finished, laughing as their house receded into the distance.

–o–

The click of the outside door lock and the protesting whine of its hinges, drew their attention to the lounge doorway.

"Hello," a familiar voice bounced into the front room, "Irene and Jessie and Imogen Rose. I'm home. Hello … Jack and Jenny and Jessie, again, and Flo. Lovely to see you. Didn't know you were coming. Or else I would have got back … two minutes earlier."

"Tea's almost ready," Irene promised, as she kissed her husband on her way to the kitchen. "Drinks are poured, and would you please open this bottle of Champagne I have here, in my chilled hand?"

"Champagne?" Jack queried. "I didn't realise we had become so important."

"There is a reason," Irene answered quickly, "that David will tell you, once he has changed and washed and … opened the bottle."

Jenny tossed a surprised and intrigued glance across to her husband, which he batted straight back at her. His arched eyebrows and slightly inclined head told her he hadn't the slightest inkling what was going on. Another child? She didn't *look* pregnant. Then, what?

"Irene?" Jenny asked, once Jack's cousin had returned to the room.

"Sorry," Irene said, a huge smile betraying her excitement at the news David was about to deliver, "but you'll have to wait until…"

"I'm here, my friends," David announced, as he burst through the door. "I know you've missed me – now, where's that bottle?"

"Finished work at three o'clock on a Sunday afternoon in the holidays, David?" Jack asked, glass of Champagne in his hand. "Come on. What gives? And Champagne?"

"Well, actually," David started, settling into his chair by the roaring log fire, "it's a lengthy story, but..."

His voice tailed away to that comfortable drone he dropped into when telling a tale, as children's happy laughter from upstairs mingled with the cracking and hissing logs that spat their yellow flames up the chimney, lighting up the little globes of soot, plugged into the fireback as they passed like some ethereal lamplighter. Icy February rain had started to lace the windows, harbinger of snow that might follow.

"...and because Mr Barchester can't tell how long looking after his mother might take," his voice faded back in to the room, "that leaves me in charge."

"When does this take effect?" Jenny asked, both pleased and concerned for their friend in equal measures. "It's a lot of work to drop on your shoulders, isn't it?"

"It takes effect as of ... now," he answered, his hallmark huge grin spreading across his face. "He's taking sabbatical leave on compassionate grounds, and the Authority is prepared to let him, because he's so good at what he does."

"What will he do for money?" Jenny asked again, ignorant of the machinations of education authority workings. "Will he get paid?"

"The usual, I should think," Jack said. "Hundred days full pay, hundred days half pay, and then bugger all, as if he were on sick, I should imagine."

"But, what about you, David?" Jenny puzzled again, not able to come to terms with all these shenanigans.

"Well," he grinned again, "that's where it gets interesting. I take over next week ... on a permanent contract. So, that makes me—"

"Substantive Head teacher of Broughton County Junior School," Jack whooped. "About time, too, if you ask me … and nobody has."

"The next interesting bit," David went on, sliding to the edge of his chair and looking directly at Jack, eyebrows raised and eyes unblinking, "is that there will be a vacancy, from next September, for a permanent, substantive deputy head teacher at … Broughton County Junior School."

"And your reason for looking at me in that expectant sort of a way is?" Jack responded, a tantalising grin appearing, daring his friend to go further. He hadn't been sure about this new school he inhabited from day one, thinking many a time that he had made a huge mistake. How he wished he had stayed at Broughton. And now…

"The only way I can make my actions any clearer," David said, with an indulgent smile, "is to say very pointedly, that the job is yours … if you want it. Ninety-nine-point-nine percent stitched on."

"Mmm," Jack murmured, a seriously thoughtful look invading his eyes. "Salary?"

"A reasonable amount more than you are getting now," David answered him, knowing how important was providing a good life for his family.

"Jenny?" Jack said, turning to his wife for her opinion.

"Don't ask *me*," she replied carefully. "You will make the right decision for us, I'm certain. If it were up to me, I know what I would do."

"And that is?" Jack laughed, knowing what her answer would be. "You're going to tell me … when I've made my decision, aren't you?"

"You know me *so* well," she replied, raising her eyebrows.

"Can I have time to think about it, old chap?" Jack asked David. "Only…"

"Course you can," he replied, "but don't leave it too long.

Closing date is a week on Friday."

"OK," Jack drawled, after a moment's pregnant silence. "I've thought about it, and … I'll take it. Jenny?"

"My answer exactly," she laughed, throwing herself at him, excitement oozing from every pore. "At last, something to get your teeth into."

"Excellent," David enthused. "This calls for a *real* celebration."

–o–

"Are you sure this change of school is what you want?" Jenny asked as they left Scott Hall behind. "I mean, middle schooling was what you always wanted, wasn't it?"

"Aye, lass, it was," Jack sighed, "but I wasn't to know I'd be ruled by the dictatorial dodo I have now, or that the school would turn out to be a cold, heartless and forbidding wasteland. You know me, Jenny. I never give up, but I simply can't work under such boorish conditions and give my best."

"I understand, my lovely," she answered, "but you don't have to explain to me. As you've not been there long, will there be a problem? I mean, will he try to stop you leaving?"

"Head teachers have the power to stop teachers from leaving only if the prospective *new* head believes the telephoned lies the old head gives," Jack said disdainfully.

"Don't they *have* to give a written reference, then?" Jenny puzzled.

"They don't have to give a reference at all," he replied with a shrug, "except that if they wish to stop you, they pick up the telephone and pour a litany of lies down the receiver. No proof of what they've said. Unwritten tradition that's supported by all of them. Except for one. David Aston *wants* to be my new head teacher."

"So, when will you tell your present head?" Jenny asked, as the traffic lights on the junction with Street Lane at

Moortown Corner slowed them to a brief standstill.

"The last date for handing in notice for a September start," Jack explained, "is the end of May. So, David's set the interviews for the week before we break up for our Whitsuntide holiday. I'll tell Byrne I have an interview the day before, and David's decided not to ask for a reference. That way, I can hand in my notice just before we break up, as the last day of May falls within the holiday week, leaving Byrne in a cul-de-sac. No room to manoeuvre."

"Clever," she said, a smile skirting her lips. "Whose idea was that? As if I didn't know."

"Well," he replied, "I had a bit of a part to play, I think. Serves him right. I'm a good teacher. *I* know that, and I was prepared to stay and give it my best. I've done that, but things have to be done his way, without question, and it's that last bit I can't stomach. Me and my principles, eh?"

"It's those principles that make you my Jack, lovely man," Jenny said quietly. "Don't ever change that."

"Mammy?" a little voice from the back of the car crept into their conversation. "Are we home yet? Only, I feel a little sleepy and I need a wee."

"OK, little one," Jenny said, turning round to attend to her daughter, "we'll be home and ready for bed in a few minutes. Can you hold on?"

"Think so," Jessie said, through a yawn and a jiggle.

–o–

"Just about time for a cup of tea and a nibble before bed, eh, Jen?" Jack suggested as he locked and bolted the front door.

"Done a lot this week," she replied. "Shame it's back to work for you tomorrow, even if the children aren't there."

"Going to be another boring and cold day at the office, I'm afraid," he said, a heavy sigh emphasising his feelings. "Roll on Christmas."

# Chapter 11

"**B**loody hell!" Jack gasped as he shouldered his way into school on Monday morning. "It's like a flaming ice box in here."

His breath spurted from his mouth, almost turning to icicles as he uttered his greeting to the freezing crush hall. The weather had been uncharacteristically mild for February during the half-term break, and now the forecasters' guesses had begun to coincide with reality.

"Winter drawers on, eh, Jack?" Big Brian guffawed as he followed him into the fridge they laughingly called a staff room. "I hope you've brought your long johns, a few extra layers, and a hot water bottle?"

"Didn't expect it to be *this* cold," Jack uttered, an involuntary shiver convulsing his body. "Have we no heat at all?"

"Ladies and gentlemen, please," the deputy's voice drew everyone's attention. "You will have noticed already that the school isn't quite as warm as it might be, coming back from our half-term break. Parents have been asked to keep their children at home today – except for those in the huts. *Those* classrooms have their own independent electric heaters, and so teaching should be possible there. It does mean, however, that they can't come into main school for any lessons they might be due to have."

"Normal timetable, then, as near as possible, for those of us out there?" Jack asked, careful not to ruffle any feathers by being *too* direct.

"That's right," Tom answered slowly, wondering what might be coming next. "Register as usual, and do what you can."

"And if *those* children don't turn up?" Jack went on.

"Let us know," Tom answered quickly, "and we'll reassign."

"Reassign?" an anonymous voice from the depths of the staff room spat out. "What does that mean?"

"We'll sort it out if it happens," the deputy answered. "You'll notice that each classroom on the ground floor has a large calor gas heater installed that should provide enough working heat for—"

"For what?" the same voice insisted. "All bloody day doing—?"

"Work, preparation, marking, and—" Connie, the senior mistress butted in urgently, seeing that Tom was about to take a verbal beating.

"Couldn't we have done that at home?" Miss Tidy's little voice chipped in. "Is it because either we can't be trusted or, worse, we can't be seen to be having a few days off more than our quota?"

"Head's orders, I'm afraid," Tom jumped in lamely.

"And where's he today?" Anonymous Voice piped in to huge guffaws. "Offices? Somewhere warm? Won't see him until May, *I* bet."

"I'm sorry, Tom," Keith Cadbury, the science teacher, added, "but if I begin to get chilly, I'm off. My condition won't allow me to stay."

"And what condition's that, Keith?" Big Brian piped up.

"I'm allergic to ... cold," Keith replied, deadpan. "It makes me feel ... less warm."

That sentiment resonated among the whole staff,

with 'hear hear' and huge guffaws supporting his feelings throughout. It seemed that more than Jack shared his principles – when their well-being was affected. Then why hadn't they supported him earlier, when he had articulated *his* thoughts? He couldn't help feeling that today's events had cemented his pending move and had expunged any doubts he might have harboured.

"I take it *your* room is warm, Tom?" Big Brian said again, a huge smile and twinkle daring the deputy and senior mistress to deny it. Tom smiled nervously, as he threaded his way through a muttering and disgruntled staff throng.

"I don't know whether any of you have seen the thumping great gas heaters in the downstairs rooms?" John Franklyn interrupted. "I don't know which ark they came out of but they give out little heat, create a huge amount of condensation and are, frankly, dangerous. I for one won't be spending much time in there. I've called the union area rep in to give an opinion."

Faint applause mixed with cries of 'good man' and 'attaboy' greeted his words, setting a tentative base for militancy. Bob Byrne had his first insurrection in the making and Jack had had nothing to do with it. So, there *was* life in this otherwise inanimate body of introspective and seemingly uncaring people – but only when matters affected them.

–o–

"How was your day today, lovely man?" Jenny asked, as they sat in the lounge together, wisps of steam spiralling from their mugs and the teapot spout.

"Damnably cold and uncomfortable," he answered, glad to be settling in the one place of sanity for him, in the whole world. "No central heating, no children, and no head teacher."

"Then, why weren't you allowed to come home sooner?" she puzzled. "Bit inhumane, isn't it?"

"Not only inhumane," Jack continued, a cloud nestling in his face, "but unsafe and illegal, too. The union rep on the staff brought in the area union organiser to look at the situation and, after consultation with head office, he called everyone out, and informed the education department that nobody would be back in school until the boiler has been fixed."

"Jack?" she drawled, a smile sneaking up on her.

"None of my doing," he laughed. "It seems the rest of the staff has grown a spine. To make matters worse, that toad of a head teacher hasn't been in school all day. Important meetings, the deputy said. Nobody believed a word of it."

"Does that mean you don't have to go back tomorrow?" she said, on the point of jumping up and down with glee.

"Indeed, it does, my little pixie," he said, nestling back into the settee's cushions, a huge grin creeping up on Jenny and Jack slowly.

"OK," she whooped. "Where are you going to take us?"

"Nowhere, I'm afraid," he said, screwing up his face in a disappointed grimace. "The agreement is that we stay at home to do work in preparation for when the school reopens. Now, as I have already done that, it means we can just … be together."

"You do realise what this means, I hope?" she warned. "When I've taken our Jessie to school?"

Jack grinned in anticipation and approval at the suggestion he knew she was making. For once, they could spend *quality* time together, on their own. No interruptions. No seeing to anyone, save Flo. No disturbances. No distractions. No way!

–o–

"Half past eight?" Jenny said, slightly startled by the tight clack of the letterbox, as she sat to welcome her porridge into her life. "He's early, isn't he?"

"You never know these days," Jack replied, as he dished his idea of the best meal of the day. "I wonder if it's anything to do with the time they get up? Late up, late post."

"I wouldn't let postman Derek, across the road, hear you say that," Jenny laughed. "He's always up and out by half five."

"I don't think I could finish *my* breakfast by school time, Mammy," Jessie's thin little voice warned, "so can I stay at home to try to finish it, please?"

"And why is that, then?" Jenny asked, suppressing a giggle and throwing a knowing wink at Jack. "You feeling poorly, too?"

"Er, well, I think so," her little voice started to waver in sympathy. "I *think* I feel poorly."

"Then, if you feel poorly," Jenny said slowly, "perhaps we need to take you to see Dr Blomfield, who will have to give you some nasty-tasting medicine, and you will have to stay in bed."

"I don't think I feel poorly anymore," Jessie said, changing her mind about that medicine stuff. "Can I stay anyway…?"

"Because?" Jenny asked, a slight creasing of her mouth corners betraying her mirth.

"Because … Daddy's staying at home, and—" Jessie blurted out.

"How about if *I* take you to school," Jack suggested, plucking her from her chair, "and collect you again at lunchtime? The bit in between will go by very quickly, and it won't seem like you've been away at all. How does that sound?"

"Yes, please," she replied, excitedly bouncing up and down in his arms. "*Then* can I stay at home?"

They laughed happily together as Jenny readied her for her usual half day at nursery.

"I'll be back in no time, Jen," Jack promised his wife as

he reversed on to the road. "Have that kettle on, see what the postman's brought, and then…"

–o–

"You're not going to like this," Jenny said, once he was back in the lounge.

"Why's that, then, my lovely?" Jack sighed, smiling at what she might say at his expense. "Have you spent *all* our fortune, leaving us having to raid the children's piggy banks?"

"Solicitor's letter, I'm afraid," Jenny replied, a grimace disfiguring her face.

"Don't tell me," he said, a deep frown betraying his disdain. "Lee?"

"'Fraid so, my lovely," she sighed, watching his reaction.

"And?" he answered, the disdain melting quickly. "Don't keep me in suspenders. She's offering me money? A share of her dad's estate, perhaps?"

"Mmm," he mumbled, once he had read the official letter. "I knew we'd have to pay *something* towards Sam's upkeep, but it has to be proportionate – and those demands are definitely *not* proportionate. We'll have to fight what she is claiming."

"Do we have enough money to employ a solicitor, though?" Jenny asked, not too sure where this was leading.

"Who said anything about paying a legal leech?" Jack guffawed. "I'll conduct our attack myself. Fortunately, I know enough about the law to know where our rights lie, and I have kept chapter and verse on everything that's gone on. It should be a slam dunk."

"Slam dunk?" Jenny puzzled. "Legal terminology? You are so clever."

"Yes, I am, aren't I," he smiled, puffing out his chest and twanging his imaginary trouser bracers with his thumbs. "Basketball, actually. Easy shot at goal. Certain score."

"Then, how are you going to go about raising our case?" she wondered. "Won't you need some advice at least?"

"We'll employ the time-honoured principles of haggling, my sweet," he explained. "We start from the point we consider is a fair and equitable amount, and that's not the two hundred pounds a month she's asking for."

"Plus," Jenny chipped in, warming to the fray, "she's quite able to work, particularly when Sam's at school."

"If he ever *goes* to school," Jack answered sceptically.

"Not like you to be so cynical, Jack," she replied with a smile.

"I thought I knew her when I was married to her," Jack snorted, "but I found, to my cost, how wrong I was. It turns out she has always been secretive and sly."

"Apart from how she treated you," Jenny asked, surprised at the conclusion he had reached, "how do you know? I always knew you worked stuff out that us mere mortals would have no idea about, but I never had you down for a mind reader."

"I forgot to tell you, didn't I," he explained, a light bulb flashing in his brain. "How he knew where I was I don't know, but I got a quick telephone call at school from her brother, John Pierre, a week or so ago, just before half-term break. All the stuff about Florence May's celebrations pushed it out of my mind."

"I don't know anything about him," Jenny said, lips pursing and a puzzled look lowering her brow. "Do I?"

Jack's explanation about the blazing rows they'd had surrounding her brother helped to paint her a graphic picture of Lee's unbalanced nature.

"He'd heard from his dad about the problems with this English dude," Jack explained further, "which set alarm bells jangling. He's coming to England for a few weeks sometime soon on business, and suggested we meet."

"Turn up for the books and no mistake," Jenny said with

a sharp laugh.

–o–

Unfortunately for Jack and his family, the 'extra' holiday didn't last long. Within a couple of days the old boiler had been fixed and everyone was ushered back to normality. If the head had had his way everyone would have been docked an appropriate amount of pay, but he had been advised by his deputy that not only was that illegal but also he would have had a full-scale mutiny on his hands. Lynching drifted into mind.

Not a nice man at the best of times, rumour had it that Byrne had been caught in *flagrante delicto* with a local librarian in her store room. Whether this bore any truth or was apocryphal, it left a reasonable doubt in most minds. However, Jack was still unsure as to whether this head was the right man for this job. He supposed that experience, as such, and significant connections were the sole prerequisites for being a head teacher. *He* would be judged, no doubt, on how his staff acquitted themselves within *their* roles.

His boast had always been that in his previous schools all his teachers were so happy they never wanted to leave. However, a further rumour bouncing along with the other told of a man who never provided a reference for any teacher who wanted to leave. The apocryphal epilogue to this saga told of the only young teacher to escape because of a fortnight's illness, which kept Mr Byrne from school. During that time, because no one was available to bar his way, that bright young man was able to forge a successful career elsewhere.

"Linda?" Jack said, as he caught up with the young French teacher on their way to morning break coffee.

"Jack," she replied. "What can I do you for?"

"I've been thinking about *you* for a while now," he said, a studied frown giving nothing away.

"Oo, I say," she laughed. "Careful. People will talk."

Ignoring her sense of humour, he said, "I have a huge amount to do these days, what with head of year, head of French, teaching French, and teaching class, all with precious little free time. So, I was wondering how you might be fixed for taking over the French department?"

"You cannot be serious," she gasped, after a moment's stunned silence.

"Oh yes I can be," he replied, trying not to appear *too* eager. "If you might be up for it, I'll have a word with Tom to square it with the head."

"Hang on a bit," she interrupted, unsure what he was asking. "Pay? Promotion? How would they all hang together?"

"I should need to know whether you would be interested in taking it off my hands first," he insisted. "If we could work something out it would be good for you, and I would get to focus on what was important to *me*. That is definitely not being in charge of a department, as well as all the other stuff I have to do."

"What about Chris?" she replied, just before the staff room door.

"What about him?" Jack went on. "He's happy with his lot; to be honest, he's finding life a bit of a challenge as it is."

"Did you ask him about this?" she probed, ever on the offensive.

"Heavens, no," he said, a little perturbed by her aggressive attitude. "Look, if you're not interested, just forget what I've said, and we'll carry on as we are – me overburdened, and you, well, going nowhere."

"I wasn't meaning that," she butted in quickly, not wishing to let half an opportunity slip by. "It's just that I need to be certain."

"Of?" he said, becoming bored with this conversation,

which seemed to be heading into the ether.

"That it's a *genuine* possibility," she added, "and not a throw-away chat line."

"Cynical bugger," he said, an indulgent half-smile forcing its way into his face. "Even though we've not known each other long, I would have thought by now you would have realised I don't say stuff just as conversation fillers. Yes or no? Make up your mind."

"Yes!" she replied forcefully, open, eager face re-emphasising her enthusiasm, much to the surprise of the senior mistress, who passed them on the staff-room threshold.

–o–

"And it makes complete sense," Jack explained in Tom's office that lunchtime. "You're giving a young and talented teacher the incentive to want to stay here, and allowing me the space to attend to what's important without being overburdened. I know there's room on the promotion ladder to reward this sort of incentive. The only thing I want out of this is to know I can devote *all* my time and energy into my area of expertise."

"Sounds sense to me, Jack," Tom replied. "I'll take your proposal to the head tomorrow, along with my backing."

"Thanks, Tom," Jack said. "It means a lot."

"And," the deputy continued, "thank *you*."

"For what?" Jack puzzled. "Not done owt to warrant anybody's thanks, least of all yours."

"For bringing your ideas to *me*, rather than taking them to the head," Tom explained. "If you had gone straight to the top, like as not he would have refused. This way, there's a much greater chance it will be listened to, at least."

Then, after a moment's silence, he said, "You know, Jack, the head has a high regard for your abilities, despite what you might think about him."

"He has a funny way of showing it," Jack replied, a resigned smile betraying his scepticism.

"Your movement through the ranks would be swift with his backing," Tom went on.

"Do I detect the presence of an 'if' about to fall from your lips?" Jack butted in.

"Professional progress in this job has always been down to doing the 'necessary extra', given that performance in the classroom etc is up to scratch, of course," Tom added.

"Necessary extra?" Jack puzzled.

"Football team, swimming lessons after school," Tom explained. "Something that shows you are committed to the school's community in its widest sense."

"So, managing in-school educational developments to ensure best practice for the benefit of the vast *majority* of the children, isn't enough?" Jack continued, sharply.

"Put whatever spin on it that you will," Tom re-emphasised firmly, "you won't progress very far without, at least not under *this* head, anyway."

"So, football team and stamp club here I come, then," Jack said, with a degree of sarcasm, as he headed for the door. "Anyway, thanks for the advice, Tom. Sound, pragmatic and honest, as ever. Just how I like it."

# *Chapter 12*

"Well, my sweet lady," Jack cooed, as he settled in his palace, next to his queen, in their soft poofy thrones, Saturday morning after porridge, "this past week has made me more determined than ever to set up shop in David's camp."

"What have they done to you now, my man?" Jenny said, squinting at him over the edge of her tea mug as she sipped. She had no idea how Jack could drink such hot fluid so quickly. 'Suffer wi' thi stomach,' Marion had always said, 'drinking it too 'ot'.

"Don't you do enough to justify your pay in that place?" Jenny said, once she had heard his reasoning. She was in danger of becoming incensed at the demands being placed on his broad but accepting shoulders. "And for what? I know what you do and how much thought and effort you put into it. And now they want you to do—?"

"The 'necessary extra'," he spat out with disdain and disgust. "I don't know what it is with this teaching lark, but the powers that be always seem to want to squeeze the last ounce out of you before they allow you to move on. In the forties and fifties, it was who you knew and which local councillors you chose as drinking buddies – certainly where *we* came from that moved along your career. Now it's all this unnecessary *extra* stuff you are expected to do, which is irrelevant to the prime reason for teaching in the first place and, in some cases, *counter*-productive…"

"Children," she added, a slight smile of pride recognising his worth.

"…and how would my running an out-of-hours football team help some of the maths strugglers or social misfits in my class?" he growled disdainfully.

"Has David heard from your present head yet?" Jenny asked, confused by this mélange of incomprehensible jargon.

"He hasn't said, but I don't think so," Jack replied, as he finished his tea and scone. "It'll be Easter holidays before long, so that means just over a month and a half to resignation day. David and I agreed that I should hand it in a few days before the end of May, shortly after the interview."

"But," she said, puzzled by a very important question that had occurred to her on one or two occasions, "what if you don't get an interview? Or worse, you don't get the job at interview? Could *that* happen?"

"Anything could happen, I suppose," he replied. "Nothing's stitched on in this crazy world. Ninety-nine-point-nine percent, David assures me, but even *he* can't guarantee it. All I can do is my best and hope sense prevails."

"Who on earth's that?" Jenny said, as a tentative tap at the front door heralded an intruder.

"I'll go, sweetness," he replied. "I'll get rid of them with one of my stern looks."

She laughed at the funny face he pulled, as he prised himself out of his warm and comfortable settee corner. He was funny, her Jack, although sometimes the humour *was* unintentional and unexpected. She heard good-humoured mutterings, and then … silence, before Jack's voice re-entered the room, to say…

"Jenny, I should like you to meet John Pierre Genet, all the way from Canada."

"Phew," Jenny exhaled deeply once their visitor had gone. "What just happened?"

"Fortune just dropped a gold nugget in our lap, that's what happened," Jack replied, a satisfied smile plastered across his face.

"The cheating, lying…" Jenny started. "To think she could do that to *you*."

"I was duped," he said, a resigned look taking over. "How naïve was that?"

"She was clever, Jack," Jenny explained, "making you think she was innocent and would do all the stuff you both agreed to. I was taken in, too, by that toad that got me pregnant. Promises, eh?"

"What John Pierre told us gives us a rather large stick with which to whack his sister," Jack replied, "and whack her I will, if she tries any funny business."

"Door again," Jenny interrupted, to the insistent rattle of the letter flap. "Like bloomin' Briggate today, we are so much in demand."

Jack was at the hall doorway before she could remove the mug from her lips, and he was back in half the time. "Somebody a bit more important, my love," he said, a huge grin joining his ears. "I'll put the kettle on while you entertain our 'new' guests."

"Irene! David!" Jenny burst out, joy in her eyes. "Good to see you both. No offspring today?"

"Mum's got them," Irene sighed, as she plopped into the armchair. "Says she doesn't see them half often enough, so who are we to argue? Yours?"

"Playing upstairs in their playroom," Jenny replied. "How long have we got you for?"

"As long as you can cope with my acerbic wit and damned good looks," David butted in.

"You're staying only ten minutes, then?" Jack quipped, as he put down his tray on the coffee table.

Their collective mirth wiped the tense situation with Jack's ex-wife's family, and reminded him of the joy of having good friends and true family around. The two couples were very similar in many ways, with shared values, experiences, and an overriding urge to provide for their families. They had a great deal to thank each other for, not the least of which was a sixth sense that allowed them to draw each other out of stressful situations.

Irene and David were members of that select band to whom their door was always open without the need for invitation.

"Staying over tonight?" Jack asked as he poured a wee dram of malt whisky for David and himself. The only thing Jack loved more than a dram was sharing it with good friends, and he knew well how much this particular friend enjoyed a dram or two of Jack's favourite Islay malts with him.

"Are you asking?" David grinned.

"I'm asking," Jack replied, with a shrug and an even bigger grin.

"Then, we're staying," Irene butted in quickly.

Their laughter heralded the onset of another weekend's enjoyment of each other's company, and the setting of a basis for many more in the years ahead.

David's offer of the job Jack needed had made a significant difference to his view of, and excitement for, the months ahead that Jenny hadn't seen for sometime. Her husband was a good man and an excellent teacher, and it seemed that he was about to show his worth – at last – to the world.

"How's our subterfuge going to work then, old chap?" Jack asked of his pal and prospective boss, over an after-dinner coffee and glass of Laphroaig as Jenny and Irene were seeing to Flo and Jess.

"Well," David started, as he nibbled nuts and sipped his coffee, "your application has to be in very soon."

"It's finished," Jack said, a self-satisfied grin telling his pal he was pleased with its outcome. "Work of art, I think."

"Then, make sure you *send* it in on Monday," David advised carefully. "It has to be sent because I need to show total impartiality in all matters to do with any job advertised. Once I have all the applications from the education offices in Great George Street, I can start the sifting process. Interviews will be set probably early during the week before the fortnight's Whit holiday, to give time to resign before the end of that half term."

"And if my head decides he doesn't want me to go?" Jack asked.

"He can't stop you, if we decide to appoint," David reassured him. "He can't stop you because, don't forget, you are still employed by the local education authority and not by him."

"OK," Jack replied slowly. "If you say so."

"Did you manage to arrange Flo's christening?" Irene asked, as the two came back into the room.

"Afraid not," Jenny said, with a resigned shrug. "The vicar couldn't christen her on her birthday – another arrangement – so we've opted for the first Sunday in June. Do you fancy a joint knees-up for your Imogen Rose and our Florence May a week on Sunday?"

"That would be fantastic," David agreed. "A joint first birthday."

–o–

"Come in," a gruff voice ordered, once the silence had been broken by an insistent and confident rattle on the door. It opened purposefully as Jack strode into the office. "Close the door."

131

"Mr Ingles," the head started, his unpleasantly aggressive voice attacking Jack as he stood by his desk, "what can I do for you?" The head looked up at him only once, before continuing his scribbling in an oversized diary, with a gold-coloured Sheaffer fountain pen.

"I have an interview in a week's time, on Tuesday 21st May," Jack started, confidently, "at the education offices in Great George Street."

"An interview?" the head growled, stopping writing mid-word. "And why didn't I know about this?"

"Rush job," Jack explained. "Came up only a short while ago. So I need to have the morning off."

"'Fraid not, young man," the head growled again, lidding his pen carefully before clipping it into his inside pocket. "I can't sanction that at all. You've only been here five minutes."

"You can't stop me, I'm afraid," Jack insisted, firmly, "and you know that as well as I do. So, now I'm *telling* you that I won't be in on that morning. I've already informed the senior mistress so she can make arrangements. There are only two lessons to cover as my two free lessons for the week happen on that morning."

"So, you're wanting to leave, eh?" Mr Byrne snarled, his face showing his true character. "Well, it's not going to happen, son."

"The process is under way, I'm afraid," Jack said, standing his ground, "and there's nothing you can do to stop it – Bob. I'm sorry for mentioning this, but you're not above the law."

"I'll blacken your bloody name in every school in this bloody authority, whipper-snapper," the head exploded, drawing as much venom and threat as he could into his words from his impoverished vocabulary, "and then see where that'll get you. Bloody upstart."

"Do your worst, *old man*," Jack replied, sure of himself, "but I shall be at that interview whether you like it or not.

Oh, and, I *am* prepared to see you in court – if necessary. No need to get up. I'll see myself out."

He turned smartly on his heels and clicked the door behind him, leaving the older man fuming in his chair. "Bloody cheek," he muttered, reaching for the telephone. "We'll see about you, young bugger."

Once he had made the call to his contact at Great George Street, he sat back in his chair, a murderous scowl crossing his jowls, his mind sliding back to *his* time as a young teacher with *his* old head's face drawing into sharp focus.

"Broughton County Junior School, eh?" he muttered. "We'll see what his prospective new head's going to say, shall we?"

–o–

"Risky path you're treading there, Jack," Tom, the deputy, warned over lunchtime supervision in the canteen.

"How come, Tom?" Jack replied. "In what way?"

"I admire your balls, standing up for your principles," Tom said, concern for the young man etched on his genuinely compassionate face, "but you've chosen a hard nut to pitch yourself against. His reputation is infamous authority-wide, and he's not got where he is today without extinguishing many a young budding career."

"Then it's about time somebody stood up to him," Jack harrumphed, feeling his hackles prickling at the mention. "He's not a god, Tom, or do I need to remind you of that? I was taught as a nipper, by the best teacher imaginable, to stand up for what I believe to be right, and *this* is one of those defining moments. I'm not afraid of him, Tom."

"Who was the teacher, then?" Tom asked, genuinely admiring his principled stance.

"Mi mam, Tom," Jack replied quietly, her face jumping in to his mind, "and I will always live by what she taught me, and part of that was standing up to bullies."

"I hope for your sake you're proved right," Tom said wistfully. "You'll go far, young Jack, but I hope this won't be a step *too* far for you."

"You're a good man, Tom," Jack threw back, a gleam sparkling, "despite what anyone else might say."

They both laughed, as the dining hall began to empty, leaving litter in the bins from sandwich eaters and an enormous amount of food waste to tickle the fancy of the local farmers' pig population. No wonder *they* were so fat.

Would Jack miss this school? No. The myriad people on the staff he didn't *yet* know? No. The dire way in which the head treated his staff? No. The children, particularly those who needed his support and care? Undoubtedly, yes. This had been the only reason he had made himself jump through all the hoops placed in his way – the only reason he troubled to continue in *this* particular hell-hole.

Big Brian's art room, opposite the main boys' toilet, around the corner of the main corridor from light and sanity, was busy – not with bodies, but with an enormous range of arty-farty stuff, both on display and in every corner. His room had one long wall of glass that made it heaven to work in on a dull day in October, but – south facing – was hell incarnate on a hot sunny day in July.

"Hello, young Jack," Brian grinned, his big ginger beard making it seem like he wasn't moving his lips, "to what do I owe the honour of this visit?"

"Just thought I'd drop in to say hello," Jack replied, eyeing all his artistic offerings. "All these yours?"

"Mostly from the youngsters," he boasted, puffing out his ample chest in mock pride, "but I always taught them how to do it. Do you have any children of your own, Jack?" Brian continued.

"Two girls," Jack said. "You?"

"Two boys," Brian replied. "Justin, who's ten, and Quentin, who's eight."

"Any reason for those names?" Jack asked. "They are rather ... er ... exotic. Family tradition?"

"Well," Brian started, "the elder of the two, was born on April 4th, so we were able to claim a full year's child tax rebate before the end of the financial year. So, we called him Justin..."

"Time?" Jack butted in, his huge guffaw joining Brian's wicked laugh. "I get it. Excellent."

"So, you want to leave us, then?" Brian asked, quietly.

Jack stopped, raised his eyebrows and tipped his head slightly in that quizzical way as he waited for his friend to finish his question.

"Or so I've heard," Big Beardy Brian finished.

"The only people to know that in this school, at this time, are the senior management triumvirate," Jack replied slowly. "Out of the three, I would lay the leak at Connie's door."

"You could be right," he admitted, "but..."

"No buts, Brian," Jack remonstrated. "I told that one little nugget to one person only, and he..."

"Shared it with his senior management team, no doubt," Brian replied with a grin, "as you would expect. Connie, I have known for years, and..."

"Is there anyone you didn't know before you came here?" Jack laughed.

"She simply dropped it into the conversation," Brian went on, "with a word of caution."

"That he makes a bad enemy, by any chance?" Jack suggested. "I've had that one already from Tom."

"Well, you'd better believe it," his friend reiterated. "All heads are the same, young Jack. The head I left at St Kevin's was so reluctant to let me go, when all else failed trying to persuade *this* head not to appoint me, he exclaimed, 'You can't take him, he's got piles!'"

"Ha ha! Typical," Jack smiled. "Don't you worry about me, Big Brian. For goodness' sake, all I want is to find a job I'm sure I'll like, and all I get is grief. Please keep this to yourself – for now?"

"Of course," Brian agreed, "but I'll be sorry to see you go. There aren't many folks on *this* staff I should like to spend more than a few minutes with."

"I'll keep you posted," Jack promised, as he turned to leave. "Now it's time for a cup of tea before this afternoon's fray. Swimming, with Enid Buckby."

Now, *she* was an excellent teacher who had started *her* career in junior school, a few years before Jack, and had taken it upon herself, single-handedly, to teach the whole of North Leeds to swim. To be honest, although Jack would have made an excellent fish, he had no illusions about his role. He made a first-class helper and support, but *she* had the skills, qualifications, and experience – and *he* did as he was told.

The pool itself was nothing grand, simply housed inside a curved fibreglass tunnel fifteen feet high by thirty feet wide by twenty-five yards long. Separate boys' and girls' facilities allowed private changing and showering, giving a very perfunctory but valuable resource within which to provide required swimming lessons without leaving the campus. Commensurate with the school's status as the biggest middle school in the country, it was also the only one with its own swimming facility – apart from the local canal.

Although the coming lesson took away one of the non-contact sessions he should have enjoyed, it was fortunate that his own class shared this session with him, giving him a different perspective on how they functioned out of their academic straightjacket.

It was always a relief when the swimming lesson was over, however, because the lack of an effective ventilation system concentrated chlorine vapour in the pool's atmosphere, which in turn affected his eyes and breathing.

Walking through his own front door at the end of *this* particular day was such a joy that a long deep sigh signalled his relief at being back where he belonged.

"Hard day, my sweet man?" Jenny asked, once all his girls had smothered his face with joyful and welcoming kisses.

"You wouldn't believe..." his voice tailed away into an explanation as the kettle whistled its readiness to offer his favourite tipple and nibble. Florence May busied herself tucking a favourite doll up in a tiny toy pram, and Jessie sat in *her* armchair, reading one of the fantasy stories Jack had written especially for her. How she loved *his* stories that no other child in her nursery had.

# *Chapter 13*

Jack was convinced there was something psychologically and emotionally wrong with him. He had seen many people lined up for interviews and they all had shared the same, almost debilitating condition. They suffered from pre-interview nerves.

He didn't – ever, and he always wondered why.

Half past seven on the morning of the interview that would change the course of his life forever and he sat at his own table, in his own home, with his family around him cocooning him from Judgement Day, eating … porridge.

Nothing could divert him from *this* meal. It had often been said that, when he received the call from beyond, he would shuffle off his particular mortal coil *only* when he had had his dish of porridge and his mug of Yorkshire tea. A life well lived, but unrushed.

"You all right, love?" Jenny said, by his side as ever. "Big day – big breakfast."

"Aye, lass," he replied, as unhurried as ever. Although he was a very quick talker, none of his thoughts was ever ill-considered or poorly formed in that over-revving mind of his. "Not toning mi breakfast down, nor rushing it for anybody. Just another day that's got another meeting in it, that's all. No big deal. If I get it, I get it. If I don't, I'm not off to lose any sleep ower it. What's meant for me won't go by me."

"Your mam?" Jenny asked.

"It is that," he emphasised. "One of her usual 'home lies'."

"That's it," he added, after a moment's pause. "Done and dusted."

"Then you'll be off in a bit?" she replied, as she finished clearing up after Jessie and Florence May.

"Just off to have a minute wi mi family, my lovely," he offered, smiling broadly as he drew Jenny to his chest. "Can't go off without a love and a kiss or two from my lovely ladies."

"Me next, Daddy," Jessie insisted, squeezing her way between her parents and wrapping her arms as far round him as her short limbs would allow her to reach.

They both laughed as he kissed the top of Jessie's head before throwing her into the air and catching her with a mock groan, as if he was about to drop her. Jessie chuckled heartily as she had done many times before at the same scenario.

"Nearly dropped you there, my poppet," Jack gasped in mock shock as he put her down.

"Silly Daddy," Jessie laughed, holding him tightly for all she was worth. "I *know* you wouldn't let me drop."

"That's me done then," he sighed. "Can't delay any longer. Have to be out for that bus."

"You sure I can't take you down?" Jenny asked, concerned that he would have to use public transport.

"I'm OK, love," he replied. "Really. At this time of day, the X255 takes me virtually from the end of the street into City Square in ten minutes, and from there it's just a shortish amble up Park Row to Cookridge Street and Great George Street beyond."

"Great George Street?" she puzzled. "Why Great George Street?"

"Education offices," he replied, with an indulgent smile.

"Been there three time before – all for interviews. Hundred percent success so far, so cross everything for me, will you? I could find my way there almost blindfold. Bus is best anyway, because there'll be no chance of finding a parking spot anywhere close by."

"Will you be home after the interview or back in school?" Jenny asked, hoping for the former.

"Home, hopefully," he answered, with a heartfelt sigh. "Apparently Byrne wanted me back the minute the interview was over but good old David told me he had suggested to him that, if I am appointed, he would need me for the rest of the day."

–o–

The X255 was crowded, with almost all the seats taken. A large, beautifully dressed and scented lady moved her shopping bag from the seat next to her to allow Jack to sit. Her perfume lingered delightfully in his nostrils, reminding him of the little blue bottle of 'Soir de Paris' scent he always bought for his mam from Woolies in Normanton's High Street.

One more stop north of the Outer Ring Road, and then the journey took only a further seven minutes because of the non-stop 'bus only' lanes recently introduced.

This was a new experience for him but one he would need to replicate daily from September – should he be lucky this day. He had that feeling he always had in situations such as this: no nerves, but the same questions growing on him every time. Was he doing the right thing? Should he have toughed it out and allowed himself to grow into Byrne's organisation at Merton Grange? He knew the answer to that one without too much thought. Still – not taking anything for granted – he might, by the end of this morning, have to mek t'best on a bad job. Good old Jud. He were allus thiyer wi"is sound pragmatical advice.

City Square was always busy at this time of day. The station next to the Queen's Hotel disgorged its incoming passengers at the same time as road traffic spewed on to the Square from Bishopgate Street and Boar Lane to make its ponderous way around its road past the Majestic cinema and the GPO. Edward the Black Prince, astride his pedestalled bronze steed, surveyed his island realm as he urged the ant-like pedestrians forward into battle for another day.

Even though early summer's furnaces were only just beginning to get into their stride, a chill breeze always eddied along the two hundred yards of Park Row's high-rise office blocks, from its intersection with the Headrow and Cookridge Street five minutes or so walk away.

The education offices on Great George Street hadn't changed over time, with yesterday's paint still clinging tenuously to its frames and sills. The offices' distinctive smell greeted him as the loose carousel doors spat him unceremoniously into the foyer – a replay of the last time he was there.

"Stick? Stick Walker?" Jack said, recognising the back of a young man trying not to look too uncomfortable in the usual leatherette chairs.

The young man swung round, surprised to hear his wife's term of endearment there of all places. "Jack Ingles," he beamed. "What a fantastic surprise. Do you work here?"

"In a manner of speaking, I suppose you could say that," Jack replied, interested at the reference. "I teach in a middle school in the north of the city but am here on interview."

"Me, too," Stick replied.

"But I thought you had a job at Martin Frobisher in Altofts," Jack puzzled. "You were having a new house built on Church Lane, weren't you?"

"Built and lived in," Stick replied, a great puff of pride and pleasure framing his face. "A junior school deputy headship came up in Beeston and so I thought I'd give it a go."

"Really?" Jack said, warning bells starting to ring in his head. "Me too. Would it be Broughton Junior by any vague chance?"

"Don't know where that is," Stick said, "but mine's called Albion Terrace Junior, off Old Lane."

"I know it well," Jack said, a wave of relief wafting across *his* face. "It's just around the corner from Moorhouse's jam factory."

Jack watched the look of bewilderment creeping into is companion's eyes, as he trotted out details of an area as if he had known it forever. Was it a ploy to unsettle him?

"Don't worry," Jack smiled, trying to reassure him. "I know the area because I taught there for a couple of years what seems like a century ago, in a school called—"

"Broughton Junior School," Stick said, twigging the reference.

"Correct," Jack laughed. "Like you, I'm here for a deputy's job – the one at Broughton."

"Mr Walker, please," a stentorian voice muscled its way into their conversation.

"That's me," Stick replied, prising himself from his uncomfortable little prison.

"Good luck, mate," Jack shouted, as his friend reached the beginning of the dark corridor to the back o' beyond.

"You, too," Stick's voice drifted back to him, as his body faded into the gloom.

Jack perched on the edge of what seemed to be a new, more comfortable chair he hadn't seen the last time he was there, a satisfied smile playing around his mouth corners. What sort of a coincidence was that, seeing—

"Mr Ingles, please," a quiet, softly-spoken voice brought him back to reality.

Now for it…

−o−

"Jack," Jenny whooped, "you're back home, and that can mean only one thing…"

"You are now married to the deputy head of Broughton County Junior School," he announced grandly. "I've been in school with David for most of this aft, but I couldn't let you know because the phone was down."

"You clever man," she added, pride oozing as she hugged and kissed him. "Does this mean—?"

"It means that, at last, I have the job I wanted," he assured her, "and that we will have enough spare money to save up for a bigger car, perhaps, or even a holiday or two on the lovely Costa Notalotta."

"What about your resignation from Merton?" Jenny asked, concerned there should be no obstacles.

"The official letter of appointment will be with me tomorrow, David said," Jack replied, smiling that he was within smelling distance of his new school, "and that my letters of resignation should go in, both to the authority and to the head at Merton, as soon as I receive that letter."

"Knowing you," she said, with a grin, "*your* letter will be ready for post *now*."

"You know me so well," he replied, a grin of self-satisfaction betraying his delight. "It's in my school bag – stamped – ready for that there postman's delicate touch."

"You'll never guess who I saw at the offices," Jack mumbled, through a mouthful of home-made scone.

"Stick Walker, by any chance?" she said, with the raising of one eyebrow and a slight tilting of her head.

"How on earth—?" Jack gasped, aghast at what she said.

"Joyce rang to let you know that he thinks he got the job," she replied, "and should be starting in September if he has. We had a bit of a chat and she invited us to visit before the end of the Whit holiday."

"Funny you should say that," Jack added, "but John said exactly the same, as we came out of our interviews, only he hadn't got to know the result of his before I left. I think *his* result was a bit closer than he would have liked."

"She said they might be thinking about moving over here because of his job," Jenny went on. "So, I wonder if they might like to come to us and have a look around here. What do you think?"

"Good thinking," he replied, hoping this might be a possibility so his ladies could have ready-made companions. "Might be an idea to have them stay, perhaps?"

"Fancy them wanting to come over here to live," Jack mused, between crunching his scone and enjoying his cup of Yorkshire. "She always said she wouldn't leave Normanton – too much in her life there to want to leave behind."

"She's a sensible lass, is Joyce," Jenny said, "and obviously realises travelling every day by car for John would be a chore."

"More like she would want the car for herself," Jack laughed. "You know how difficult it is to get around on foot, especially with a nipper or two in tow."

"On second thoughts," Jenny went on, "perhaps we *will* go to them and invite them back one weekend before finishing for the summer. That way, we can not only wait to see whether a move is on the cards but we can call off at Mum's before seeing to the graves in Normanton."

"Sounds like a plan, my beloved," Jack agreed.

"Mum has often suggested we should go and stay with them sometime soon," she pointed out. "It would be lovely."

"Pinfold Lane, eh?" Jack drooled. "I always wanted to live there. So many plush houses and bungalows. It would be good to get to know Jim a bit better, too."

"I'll phone her tomorrow," Jenny said, with a grin, "when

you're back at school."

"Thanks for that," he said with a grimace. "Not looking forward to being there at all. I've no idea what Byrne will be like with me but I can hazard a reasonably good guess. War of attrition, I should imagine."

"You going to be all right, then?" she replied, a seriously worried cloud passing over her otherwise clear blue skies. "I mean…"

"Broad shoulders, love," he laughed. "I've not got where I am today—"

"I know," she interrupted, clearing the cloud. "Without having broad shoulders."

They laughed at the face she pulled, and at the closeness they enjoyed, taking everything in their stride that life had to throw at them.

–o–

"You're a dark horse," Big Beardy Brian said as they both headed from his art room towards a hot cup of tea.

"Heard from the gods already, eh?" Jack smiled, rounding the corner, towards the Crush Hall, to be met by the ominous figure of the head teacher lurking at the bottom of the open stair well.

"Can I see you in my office now, Mr Ingles?" Mr Byrne growled, when Jack and Brian drew near. The head turned on his heels and led the way to his goldfish bowl on the corner.

"See you later," Big Brian said with a knowing smile, a raised single eyebrow and a cocked head.

Jack left the office door open deliberately as he strode into its hallowed interior, handing the head a typed envelope as *he* took to the swivel chair behind his huge oak desk.

"What's this?" he snarled.

"It's a courtesy, Mr Byrne," Jack answered quietly but

firmly, "which is more than you showed to me the last time we spoke. I have received official acknowledgement this morning that I have been offered the post of deputy head teacher at Broughton County Junior School. The only thing needed now is my official acceptance, which I put in the post on the way here this morning."

"I was perhaps a bit hasty in what I said to you the other day," the head growled. "So, come on, what do I need to offer you to stay?"

"In a word, Mr Byrne – Bob – nothing," Jack replied, a slight smile on his face. "Now, if you'll excuse me, there is a hot cup of tea waiting for me in the staff room before I attend to my duties."

The door snecked quietly as Jack swept out of the room leaving the head, mouth open, aghast at how quietly, efficiently and cleverly he had just been slapped down.

"Now for that tea," Jack muttered, a self-satisfied smile spreading as he strode across the Crush Hall with a purpose he'd not experienced in this school for some time.

The ordinary school day turned into an extraordinary school day as his shoulders bore the weight of so many congratulatory hands, and his back became sore with as many well-wishing slaps.

Jack was pleased by the end of the day when the bonhomie had worn itself out and thoughts of his escape returned to their rightful place – his own head. School life at Merton would return to its normal, tedious self, lasting only one more day until he finished for his Whitsuntide break of two wonderful weeks.

He couldn't wait.

# Chapter 14

"He didn't know what to say," Jack grinned, happy that the status quo had been re-established at work. "Left him quietly with his mouth sagging, gasping like a fish out of its bowl."

"Poor thing," Jenny laughed. "I hope he'll be all right."

"Poor thing be buggered!" he harrumphed. "He got what he deserved. You can't speak to people like he spoke to me last week and hope to get away with it. I was calm – not a bit bombastic – told him what I was about to do and left him with *no* answers to his desperate questions."

"Good for you, Our Jack," Jenny said, proud of the way he handled the world and its difficulties. "So, what are we going to do over the next couple of weeks?"

"You mean, apart from enjoying every day wi'out school?" he replied with conviction and obvious relish. "And our Flo's christening?"

"Week today," she replied quickly. "Saturday 25th. We had to book it early because we needed to give everybody enough time to organise themselves to clear the day in their diaries."

"I propose this weekend, as the weather's picking up," he said, "that we enjoy being together, with the occasional trip to Roundhay Park and Golden Acre Park to feed the ducks. What do you say, Jessie?"

"Yay," she answered, briefly and reluctantly lifting her eyes from her book. "I like feeding the ducks. Can we go now?"

"After lunch, poppet," Jenny agreed, casting a glance across at her husband's grinning face. "Daddy needs a little rest to get used to not being in school, and then we'll go after we've eaten."

"Lunch soon, I hope," Jack laughed. "I feel strangely hungry."

"It's only ten past twelve," Jenny protested. "I thought we'd start having our lunches when we feel like it rather being dictated by the clock – you feel like it now, don't you?"

"Course I do," he agreed, happily peckish. "I've usually finished mi snap by this time, when I'm in school."

"But you don't finish morning school until twelve," she replied, puzzled by his response. "Don't you?"

"Well," he drawled, almost apologetically, "I can't help having a healthy hunger. If I leave it *too* much longer, I begin to feel faint and mi past life flashes before mi eyes."

"All right, all right," she agreed, capitulating in view of her husband's and daughter's open faces urging her to turn the key in the metaphorical lock on the pantry door. "You've twisted my arm."

"No, we didn't, Mummy," Jessie replied, a look of serious consternation overtaking her little face. "We didn't touch your arm. I promise."

Jack and Jenny burst out laughing at Jessie's naïve but earnest observation. Jack picked her up and threatened to throw her in the air, to her wild screams of joy and demands for 'again', as they made for the kitchen and its brown, Formica-topped table, ready for the next instalment of feeding.

"It would be nice to sit outside for lunch with the weather as warm as this, Jack, don't you think?" Jenny said, as she mashed the tea.

"During the summer holidays, our lass," he replied, once the first mouthful of his corned-beef sandwich had slid down his throat, "I intend to extend that tiny apology of a patio at the back door into one big and fit enough to take a table and chairs, and the occasional lounger, all fitted around yon grand conservatory we'll be having done."

"Really?" she answered, more than a little puzzled. "But we can't afford to have someone in to do the work, can we?"

"No," he replied, "but we *can* afford for *me* to do it. Materials aren't that dear, and my labour carries a negligible cost. Luckily, we got t'conservatory at onny a bit ower cost, which will save us a fair bit."

"But, you've never done that sort of thing before," she continued. "Surely—"

"Then it's about time I did," he insisted. "I've thought it all through, and it shouldn't prove to be too difficult."

"I've no doubt you have, my lovely man," Jenny said, a little concerned he might be taking on a bit more than he was capable of delivering, "but won't it be hard work and…"

"Be rayt," he replied. "I've ordered t'slabs already from Mone's quarry, and all I have to do then is hire a mixer and buy sand and cement to mix mi compo, so I can slap 'em down. We *will* have somewhere to sit outside properly this year. Trust me."

"Oh, by the way," Jenny said, as she cleared away the debris from lunch, "I'd forgotten that we've agreed to visit Joyce and Stick Walker week after next – probably Wednesday – after the christening, if that's OK with you?"

"Sounds grand to me," he replied. "We can kill two birds with one stone – mi mam's and your dad's graves, perhaps, as we said before."

"Perhaps we can call in and see my mum on our way there," she offered. "Do you think?"

"Aye, course we can," he replied, "and then we…" His voice tailed away as the clock's loud tick gradually faded in, joined by Flo's gurgling play in her playpen, Jessie's mouthing of slightly longer words in her story, and the happy chirruping of the hoard of sparrows in the garden pecking their way to full bellies once more. Both Flo and Jessie loved to sit in the dining room to watch the antics of the birds in their soon-to-be better garden.

Jenny had such high plans for her back garden that would never be just a back yard. She'd been frustrated by one of those for the best part of five years, and now she was determined to have something proper – somewhere she could smell her flowers and … potter. How she would love to be able to 'play out' in her garden, particularly during this unusually lovely spell they were experiencing now.

Jack wasn't a gardener in *her* sense of the word, but he was clever with his head and his hands and he would make her a place she could do things in and grow the sort of stuff she'd always wanted to grow. Whatever structures she needed to have to make her garden beautiful, she knew he would build. He was one of life's planners and doers was her Jack. A grafter. A perfectionist. Her lovely man.

–o–

The rose garden in Roundhay Park was beginning to come into its own at this time of the year and, as with many places, it seemed to be in a constant state of change and improvement. Of course, over the years many changes – most of them good – had been introduced. Jack had been brought here by his grandma and granddad on one or two occasions when he was a nipper.

Bus, train, and tram – how good did it get? He could even remember being deposited on the huge terminus turn-around near the rose garden by one of the last trams to service the area. Those trams, unfortunately, were long-gone, being replaced by blue double-decker Samuel Ledgard buses, which were nowhere near as exciting – or uncomfortable.

"Can we go on the swings, please, Daddy?" Jessie asked, excited at the prospect.

"Course you can, my lovely," Jack replied. "Tell you what. There's a small fairground down near Waterloo Lake for Whitsuntide. Would you like to have a go on the swings and the helter-skelter?"

"Ooh, yes please. Goody," she whooped, clapping her hands in glee. "What's hell-ter-skell-ter?"

"You'll have to wait and see," he said, smiling at her drawled mispronunciation. "It's just down the hill and round the next corner."

Jessie's excitement began to overwhelm her, almost to the point of tears, and Jenny had to draw her close to calm and settle her. She'd never seen a fairground, never mind such a small one. She had always resisted taking her daughter to the Heath Common fairs at Easter time, which Jack had so enjoyed as a youngster, because *she* didn't enjoy what they had to offer. Although the smells and sounds were to *his* taste, they weren't to hers.

"Do you think this is really such a good idea, Jack?" Jenny asked, a little concerned that the fair seemed to be quite run-down, and maybe a bit ... unsafe.

"Don't worry, Jenny," Jack tried to reassure her. "She'll be rayt. Perhaps the helter-skelter might not be up to scratch but those swing-boat type swings are meant for two and I'll go on with her. You can't disappoint her now."

"Daddy?" Jessie asked quietly.

"Yes, my poppet," Jack replied, catching a note of fear in her voice.

"Can we not do the helter-skelter, please?" she said. "Don't like the look."

"Of course, you don't have to," he told her. "How about the swing? It's—"

"Not what I want to do, either," she said, bottom lip quivering. "Can we go home now? I would like to see that my dolly, Tossy, is all right."

Jack looked across at Jenny, and they both smiled, realising that *this* experience was perhaps a bit too … extreme, for now. Jack picked her up, and swung her around onto his shoulders, reminiscent of their stay at the White Lodge in Filey, to her whoops of joy, as Jenny pushed Florence May's snoozing form in her pushchair towards the car.

"Cup of tea and a scone, everybody?" Jenny suggested, as they left the rose garden behind them.

–o–

"What's this 'ere conservatory lark, then, our Jack?" Jenny asked, as they sat around the dining room table, chomping on scones and drinking Yorkshire tea, whilst watching the antics of a myriad birds in their embryo garden.

"It's a new-fangled way of sitting in the back garden," he explained, his brow furrowed in thought as he searched for the right words, "without sitting … in the back garden. Like a big lean-to greenhouse, onny more comfortable like – with no staging or tomato plants – with proper chairs and a rug. Double doors – what do they call 'em? French doors? – where that big, useless window is now, so we can open it up to go through, or lock up and not. I *like* choice."

"And there's an outside door in this 'ere conservatory," Jenny asked, a little unsure, "so we can get out into yon garden if we need to?"

"Of course there is," he laughed, "otherwise it'd just be a glass room."

"Do you know," Jenny mused, after a moment or two's quiet contemplation, "when I think back to only a year or two ago, I'd never have believed the luxury we live in now – conservatories an' all, Our Jack. Queen Street to a king's palace."

"We deserve it, my beautiful lady," he laughed. "I have graveyards a lot to be thankful for, I must say."

The strident insistence of the telephone interrupted their conversation, urging them to pick it up.

"Well?" Jack said, once the telephone and conversation had stopped jangling. "Your Val, I assume."

"Actually, no," she replied, with a surprised smile. "It was your William."

"Our William?" Jack puzzled, with a slight inclination of his head and a quizzical raising of one eyebrow. "Is he poorly? Has Val run off wi' yon college friend? Has…?"

"They would like to come over to stay for a little while next week," she went on, ignoring his weedy attempts at humour. "The two boys are off on school trips for a day or two, and so it would be just the three of them."

"Any reason?" Jack asked, mildly intrigued.

"None offered," she replied, "and I didn't ask."

"I like cousin Mary," Jessie said, putting her glass of milk on the table, and leaving a pencil-thin white moustache on her top lip, "…sometimes."

"And why is that, my little kitten?" Jack asked, trying not to show his mirth at her pert answer.

"*Nearly* all the time we can play," Jessie replied, after a moment or two of consideration, "but sometimes she can be bossy, telling me what to do because she's a bit older than me."

"Well, we can't have that, Our Jessie," Jack replied.

"I'm being serious, Our Daddy Jack," Jessie remonstrated, hands on hips, looking steadfastly into his face.

"And so am I, my little one," Jack replied, suitably chastened, with a serious smile on his face and trying not to laugh.

Jenny turned away to hide her smile as her daughter swung her way into the lounge to what she called her 'book corner'. Jack and Jenny found her there moments later, in her little chair, eyes buried in her present favourite book, mouthing its contents silently as she slid her guiding forefinger along the page.

"Our little girl's growing up, Jenny," Jack said, catching the occasional glimpse of their daughter concentrating on her story.

"Frighteningly inevitable, I'm afraid," she replied. "All we can do is give her lots of love and the tools to do it as safely and as smoothly as we can."

"She'll be rayt," Jack said, in his usual Yorkshire pragmatic way. "Bound to be, she's ours."

–o–

"It's lovely to see you and have you stay and all that, Our Val," Jenny said pointedly, once Jack and his brother were out of the way on a walk to the Jockey pub. The boys had asked them to come along but they had declined in favour of a cup of tea and some new oaty biscuits. "But why did *William* phone? He never phones Jack, let alone me."

"Because I told him to," Val smiled as she dipped her oatmeal biscuit in her Yorkshire tea. Cleverly constructed, those oaty biscuits. They would stand up to *five* dunks before they would become even a bit soft. No fear of them collapsing and forming a biscuity sludge in the bottom of the mug. "He needs at least to try to become part of this family again … to take responsibility for his – our – life. Anyway, he has something to tell you – himself."

"Do tell," Jenny urged, swivelling to face her sister, excited anticipation in her eyes. "I *love* an intrigue."

"Well," Val replied slowly, "you'll just have to wait and

see. I'm glad we could come a for a day or two so *we* might spend a bit of time together – stuff we rarely do without others orbiting around *our* little world."

-o-

"Do you mind if we just walk?" William asked his brother as they strolled towards the Jockey. "I don't feel too much like beer at the moment."

"Suits me fine, Bro," Jack replied, rather relieved. He wasn't a big beer drinker and a pint of wallop would spoil his corned-beef sandwich and coffee, truth be known. "We can take a turn around the golf course up Nursery Lane and back in time for lunch, if you like?"

"Perfect," William agreed, with an emphatic heart-felt sigh.

Never one to pry or to bring up personal stuff with his brother, Jack's conversation turned to school in general and to William's perceived wish to return to his professional roots.

"I can't say this last few weeks haven't been hard," William started hesitantly. He wasn't as fluent a thinker as Jack and he found it difficult to articulate his thoughts and feelings, especially to his little brother.

"I know it's not going to be easy," he went on, "both to go back into school, and to prove to my family that *they* are my only concern."

"I've always been here, you know, William," Jack assured him with honesty, "but we've never been close enough to confide."

"Distance and time, really, I suppose," his brother replied.

"In more ways than one, eh, Bro?" Jack said, a rueful smile overcoming his face.

"Anyway," William replied, after a few moments of thought, "I've come to one or two fairly important decisions that … you'll have to wait to find out."

"Find out what, O Brother Mine?" Jack interrupted, a cleverly mischievous twinkle in his eye.

"You might be smarter and quicker than me," William laughed, "but you don't trick me that easily. You'll just have to wait until this evening – or thereabouts."

The housing estate they regained through a tiny snicket between two pairs of 1920s semis, was a hotch-potch jigsaw of styles and levels of building, offering prospective purchasers the chance to watch *their* house at all stages of its growth.

"A lot still to be built, then," William said, as they threaded their way through strewn building materials and equipment – planks, ladders, barrows half-full of mortar hardening around brick-laying trowels and piles of new red bricks littering the landscape, like so many truncated ruddy smoke stacks.

"You could do worse than move back up here, Our William," Jack replied, causing his brother to stop and think.

"All well and good for you," he replied, a wry smile giving nothing away. "You're already here and well-known in this education authority. I'm not – and besides, we have a house already, as you well know."

Jack fell quiet as they walked. For some reason, his instinct started to scream at him that something here didn't ring true. There was something his brother wasn't telling him. Perhaps…

"Look," William urged, a great grin splitting his face, "Mary and Jessie at the front room window. This smacks of a cup of tea and a bun, I think. What do you say, Jack?"

"Mmm," Jack muttered, not sure about what his brother might be hiding, but he was sure they'd find out before long.

–o–

"And now I feel sure you're about to tell us what it is you're hiding," Jack said, pointedly, between bites of his wife's wonderful waffles and super-soft sultana scones and mouthfuls of her magnificently mashed tea.

"Jack," Jenny urged, a look of surprised encouragement ricocheting around his ears. "In their own time."

"No," Val interrupted, the first genuine smile for a long time beginning to surface, "Jack's right. We do have some news to share with you. William's got—"

"An interview – in Leeds," William burst in.

"Tomorrow," Val continued. "There. Done. Now you know it all."

"Interview?" Jack gasped, so flabbergasted he had to sit down.

"In Leeds?" Jenny echoed.

"But—" they chorused.

"Time I got a proper job," William explained. "One that will pay our bills regularly and give us a future, with none of your airy-fairy stuff any longer. Besides, I've realised at last that being close to family is more important than anything else."

"Well, William, old chap," Jack continued. "I'm impressed. Where are you hoping to live?"

"House is sold, subject to contract," Val added, "and we've got our eye on one of the new ones round the corner from here."

"Yes!" Jenny whooped, grabbing her sister in joy and doing a jig around the lounge.

"Isn't that a bit cart and horse-ish?" Jack cautioned. "I mean, what if you don't get the job?"

"Actually," William said quietly, "I have two others in the pipeline over the next week or two, so you'll be seeing a bit more of us."

"You … dark horse, you," Jack laughed. "We'll make a

family man of you yet."

"Start September," his brother went on. "So that means renting around here, as the house won't be ready until early October. So…"

"You'll put your furniture into storage at Turnbull's and stay here with us," Jenny insisted. "No argument. Right, Our Jack?"

"As long as we hurry the builders along," Jack grinned.

They laughed that easy sighed laugh, relaxing into the comfortable knowledge that, at last, all would be well again in the Ingles clan.

*This* prodigal son was about to return.

# Chapter 15

Little Flo's christening was a tiny, quiet affair, celebrated in Normanton's All Saints' Parish Church, with just family – present and past – as guests. Jenny's mum had asked them all to go back to hers to join in a buffet to which Jenny had offered to contribute to the fare but which her mum had emphatically refused. David and Irene weren't able to join the party because of a clash of family commitments.

"My treat," her mum had explained. "She is the only one of my grandchildren to invite me to her do, so it is *mine* to cater for – and no arguments."

The bungalow didn't seem large enough from the outside, set in a third of an acre of beautifully tended gardens – front and back. It was the sort of garden Jenny aspired to, and was very similar to the one she had grown up in. Although her plot was nowhere near as big, the lawns back and front and their herbaceous borders she could replicate to a certain degree.

The inside, however, was a different matter. Large by anybody's standards, and well set out by Jim, it still needed a 'woman's touch' to make it *outstandingly* comfortable.

The enormous dining room had been laid out with the choicest finger foods that any buffet might offer. Mary liked the look of everything she saw but Jessie wasn't so sure. She was at that awkward age that made everything suspect and unsure. Jack never forced the issue because he knew she wouldn't starve herself.

The southern Ingleses had to leave as soon as they had had their fill to allow them to welcome their sons back home from their school trips the day after. They had, however, spent several very productive days in Leeds, settling a few ghosts and reacquainting themselves with the areas they had explored and enjoyed when they were students, and where Val had started her teaching career.

"You are staying overnight, we hope?" Jenny's mum asked Jack. "We need some urgent help to shift all this food."

"Put like that, Flo," Jack answered with an obliging grin, "how could we refuse and not appear rude? We shall have to be off in reasonable time tomorrow, though, as we're sorting mi mam and Jenny's dad's graves out, as well as calling in on some friends, Joyce and Stick, in Altofts."

"Stick?" Flo puzzled. "What sort of a name is that? Is he a Swede?"

"He was called a cabbage on many an occasion by Maxi Machin at the Grammar School," Jack quipped, a huge grin betraying his humour, "but never a turnip."

Jenny's mum laughed at Jack's quick humour. She loved this young man for his wit, his compassion and his fearlessness. Never one to shy away from big decisions and hard work, he was much more than his elder brother could ever be – and he was always there. She was so glad Jenny had brought him into their lives because, not only was he the centre of their family, he was the centre of *her* universe too.

"He is called Stick, Mum, because his surname's Walker," Jenny explained.

"I once knew a boy called Floury Miller when *I* was at school," Flo added, "though I can only guess why."

"Dusty, Flo," Jack corrected with a guffaw. "Anyone called Miller always has the nickname 'Dusty'."

Jim sat quietly in his favourite armchair, listening to all this good-humoured banter, a smile etched on his face. He'd never experienced such lively and funny exchanges before he had got to know Flora Mae McDermot, and now he was in the thick of it, an outsider no more. He was going to love being a member of this lively gang and he saw no reason why that shouldn't happen as often as possible. This young man was a very different kettle of fish from his trouble-causing father, whom he had encountered briefly on the odd occasion their paths had crossed at collieries they had both inhabited. Flora Mae had opened up a whole new vista of life he hadn't known existed, and his life had changed very much for the better.

The one thing that *really* tickled him was that instantly he had become grandpa to five youngsters of varying ages from one year. He'd never been a grandpa before and … he loved it.

"Is there any chance," Jim ventured tentatively, "that you might leave yon bairns with us ower night, like, while you are at your friends' place? Onny, I don't have any other grandchildren and they're great … fun."

"Well, I never did," Flo said, turning to him with a surprised if compassionate look in her eyes. "And I thought you wouldn't be too sure about youngsters rushing about in your bungalow."

"*Our* bungalow," he corrected, slipping his arm around her shoulders. "Anyway, it would be good for them, too. We could…"

"Done!" Jack butted in quickly, after a nod of assent from Jenny. "We'll collect them on our way back on Tuesday. If that's all right with you?"

–o–

"Fancy that," Jenny said, a satisfied smile on her face as they turned into Barnsdale Road from Pinfold Lane, on their way to Methley Bridge and the Three Lane Ends. "I would never have had Jim as an old softy for children. I think it's lovely he should want to spend time with our kids, who are not 'his' kids."

"Hey, don't knock it," Jack replied. "things are just beginning to look up, what with our William and your Val, and now Flo and Jim."

Four Lane Ends was quite busy, even for Whit Monday. Bank holiday always drew out the crowds as there was usually something to do and see in most areas.

"Did *you* wear something new at Whitsuntide, Our Jen?" Jack asked, as they chugged past Whitwood Common towards The Rising Sun. "I mean, some new item of clothing you'd been saving just for *that* day, when you were little?"

"Not really," Jenny replied, slightly puzzled at the question. "We got something new all the time. Obsessive parents, you see. Why?"

"Well," he went on slowly, sliding back to being seven again, "mi mam would use her corp cheques she'd saved up to buy us a new coat or pair of trousers or pumps, just to wear at Whit."

"I don't recognise that one, my man," she said, searching her mind. "What are 'corp cheques'?"

"The amount she spent at the Co-op on Wakefield Road near t'Mopsey, counted towards her Co-op divi – or dividend," he began to explain. "Because everyone who shopped there regularly became a member of this 'Co-operative Wholesale Society', they got money back every year. This was her divi, which she spent on clothes for us at the main branch in Wakefield. I can remember traipsing to Wakefield on a Saturday early in May to see what to get."

"You're a walking social history and no mistake," she laughed. "And was that the only time you got something new to wear?"

"Aye, it was that," he replied. "That, and when I earned money in the pea fields when I was fifteen or sixteen."

"Pea fields?" she puzzled. "Do I know that one?"

"Probably not," he said. "I'll tell you about it later. We're just coming to our turning."

"But," she said, a puzzled frown descending, "we've not got to Normy yet, and…"

"A quicker way, my lovely," he cut in, a wicked smile crossing his eyes, as he turned right into Whitwood Lane. "If you've never been on my magical mystery way, you've never lived."

Whitwood Lane wasn't the epitome of suave living he used to enjoy at Garth Avenue, or Scarborough Row for that matter. Terraced houses and intermittent dereliction led them to the double right-angle road that took them past the Wheatsheaf pub and the dog track, onto Altofts Lane.

"Not been down this way since I was fifteen," Jack said, once they'd passed the terraced houses below the station, opposite to where Pope and Pearson's pit used to be.

"I've not been down here at all," Jenny said. "I know there used to be a colliery here, because Dad used to mention it when he'd had to do a shift here."

"The row of houses we've just passed," he continued, "was called Pope Street, I think – houses built for the colliers, by the pit owners. The railway station up yonder was quite important as well, even though the platforms were med out o' wood, and the ticket office were a bit rickety, too. The pit closed in 1966, I think – or thereabouts."

"You said something about being down here when you were fifteen," she asked. "Why?"

"Well," he explained, as they passed St Mary's Church, "when I was fifteen, I started courting an Altofts lass called Margaret. Her mam had Chadwick's shop at the corner of

High Green Road and Church Road – a nice little general-purpose store that was part of her house. Anyway, Margaret was a couple of years older than me, and worked in an office in Leeds, I think. She went to Whitwood Tech on Monday evenings – to do shorthand, or summat – and I walked from home every Monday to meet her out of college, to walk her back home. Highlight of my week."

"From Garth Avenue?" Jenny said, surprised at the distance. "You must have been smitten."

"I was," he went on, a twinkle in his eye. "It lasted six months."

"Then what?" she asked, eager to know everything about him she didn't already know.

"She dumped me, for an older man," he said with a smile, "of eighteen."

"Aww," she laughed. "What a shame."

"Always happens to me," he joined in. "When I was seventeen, I took up with a fifteen-year-old High School lass called Linda. Her dad had a shop Wheatley Avenue way on in Normanton – Howarth, I think they were called. She dumped me four months on – for a lad two years younger than me. What is it wi' me and shops, eh?"

"You poor lad," she cooed, stroking the back of his head.

"Funny thing was, both sets of parents *liked* me," he laughed. "Had me measured up for a son-in-law, I'm sure. Anyway, we're here."

"That enormous house, beyond that tiny … library?" she asked, with a cosy, if surprised look playing around her eyes. "Next to a … cemetery. I like cemeteries."

She linked her arm through his as he drew to a halt on the lengthy drive, and kissed his cheek tenderly. She loved this man – this man she had known almost all her life, and the longer she knew him, the deeper the roots of that love spread.

Stick and Joyce were waiting on the top step to greet their guests, both beaming excitedly, the proud owners of a bespoke property fit to house a minor dignitary.

"I'd like my front garden to be like this one, Our Jack," Jenny said, as they linked arms to the front door, pointing out the immaculate lawn framed by delicately coloured flowers and shrubs.

"Joyce. Stick. How lovely to see you," Jack said, as he hugged and shook hands. "What a fantastic garden … and house."

"No Valerie?" Jenny asked.

"Out on the razzle wi' her pals?" Jack quipped.

"She's at Stick's mum's," Joyce laughed. "They wanted to have her for a day or two, and she couldn't go to mine for obvious reasons."

"For obvious reasons?" Jenny puzzled.

"Dotty French," Jack started to explain. "Remember?"

"Dotty Ingles now, of course," Joyce corrected, "and has been for quite some time. They live Rothwell way on, and Eric, their son, is probably four or five years younger than you and me, Our Jack. We *don't* see them."

"Anyway," John chipped in, "are we going to have coffee on the front step or should we go inside. Lots to talk about, Jack, and here's not the place to do it. Your new job in…"

The swish new solid-oak door whispered shut behind them, taking their long-awaited conversation and banter away from those who didn't need to be party to them. It was a lovely house, with a smell of warmth, love, and new baking drifting throughout, where dreams and happiness and contentment lay in thick abundant layers, drawing callers-in to share in their magic.

–o–

"And do you remember Saturday dances at Normy baths,

Our Jack?" Joyce said, a misty-eyed reminiscence oozing over her. "You were quite a mover, if memory serves."

"Oh, the excesses of crazy youth," he replied, grinning as the memory hoofed its way heavily back into his consciousness. "It took some courage, I can tell you, breaking into that circle of bouffanted hairstacks, dancing around their handbags."

"Ha ha," Joyce laughed. "You seemed to do all right, exuding your usual confidence."

"Practice born of terror, I can assure you," he said, mock fear printed on his face. "It stood me in good stead for bopping at the youth club just up the road here, next to the Robin Hood pub on Birkwood Road. Much smaller, and so you stood out more. Best part of fifteen years ago."

"You, Our Jack? A dancer?" Jenny sniggered. "I'd love to have seen that, with your slicked-back Brillcreamed hair and your collar and tie."

"Don't forget the DA," he added, "and dancing strides."

"DA?" she asked, puzzled at the reference.

"Duck's arse," Stick said, filling the gap.

"Duck's…?" she asked again. "I don't under—"

"Both sides of the hair, at the back of the head, combed towards each other," Jack explained, "to make it look like a duck's…"

"Arse," she added with a grin. "I get it. But 'strides'?"

"Trousers," he said. "Jenny! Don't you know anything from your naïve sheltered upbringing?"

They all laughed, easy in each other's company, born of years of being good friends and looking out for each other. A few tales to tell there, then.

"Albion Terrace Junior," Jack said, once he'd finished his favourite – second – dish of apple crumble. "I know where it is but I've never been. You are either lucky to have got the job from outside of Leeds, or you must be so super-talented they couldn't afford to let you go."

"It has to be the latter," Joyce butted in, as she cleared away the dessert dishes to make way for her husband's cheese, biscuits, coffee, and … brandy. This was almost a replica of some 1920s' aristocratic soirée in the depths of Knightsbridge – without the cigars and the women leaving the men to talk about stuff *they* weren't supposed to understand. But they didn't do that sort of stuff ararnd 'ere. It was Altofts, when all sed an' dun, in t'depth o' t'West Riding, where folk dint 'old wi' be'avin' like them theeyer 'oy polloy. 'Ere, it were onny a token.

"It was luck, really," Stick replied, modestly. "I happened to be in the right place at the right time. No more, no less."

"Aye, well," Jack replied, "I think it's more than that, Our Stick. Tha's a Normy lad, and they'll allus be worth 'aving ower anybody else."

"Where did you train?" Jack added, intrigued by his new fellow deputy head. How coincidental could that have been – colleagues in schools only half a mile apart, and his best friend's husband, too?

"St John's College, Oxford," Stick replied, equally respectfully. "You?"

"Part of…?" Jack ventured.

"*Affiliated* to Oxford University," Stick said. "A teacher training college but otherwise nothing to do with the grandiose up at the university. It was a good course, which prepared me well for what I'm about to do."

"Me, too," Jack piped in. "Three-year course? I…"

Their conversation faded in to the background, weaving in and out of the sound of Perry Como as it drifted from their new hi fi.

"They seem to be getting on quite well," Joyce noted from the kitchen doorway, as they washed and stacked the pots in the plate rack on the stainless-steel draining board.

"I like this new-fangled moveable mixer tap," Jenny said, as she admired Joyce's new kitchen. "My two are fixed and don't reach the middle of the bowl."

"Only problem with them is you need a specially designed sink with only one central fixing hole thingy," Joyce added. "So, if you want to change back to two taps you have to buy a new sink, and that's not going to happen."

"We ought to do this more often," Jenny said, once the washing-up had been done. "You know, leaving the nippers with their grandparents so *we* can have a relax together."

"And what made you choose the Old Lane area?" Jack's voice faded back in again.

"One very sound logical reason," Stick replied, after very little thought. "It was the only one I saw advertised."

They both laughed and relaxed back into their brandy tumblers, cutting out all vestiges of life outside of their four substantial walls, as crepuscular dark dropped gently in on them – the uninvited, inevitable, unstoppable guest.

# Chapter 16

"Are you going somewhere?" Jack said, a quizzical look in his eyes as Jenny, Joyce and John trouped back into the lounge after breakfast, fully clad as if ready for a late May morning stroll.

"Indeed, we are," Joyce said. "I thought you might like a little trip down memory lane. It's a lovely morning so come on, Our Jack, stir your stumps."

"Where are we going?" he asked, as they set foot to the front path.

"That's for me to know and for you to find out," she replied, a wicked glint flashing in the brisk morning air, "very soon."

Although heading towards the back end of May, there was enough of a chill to oblige the casual stroller to wear a light jersey or even a windcheater. Jenny had on both, what with her susceptibility to even the slightest breeze. Jack wore his long shorts and a tee-shirt and light windjammer – just in case.

"That was Mrs Chadwick's shop," Jack pointed out, a wistful look betraying his thoughts, as they passed High Green Road corner and headed past the Robin Hood pub and on towards Stanley Ferry.

"Now, that's the place I was talking about," he said, slowing to a halt opposite the Methodist Church.

"The church?" Jenny asked, frowning slightly.

"No," he replied deliberately, as if dredging the depths of his memory, "the building next to it. When I was fifteen, it was a youth club with enough of a small hall to allow dancing twice a week."

"I still can't get over the thought of you as a dancer," Jenny said, an amused smile giving away her surprise at the suggestion.

"I'll have you know that I was an excellent bopper," Jack said, smiling as he puffed out his chest in pride. "I joined about a dozen or so others regularly on Thursday evening with my former girlfriend, Margaret. This was one of the three haunts where I strutted my stuff, I'll have you know."

"And the other two were Normy baths during the winter," Joyce added. "I used to go there with my cousins. They put on the occasional local group to add to the excitement. We used to nip out under the balcony towards the emergency exit for a quick snog and smooch in between songs. The other was the Mecca  Locarno in Wakefield."

"I never went to any of 'em," Jenny said. "Didn't like bopping much because I couldn't get the timing right. So how could you dance when there was only the pool area?"

"They folded back the changing cubicles," Jack explained, "and laid sturdy boards from wall to wall to make the dance floor. Never got to know whether they drained the water first, though."

"They had a stage at the diving board end as well," Stick joined in. "We had a couple of speech nights there before I left to go to QEGS."

"QEGS?" Jenny asked. "Don't know that one. I thought you were at the Grammar School until you left to go to college?"

"Queen Elizabeth Grammar School," he added. "It was up Northgate in Wakefield – founded in 1591 by charter from QE1."

"Speech Night," Jack began to recall. "My first, in 1958, was when I realised how harsh life could be."

"Harsh?" Jenny queried. "At twelve?"

"Well, you see," he began to explain, "I was in Form 1B, and the music master – Mr Hallam, I think it might have been – needed to choose a junior choir for our first speech night. So, he chose the whole of the first year – Forms 1A and 1B – to be … it … except for Arthur Jones, Curfy Wood, and … me. I was gutted."

"My poor man," Jenny cooed, as they burst into peals of laughter.

"Can you imagine," he went on, "Arthur, Curfy, and me? The only ones sitting on the balcony."

"I remember seeing you up there," Stick guffawed. "A bit like Wilson, Keppel and Betty."

"All we needed was a bucket of sand and some Egyptian costumes," Jack threw in quickly. "Though with Arthur Jones' dancing skills and Curfy Wood's Tony Curtis hairdo, we wouldn't have got very far."

Linking arms and doing a Wizard of Oz dance down the middle of Birkwood Road, the way seemed to funnel them towards Stanley Ferry, just a short walk away.

Jack stopped suddenly, unexpectedly – farm to left and right – and walked slowly towards a rough wooden stile over a linked, barbed wire topped fence to his left. The well-trodden path the other side of the fence meandered through another field and on to a high stone wall that surrounded a wood of disparate broad-leaved trees. Jack mounted the stile in silence and trod earth the other side of the fence before his companions reacted.

"Where are you going, Our Jack?" Jenny asked urgently, not sure whether he wanted them to follow, or he had seen something he wanted to retrieve. "Jack?"

"You can either come," he answered, halfway into the field, "or wait for me there, but there's something I need to do. Coming?"

"Count us in," Stick shouted, as he ushered the girls over the fence. "Hang on a bit."

They caught up when he landed on the other side of the second stile, as they entered a dappled tunnel of intertwining, leaf-covered branches of the trees to the outside of their path and the inside of the walled wood. Jack stopped, searching the length of the bilious-green, lichen-encrusted wall for an indeterminate ... something.

"What is it, Jack?" Joyce asked slowly, an almost inaudible church whisper oozing from her lips. "What are you looking for?"

"There, just by that young oak," he said, excitedly stabbing his finger towards a slight curve in the stonework. "That's where we used to climb over when we were about nine or ten. Come on."

He leaped forward in glee, as if recovering a long-dormant memory, gaining speed as he approached his goal. Then, like a frightened gazelle, he was over the wall and disappearing into the wood beyond.

"Come on, slow coaches," Stick urged, as he shinned up the wall to wait for the girls, a look of excited anticipation on *his* face. "Tally ho!"

"This ... is ... beautiful," Jenny said, a slight catch in her voice as she drew to a slow halt on seeing her Jack.

Knee-deep in an intense blue haze, the dappling sunlight in the wood filtered through the leaves overhead, drawing a deep sigh from him like it had around twenty years before. Here and there, bare patches of compacted earth hinted at vestiges of a meandering path leading to goodness knows where. He simply stood, arms hanging loosely by his sides, memories oozing to the surface and dancing around the splashes of yellow sunlight, as his eyes flicked and flashed from bole to branch to bluebells, remembering his first awed encounter here with his mates when he was ten. *Then* he had picked an armful of flowers to take home for his mam. *Now…*

"I think we ought to take some," Jack said, quietly, "for mi mam and for yours, Our Jen. What do you say?"

"What a lovely thought," Joyce said. "Perhaps *we* ought to take some, too. What do you think, Stick?"

"We're off to see to mi mam and granddad's graves this aft," Jack continued, "and they would definitely have appreciated that. Mi granddad was a gardener, and mi mam – well, she just loved flowers, especially yon bluebells from hereabouts. They were the first flowers as ever I gave her."

"Then," Jenny urged, "let's start picking."

"Onny just enough, mind," Jack warned, ever one to conserve. "T'bees and t'bulbs need us to leave some for *them*."

"What I didn't realise at that age, Our Jenny," Jack went on, "was that this walled bluebell wood was part of the Newland Park Estate, and that by following the path we could get back onto Newland Lane and past the brickworks we saw the other week. Remember? And then on to Wakefield Road, by yon Catholic Church."

"Of course I do," Jenny said with a smile. "How could I ever forget you and your wars?"

"Wars?" Joyce asked, a puzzled frown disfiguring her brow.

"It's an involved story, Joyce love," Jenny replied with an indulgent sigh, "and I'll tell you about it when we get back."

–o–

"Been a week and a *half*, really, don't you think?" Jack said, as he turned into the road home, out of Pinfold Lane towards Leeds Road and Methley Lane beyond. "Very enjoyable, though."

Jenny smiled as she turned to check on her two beauties in the back seat, both now happily asleep. She, too, felt her eyes prickling and, although she tried to fight it, within five minutes her eyes were closed and her mouth was open, making that strange little clicking sound Jack always noticed when she was away with the fairies.

A satisfied grin stretched across his face as he settled to provide as comfortable and jerk-free a ride home as he could, road surfaces willing. This weekend had been an emotion-shredding experience, brought on by an overload of memory-nudging and wall-to-wall nostalgia – and he had loved every second. Sharing his day with friends he had known almost all his life and with the woman of his dreams was all he could ever have wished for.

Icing on the cake for the family was William coming back into the family fold – preferring warmth and family love to cold isolation with someone who didn't really care that much. His job interview the week before had gone well, he thought, and he would get to know its result within a day or two. Everyone had everything crossed, for the outcome would herald a new era in Jack's family fortunes. Yet although he was bracing himself for the influx of another three children and two adults into his home, they were *family* and this is what a real family did.

"You're looking very thoughtful, my man," Jenny whispered, as he negotiated the twin roundabout approach to John o' Gaunts and the run through to Stourton and Hunslet.

"You've not been off for very long," he replied, happy to see his wife's beautiful face. "Woke yourself up snoring?"

"I've told you before," she harrumphed, playfully, "that I *don't* snore."

"That divine intuition of yours again, is it?" he laughed.

"Or do you sleep with one ear open?"

They both laughed silently, as Jessie stirred in her sleepy cocoon.

"I'm dying for a cup of tea," he added, trying to moisten his tongue. "Can't wait to be pulling into yon driveway. Been such a long time since we've been home, I've almost forgotten what mi Yorkshire tea tastes like."

"That Typhoon stuff Mum uses, not to your discerning palate, then?" Jenny replied quickly, as she noticed his lips curling in distaste.

"It's … all rayt, I suppose," he shot back at her, "but it's not Yorkshire."

–o–

"I think I've said it afore, but I'm off to extend yon patio at t'back of t'house in the summer holidays," Jack said, as he relaxed on the lounge settee next to his wife, a mug of tea steaming on the coffee table and a chocolate digestive about to slide delicately between his lips.

His daughters were settled in the lounge near to them, one playing with her soft rag doll on the hearth rug and the other reading one of Jack's stories about a family of birds.

"I think you have a fan there," Jenny said quietly, as she nudged him in the ribs, setting up a coughing reaction as a few crumbs chased down his windpipe. "Jessie seems to like your story."

"So she should," he replied, once he had cleared all vestiges of McVities from his windpipe. "It was written for her. One of these days I'll have it turned into a real book. Then she can take it to school with her."

"Did you notice, by the way, that there's a message flashing on yon new-fangled answering machine?" Jenny said, in a lull.

"No," he replied, disinclined to move. "Then why didn't

you find out who it was from? Probably nobody of any consequence."

"I would have," she said, "but I don't know how to."

"Press the little red flashing button," he explained, "and it will talk to you. I'll come and see to it when I've finished mi tea."

"No," she insisted, "I'll do it now. I have to learn how to do all these things for myself."

"Why?" he asked, a smile creeping up on him. "In case I snuff it?"

"Jack!" she gasped. "You know what your mam would have said to that."

"Probably 'don't tempt fate'?" he ventured.

"Then don't," she agreed.

Jack detected a little beep as she pressed the answer button but, hearing an indistinct whirring whine, he caught nothing of the message on the machine.

"You'll never guess what's happened," she said, a deadpan look betraying nothing of what she had just heard.

"Some catastrophic accident or mistake our William's made, no doubt," he said, an unconcerned 'I'm drinking my tea and I don't care until I've finished' look on his face.

"Well," she went on unabashed. "I'm going to tell you whether you like it or not because it's important – and exciting."

"Well, go on then," he urged through her deliberately pregnant pause. "Now, thoo has got my interest and my attention, thou brazen hussy. Come on, spill."

"Your William..." she started.

"For goodness' sake," he sighed, "what's he done now? Not that Selina bint again?"

"Samantha," Jenny said slowly, deliberately slowing down the telling. "She's called Samantha. Anyway, that's not it."

Jack's chin slumped onto his chest, eyes closed, as he

began to snore loudly, indicating his boredom with her antics.

"He's got that job," she continued, laughing at him.

"What?" Jack gasped, jerking his head upright to catch the full import of her news. "Got a proper decent job, has he? About time he came to his senses. Does that mean they'll be coming to stay with us, then, until yon new house is built?"

"Of course it does," she said, "but I'm just about to phone Val to find out."

At last. Finally grown up to realise what's important in his life. No more philandering. No more crazy ideas on outlandish jobs that don't pay. No more daft schemes because he doesn't want to do a proper job.

–o–

"Jenny!" Jack shouted from the bottom of the stairs, before he started preparing breakfast. "Can you come down please? I've something I need to show you."

"Oh yeah," she scoffed, her toothbrush still in her mouth, "I've heard *that* one before."

"No, please," he went on. "It's important."

"What do you see outside yon sliding patio doors?" he asked, a frown of concern growing. "Well, from the back fence, across the wet soil and to the doors?"

"Oh, my God!" she gasped, clapping a hand to her mouth. "Are they … footprints?"

"They certainly are," he growled, "and you notice how the muddy prints stop at the door, before heading off in front of the garage and down the drive. They disappear about halfway down the house."

"What were they doing?" she asked, naïvely.

"The interesting and disturbing thing is when you open the door," he said, stepping outside, "you notice here, around the lock and on the metal frame, that someone has tried to force their way in."

"Oh, my goodness," she replied, concerned that they had nearly had an intruder. "So, what are we going to do? Phone the police?"

"No point," he replied. "They won't have a clue. No. I need to make the door more secure from the inside. That one lock is tiny and not too difficult to break. I reckon he only had a piddling little screwdriver. If he'd been more prepared – and more determined – it might have been a different story."

"You keep on saying 'he'," Jenny said, pursing her lips, "but how do you know it wasn't a female?"

"Just take a look at the footprints," he pointed out. "It's either a male, or a female with king-size feet."

"What would we have done if he'd got in?" Jenny said, her voice dropping to a hoarse whisper.

"Phoned for an ambulance," he replied in a flash, "because that's what he would have needed. Nobody threatens *my* family and gets away wi' it."

She smiled nervously, on the one hand proud that she had a protector who would stop at nothing to make sure they were safe but on the other concerned, as she looked at the footprints, that there were people like *that* around where they lived.

"It was probably an opportunist, on his way home from a late night," Jack tried to explain it away, so as not to frighten her. "I'm quite sure they won't be paying a return visit, so don't worry. Anyway, I'm off to the DIY shop this aft to get a couple of bolts. I won't be happy until yon door is as secure as I can meck it."

"Then, when you get back, we'll have to start to organise the sleeping arrangements," Jenny said, as she put the kettle on to help move breakfast along. "We haven't enough furniture and they'll be here on Sunday – day before your last half term at Merton starts."

"Thursday now," he replied, scratching his head, "so after breakfast we need to have a look, measure up and nip to MFI to get one or two flat packs. We don't need much. A couple of quid should sort it all out."

"Yeah, right," she scoffed. "Add a hundred on to that."

"I'll give 'im a bill when they move into their new house," Jack laughed. "Anyway, families look after each other. No problem. I just hope that this new route of his lasts. My concern is how's he going to fund all this? I mean, we can't afford to subsidise them forever."

"Val says she's got a temporary teaching job at her old school for this coming half term," Jenny said, shrugging her shoulders, "and he's prepared to do anything to fill in."

"Time to tighten *our* belts, then, as well," Jack sighed. "Roll on."

# Chapter 17

"You look buggered," Big Beardy Brian said, as Jack ambled into his art room the first day back after Whitsuntide. "Been busy?"

"You *could* say that, BBB," Jack replied, wiping the imaginary sweat from his furrowed forehead.

"How's that, then, young Jack?" Brian asked, his smiley eyes dancing to their usual tune.

"Inundated with family," he gasped, as he launched into the tale.

Two weeks away, and Beardy Brian's art room looked no different from the day they had broken up. Yet there was an endearing quality, an individuality and uniqueness about *his* works, and how his youngsters had interpreted it in *theirs*.

"You need a bloomin' holiday, young man," Beardy Brian gasped. "These here holidays are meant to be just that – *holidays*. I don't reckon much to family taking over, no matter how close, needy or homeless they are."

"They'd have done it for us in similar circumstances," Jack replied, doing what he said he'd never do – defending the indefensible. "My brother's not much good on organisation and so someone had to make sure his family don't suffer. It's not *their* fault he's so useless."

"Have they got somewhere else to live now, then," Brian asked, sure of what answer he was going to receive.

"You must be joking," Jack guffawed. "They're here for the duration, I'm afraid – at least until September."

"For goodness' sake, why?" Brian asked, incredulous at this cockeyed way of thinking. "I wouldn't do all that for *my* brother."

"Why's that, Brian?" Jack asked, surprised at what Brian was saying.

"Because I haven't got one," he said, that usual mischievous giggle bubbling up.

"Daft bugger," Jack replied, joining in the mirth. "Time to go. Briefing in ten minutes and time to see which thoughtful person has decided to extend his holiday."

"You're a dark horse," a female voice accosted him from behind, as they passed Marjorie Chamber's Home Economics room opposite the boys' toilets. Talk about a dichotomy of smells. Experienced members always hugged the Home Ec side of the corridor and burst round the corners in double-quick time.

"And how's that, then, Linda?" Jack replied, without looking back. He knew the owner of that insidious rasp without the benefit of visual corroboration.

"Half a term left," she said, as she steamed past. "You know. Leaving at the end of this term. Promotion – just not … here."

Jack ignored her jibe, realising with a smile that the promotion point she had *now* was about as far as she would go, unless she learned to control her gob. Abrasive and uncontrolled. Yuk!

Jack and Beardy Brian finally managed to shoulder their way into a crowded staff room, the steam from thirty, full, hot tea and coffee mugs vying with the blue haze from several Woodbine, Dunhill, and Peter Stuyvesant cigarettes in this wholly inadequate and inhospitable staff box. Brian's priority was joining the queue at the coffee urn, Jack's was finding a more comfortable, smokeless hole next to an open window.

"Ladies and gentlemen, if you please," Mr Byrne's soporific drone wound itself into first gear. "We have to start this briefing on a very sad note, I'm sorry to say. I have to report that our new young RE teacher, Peter Solomon, passed away yesterday, in the early hours of the morning."

Disbelieving gasps dragged a stunned silence unexpectedly into the gathering. This was not the way they either expected or wanted to start their last half term of this academic year. Peter Solomon was one of those quiet young men who seemed to remain invisible, even in a small crowded room like this one, where he never had much to say or to contribute to any gathering. A tall, pleasant young man, he kept himself to himself, always seeming to prefer his own company to joining in the ready chatter of most usual staff rooms.

"Our hearts and minds must go out to his family at this awful time," he continued. "The school will send a floral tribute and a representative to his funeral, to be held a week on Friday. All other matters are insignificant by comparison, and will be dealt with at a later time."

With that he was gone, leaving the gathering gasping and muttering in knots.

"Did I detect a slight note of compassion in the old goat?" Beardy Brian said quietly, almost in an aside.

"Probably feeling a twinge of mortality," Jack replied. "Gruff exterior somehow doesn't do it for me."

"I wonder who'll be representing the school?" Marjorie's soft Scots' lilt wafted into the conversation.

"Probably Janet Marne," John Franklyn suggested. "She is his head of department and probably the only one on the staff he either spoke or related to."

"Well," Jack sighed, as they trooped out of the staff room, "here goes, to what I hope will be an uneventful few weeks."

"Going anywhere exotic for your summer hols?" Brian asked.

"Yes," Jack enthused. "Back to the White Lodge at … Filey."

"Wow," Brian added. "Not fancy anywhere abroad?"

"Not really," Jack explained. "My two are too young for that sort of stuff – the one likes digging in the sand and the other still needs breastfeeding. So, Filey's just the ticket. A week's just long enough."

"Something you enjoy, Jack?" Brian asked, as they approached his art room.

"Yes, it is," Jack assured him. "I can dig in the sand with Jessie but breastfeeding is one of the few things I *can't* do."

The door from Linda's classroom, round the corner from Brian's studio, erupted as it spat out a red-faced little boy onto the shiny floor. He picked himself up hurriedly and turned to flee.

"Paul Ridsdale?" Jack shouted, his authoritative voice halting the fleeing boy momentarily. "You are going where?"

"I'm not stopping in this dump a minute longer – not with *her*, I'm not," he threw over his shoulder as he made for the outside door. "So, don't *you* try to stop me."

"I won't," Jack replied calmly. "I'll just see you tomorrow."

The little boy stopped mid-stride for a few seconds, a look of indecision crossing his face, before he struck out for the outside door again – and freedom.

"See you tomorrow, Paul," Jack shouted after the fleeing boy.

Beardy Brian laughed that conspiratorial, twinkly-eyed giggle that was so infectious, as he slapped Jack on the back and turned into his classroom. Unlike Jack, he was one of the three year heads who had no registration or classroom duties, so he could prepare himself for the morning's strain of trying to inculcate some degree of art appreciation into resisting twelve-year-old bodies and minds.

"Gabrielle Sarah!" Jack gasped, clapping his hand to his shocked face as he sat down in front of his class to do the register.

"What is it, Mr Ingles?" she replied, a puzzled look invading her eyes. "What have I done?"

"Well," he went on, "you're either here early, or some foreign nation has secreted an imposter into your seat."

A snigger careered around the room as all faces turned towards her. There was nothing the class liked more than Jack's wit at the beginning of morning registration. *That* was what they all waited for. It wasn't a sharp, cutting wit – just poking a bit of fun at someone's expense; gentle, almost charming, that *everyone* enjoyed.

–o–

The lunchtime staff room was busier and smokier than usual, as every few seconds the opening door spat another body into the room from the jostling throng outside.

"What's going on in here?" Freddy Hoostayn gasped, his sparkly eyes lighting the room as the door clicked behind him. "Free coffee and cakes?"

"It seems that, Hoostayn, we've had a problem here," Jack replied in his best American accent.

"Problem?" Beardy Brian said, as he ambled in.

"Apparently, all the shops around here have run out of … toilet paper," Keith Cadbury said as he sat down.

Hoots of derision greeted that announcement, accompanied by a variety of obvious and not-so-obvious toilet references and quips, giving the impression that nobody believed a word of it.

"It's true," Keith insisted. "Tell you what. All of you. Call in at your local shops and see for yourselves when you get home."

"What should we call ourselves, Keith?" Beardy Brian said. "Your s-hit squad?"

The room erupted in good-humoured banter, usually at Keith Cadbury's expense.

"You'll see," he said, with a knowing smile as he sipped his week black tea, calmly, not rising to the bait. "You'll see."

–o–

There were two things Jack always did as soon as he had clicked shut yon front door to his home after work – kiss his wife hello and sit down in the lounge, coat-free and slippered, with a steaming…

"Cup of Yorkshire and a digestive," he sighed, as he clasped his hot mug to his chest. "Bliss and heaven. Proper tea, not like that muck they serve up at school. We've just been allocated a very small locker – big enough for a mug and a box of tea bags. So, I'm going to have to teck mi own. Can't stomach it any longer, even if I have only a week or two left there. Your day?"

"Crap," she replied, laughing at her own joke. "Local shop's run out of…"

"Don't tell me," he butted in, a knowing smile growing. "Toilet rolls."

"How on earth do you know that?" she gasped.

"Crazy science teacher called Cadbury, of all names," he guffawed. "Nobody believed him, but…"

"Then we shall have to test out his theory," she said, smiling at the challenge to hand. "His is a hypothesis that needs testing to a conclusion, then we can arrive at a working theory."

"Oo, 'ark at you," Jack laughed. "I have no idea what you just said, but it sounded clever and impressive. Perhaps we ought to try to buy some at the supermarket. Grandways in Harehills might be a good place to start."

They both laughed as she jumped on him to tickle him into submission but he had anticipated her move by rolling off the settee, over its dropped arm. She wasn't to be fooled by his clumsy escape attempt because she was already on top of his writhing body before he had time to blink. He could only capitulate in a heap in the corner by the front window in fits of hysterical giggles.

"That'll learn you not to take the mick out of me," she said, a look of triumph overtaking her as she allowed him solace and the space to make her another cup of tea.

"You're a hard woman, Jenny Ingles," he gasped, a chuckle rising to his throat again as he straightened his clothes. "I pity the poor bugger who gets you when I snuff it."

"Jack," she protested quietly. "Don't say that. If *you're* not here, then neither shall I be." She flung her arms around his waist and buried her face in his chest.

"And who would look after yon bairns if we were both not here?" he said quietly, kissing the top of her head. "Your mum? Val and William? I don't think so."

"Enough of that sort of talk anyway," she insisted. "It upsets me. Don't you like it here with me?"

"Course I do," he assured her. "I was just saying."

"Then don't…" she went on.

"Tempt fate?" he added, finishing off one of his mam's well-used homilies.

"Mummy?" Jessie's squeaky little voice floated in from the hall doorway.

"Yes, my poppet," Jenny replied straightaway, recognising that urgent request she had met so many times before in so many different circumstances.

"Come on then, upstairs and…" Jenny urged, heading for the door.

"No," Jessie replied, standing her ground, hands on hips like she'd often seen her Grandma McDermot. "I don't want to use the toilet. I can do *that* on my own, anyway."

"Then what?" Jenny asked, puzzled at this new request.

"I was wondering if we might have some tea now," she replied, "only Florence May and I are a little peckish."

Jack could hardly contain his mirth at hearing this five – going on fifty – year old telling Jenny what neither had heard from her before.

"Well, my little one," Jenny replied, with a straight face, "I was just saying to your daddy that it was about time we had some dinner. What would you like?"

"Dumperlings and gravy," Jessie said, licking her lips as a smile took over. "My favourite."

"Do you know," Jack said, picking her up ready to toss her into the air to huge hoots of joy, "that's *my* favourite too, and I think I might be able to detect a slight smell of something like that squeezing its way out of the kitchen, trying to escape."

Jessie whooped again as he caught her and set her down, right way up, before marching off with her towards the smell.

"Shall we go and have a look?" he added, a conspiratorial whisper escaping his mouth as he crossed his lips with his forefinger.

"Silly Daddy," Jessie's forced whisper could be heard as they tiptoed into the kitchen. "Smells can't escape. They don't have legs."

–o–

"Tell me again," Jack said, as he finished chasing the last vestiges of meat and dumpling around his plate. "When are we to be overrun by … family?"

"They arrive this Saturday coming," Jenny replied, finishing giving Flo her share of dumplings and gravy. She was a dream to look after, was that Florence May Ingles. Never protested and always took everything offered to her with relish, always licking her lips just like her great-granddad Jud always did.

"They can please themselves when they come," he replied, leaning back happily in his chair. "Everything's ready. We've enough bed and sleeping space for a platoon from KOYLI."

"KOYLI?" Jenny puzzled. "What's that?"

"You're a Yorkshire Lass, and you don't know that?" he scoffed. "King's Own Yorkshire Light Infantry, of course. I thowt all Yorkshire folk knew that."

"Four days, then," Jack muttered again, after a moment's quiet. "Better gird mi loins."

–o–

"You'll never believe it," Jack said to Beardy Brian, as they walked into the building from the car park.

"Oh yes I will," Brian replied, knowing full well what he was about to say. "Like you, I would assume, I went to several outlets on the way home yesterday, to disprove Crazy Cadbury's cock-eyed crap, and…"

"You found you couldn't," Jack interrupted with finality.

"Exactly," Brian agreed. "Every bloody one – out of stock. Supply problem, they all said."

"Same here," John Franklyn's voice overtook them as they reached the back entrance by the Youth Centre. "And want to know something else? No sugar either."

"We don't use it, so it doesn't matter to us," Jack replied, "but what is it with this country? Makes a chap want to emigrate."

"He'll be sitting in his corner by the notice board," Beardy Brian added, "a smug self-satisfied look on his face as he sips his bloody black brew. Mark my words. Makes you want to chuck summat at him."

The first thing they *did* see as they entered the anti-crush hall was Keith Cadbury exiting the head's goldfish bowl of an office sharply, looking both ways as he did; the second thing they saw was a large pile of white toilet rolls, stacked obviously behind the head's black leather swivel chair.

"Bloody hell!" Beardy Brian gasped, as Keith bounced towards them. "So, *that's* where all the toilet rolls have gone."

"You found out I wasn't spinning a yarn, then?" Keith said, a smug smile sitting on his face. "Sensible chap, that Mr Byrne. He had heard about the shortages, both of toilet rolls and sugar, and so he asked me if I could do anything about it."

"And we can see that you could," Jack nodded towards the stack of white tissue behind the captain's chair, "but that beggars the question – how?"

"I have … contacts," Keith replied, touching the side of his nose and smiling knowingly. "Would any of you like to avail yourself of my reasonable service?"

"And how much do you get out of this 'service'?" John Franklyn asked pointedly.

"Suffice it to say that the rolls are marginally more expensive than they were," Keith advised, "but after *this* particular shortage, they'll never return to pre-shortage prices."

"How can you, a mere teacher, know *that*?" Brian scoffed, not impressed by his know-all attitude. "Unless it's you causing the shortage."

"I don't think so," he added, as he made to move away, "but my contacts tell me it's a ploy by the suppliers to force up prices – same with the sugar. Let me know when you need my assistance."

With that, he headed for the stairs, and on towards his science lab on the top floor.

"He doesn't realise, of course," John said, as they made for the staff room, "that the head has two HM Inspectors coming to see him – in about fifteen minutes. I'd love to see Byrne's face when he leads them into his office, to be confronted by a mountain of toilet rolls and bags of sugar."

They laughed as they shouldered their way through the wall of huge plate-glass doors by the aviary, where Miss Copthorne's children were already swilling out budgie deposits from the stone-flagged floor.

# Chapter 18

"**Y**ou must want *something*," William insisted on the phone the day before they were due to move in with his brother's family. "There's five of us, for goodness' sake."

"And how are you going to afford what I would need to charge you for the time you'll be here, William? Eh? Tell me that," Jack snorted, knowing his brother would have no answer. Val had secured a part-time job at her old school, and his brother had managed to persuade his new school to take him on for a couple of days a week in the run up to the summer holidays, and *that* didn't amount to a bag of beans.

"But..." William went on, seeming not to want to take no for an answer.

"But nothing, Bro," Jack insisted. "You can chip in occasionally if you like – fish and chips here, Chinese there, chek now and again."

"I..." William started again.

"The bit about the chek was a play on—" Jack began to explain.

"I know what it was," his brother harrumphed.

"Then all you need to understand, William," Jack insisted firmly and finally, "is that this is *my* house, so we play it by *my* rules. OK?"

Their conversation faded to mutterings before he replaced the receiver and shrugged his shoulders.

"Not an easy person to have a rational conversation with, Our Jack," Jenny said, watching her husband fighting his frustration.

"They can't afford even to pay their way, Our Jen," he pointed out, "so how can I take money from them they don't have?"

"Will *we* be able to manage, though?" she asked. "I know you're a wizard with our income, but…"

"It's all worked out, lovely lady," he assured her. "It'll be tight but we'll manage. Trust me. I'm a … magician. We all ready for the influx?"

"What have they done about schooling for their brood?" he added, puzzled that Val, at least, hadn't broached the subject.

"Mary's going to Prince Lane Junior, like our Jessie, only in a higher class," Jenny explained, "and so is Ed, but only until the end of this year. September, he starts at Allenby Comp with his brother. Different years, but together. That has to help them both."

"They're all smart," Jack said, nodding sagely, "so it shouldn't be a problem. They'll succeed … *despite* the efforts of their teachers."

"Well, sixteen hours and they'll be here," Jenny said. "We'd better be up in good time, to make sure everything's…"

The insistence of the telephone again shut down their conversation, urging someone – anyone – to pick up its handset. Business to attend to, folks to placate.

"No problem, mate," Jack replied, as an urgent babble hit his eardrum. "Don't worry. Just come when you're ready."

"Do I detect a problem?" Jenny asked. "Your William?"

"Something about needing to come this evening instead of tomorrow," he replied with a sigh. "He *does* make mountains out of molehills."

"Any reason?" she asked.

"Didn't ask," he said. "It would only have caused waves. They'll come when they come. Everything's aired and ready, so I'm not busting a gut. They'll just have to take things as they are, with a roof over their heads – albeit a tight one."

"I suppose I'll have to—" she said, making a move towards the kitchen.

"No need," he urged, holding her back. "They're calling off for something to eat on the way. There's plenty in the house for everyone. Both fridge and freezer are full, along with every conceivable cupboard and wardrobe, so nobody's about to starve. It ought to last best part of … two days."

She laughed at his sense of humour, but marvelled at how calmly he was taking the dam-burst that was about to be his brother and his family.

-o-

"The bedrooms are just lovely," Val said, as she hugged her sister. "I can't tell you how much of a life-saver this is for us – and an excitement for the children."

"Arrangements for ablutions are easy," Jenny said. "Although Jessie and Mary are sharing a room, Jessie will use our en-suite and Flo will be in our room."

"But William and I don't even have an en-suite at home," Val replied, a gleeful smile catching up with her. "The one here with our bedroom is just divine. The boys will share the family bathroom, and Mary can probably share ours."

"Are you sure you're not…?" Jenny went on, adding a generous slice of concern for their comfort.

"Called off at a Wimpy Bar on the way – twice," her sister said, calming her worries. "You know how hungry growing lads get. Now, we must come to some arrangement over food, and…"

"It's all sorted, Sister-in-law," Jack's voice invaded their space. "Just had the same conversation with your husband.

Your finances will be exceedingly tight until William is working full time and you are in your own place. So, you'll have to accept the boundless generosity of your munificent brother-in-law and his wonderful wife."

"I can see *you* won't need anything else to eat today," Jenny laughed, "because of that dictionary you've just swallowed."

They laughed that easy, sighed laugh that comes with the release of worry and stress. Val and William had needed help and Jack and Jenny had delivered it in huge dollops, without demur, duress, or demands. They could now look forward to cementing the rest of *their* lives, where they should have been in the first place – instead of traipsing to that dead-alive hole 'darn sarf'.

–o–

"Six weeks left to Dooms Day, eh?" Beardy Brian said, as he squeezed himself out of his wife's Hillman Minx.

"Deliverance Day, I prefer to call it, old chap," Jack quipped, taking a deep breath of clear morning air as he unclipped his trouser bottoms, before he walk his bike in to school. His exertions seemed lighter, and his rucksack less heavy, the nearer he drew to his escape door. "You're going to get varicose veins and piles driving that tiddly little machine, if you're not careful. What's wrong with your Granada?"

His companion released his infectious little giggle, which seemed incongruous for such a big man. But then he *was* an artist who was allowed so many different facets to his character. Beardy Brian claimed it made him more interesting as a person, and that it was why his wife had chosen *him* out of the crowd.

"What will you do without all this aggravation and unpleasantness, Young Jack, when you're gone?" Brian asked.

"I won't miss you at all, Brian," Jack quipped with a wicked glint in his eyes, bursting out laughing as he spoke.

194

Fortunately, Beardy Brian had a similar sense of humour and he joined in Jack's mirth.

"You are probably the only person I shall miss, old chap," Jack added, an air of seriousness invading his demeanour. "The only person who has shown me friendship and honesty, and to whom I can relate easily."

"Likewise, Jack," Brian said quietly. "Likewise. Keep in touch?"

"Undoubtedly," Jack replied, as they approached the staff-room door. "You understand, of course, that I'm not one of those folks who never carries through a promise? We *will* meet again, don't know where, don't know when, but until this afternoon…"

"Good morning, ladies and gentlemen," the deputy's voice drew everyone to order in the staff room, ready for Monday-morning briefing. "It is with great regret that I have to tell you that my union – to which most of you I know are affiliated – has informed me that, as of next week, they are calling industrial action over the government's intractability about pay and conditions."

"Does that mean," Beardy Brian asked, "that we will be getting an unpaid extra holiday?"

"There are two angles to this, Brian," Tom began to answer. "The one involves staying at home and losing pay. The other – which the union advocates – is being in school and refusing to cover things like bus and lunchtime supervision."

A disjointed and dissatisfied mutter rolled around the room, to be interrupted by Jack's pragmatic and pointed question. "Does that mean also that our disadvantaged and vulnerable youngsters – for whom a cooked midday meal is probably the only one they'll get – will have to go without?" he asked, a serious note of disquiet underlying his concern.

The room fell silent as eyes searched for the face asking

such a crucial, uncomfortable question. Minds realised, without thinking, really, the conscience behind the words. Trust him to raise such a socially searching and sensitive question at *this* time. Conscience or cash? What other conclusion could there be than that which would enhance their status and standard of living? Their salaries had been held back for too long, and surely...

"Because if it does," he continued, "you can count me out. You can't seriously be considering the rightness of *that* argument – surely?"

The ensuing deafening silence from a group of 'caring' professionals told Jack everything he needed to know about this group of sanctimonious hypocrites. He strode out of the room, leaving stunned faces gasping for air, like so many cod heads on a fishmonger's slab.

"Well said, Youngster," Beardy Brian's voice caught up with him as he rounded the boys' toilet corner. "You slapped down that group of ne'er-do-well self-servers with panache."

"Sounds like one of mi mam's teas," Jack grinned.

"One of...?" Brian puzzled.

"Pan ash is a cooking utensil containing potatoes and left-over meat and carrots and stuff," Jack explained. "We used to call it hash. So, pan – ash."

"You are *so* clever," his companion replied with a laugh, his words laced with a healthy dose of sarcasm. "So, next week you can show everybody how deep your principles run. Me? I don't do lunch anyway, so it won't affect."

"I don't either," Jack replied, puzzled at his response, "but I'll simply eat my bread and jam while I'm supervising. I assume Byrne will maintain *his* duty as head teacher. Although am I being naïve here?"

"No, Jack," Beardy Brian replied, with an approving smile beneath his beard, "you must maintain your ideals. Nothing else matters. But what about *your* union? Won't they have something to say about it?"

"Only do as your heart and mind dictate," Jack said, smiling at the memory of his last school. "I'm in AMMA, and we don't strike."

"And *that* is…?" Brian said, looking puzzled.

"Assistant Masters and Mistresses Association," Jack trotted out. "They won't support strikes, but leave the conscience thing to individuals. Fits with mine perfectly. I…"

Jack's voice faded away, as he explained his previous experiences with industrial action, to be overtaken by the clamour of excited children getting on with their last half term of this academic year. For some, it would be their first and only year spent in a middle school – ever.

–o–

"Looks like we're in for bother again," Jack said, as he settled back to a drink and a nibble after school.

"Why's that, then, Our Jack?" Val asked. "No need to worry. Family's here, and our Mary'll sort them out. Eh, Chick?"

"Got bother of my own, I think," Mary said quietly, her reluctant reply raising one or two eyebrows.

"Mary?" Val said, concern etching the name. "Bother? You didn't tell me that when I collected you from school. Mary? Spill."

Looks of consternation leaped from one adult face to the next, as Mary jiggled uncomfortably in her seat. "It's that shitty Smallpiece," she mumbled.

"Mary!" Val gasped her warning to her daughter. "Where have you learned such words?"

"It's what they all say," she pleaded uncomfortably, "and besides, it's what Dad said all the time when he was talking to Mr Grove next door at … home."

Her voice tailed off as William butted in. "What's

happened with this … Smallpiece girl to make you be in bother?" he asked hurriedly.

"Boy," Mary corrected, "and he wouldn't stop pulling my hair at playtime, so … I hit him."

"Attagirl, Our Mary! Serves him right, I say," Jack burst in, in support of his niece.

"Jack," Jenny interrupted, raising a cautionary eyebrow. "Not helping."

"If he's the one who picked on you," William said, following his brother's reasoning, "then he got what he deserved, and if the teachers make anything of it I shall tell them so."

"And where did you slap him?" Val asked, hardly daring to pursue this line of questioning much further.

"I punched him in the nose," Mary replied, a burst of confidence rising once she had seen her Uncle Jack's smile of encouragement. "He had blood on his face and he burst into tears."

She planted her feet firmly on the lounge carpet, hands glued to hips as she had seen her mum do several times lately, with pursed lips, and a deeply furrowed brow of defiance etched on her face.

"Blood?" Val gasped. "Oh, my god! What has my little girl come to?"

"Exercising her God-given right to protect herself," Jack insisted, "as she should. I'll guarantee she won't be picked on again. Way to go, Our Mary."

"And you, Our Jack?" Jenny asked, a smile beginning to form. "Not punched that Mr Byron, I hope?"

"Mr Byrne," he corrected, with a good-humoured laugh. "Not quite. For once it's not him causing disruption to my life in school."

"Come on, then," Val joined in, after a moment's pause. "Spill."

"My esteemed, compassionate and caring colleagues have decided to strike for better pay and conditions," he answered, with as much disdain and disgust as he could muster.

"Strike? Teachers?" she gasped. "But, that's against—"

"The principles of our system of education as we know it?" Jack spat back. "My thoughts, too."

"What are you going to do, lovely?" Jenny joined in, a little concerned at the unilateral action he might take.

"What I always do," he said. "Follow my principles and do what I'm paid to do – look after the youngsters in my care."

"But how can you do that when your children won't be in school?" William asked, puzzled at his reply.

"Yon teachers have been clever, you see," Jack explained. "The children *will* be in school, allowing the teachers to exercise their educational duties and not lose pay. They just won't do dinner duties, thus punishing the innocents in all this – the children who can't fight back."

"They'll go home, won't they?" William observed naïvely.

"What, when parents will be at work – or somewhere else?" Jack harrumphed, disdainfully. "They'll be turfed onto the streets – hungry until late evening. Poor buggers. The least worry in their parents' selfish lives. Not going to happen, not on my watch. Like the Windmill, the canteen *will* stay open."

"And what will your union have to say about that?" William asked again, rather pointedly.

"Non-striking union, Bro," Jack replied quickly, putting him in his place as he went on to explain the last time he was in this position "…and that's why I chose my present gang."

"I think that's what's happening at my school, Mammy," Mary said.

"Mine, too," three other voices chimed in, in unison.

"Then we'll all have to come home for lunch," Jenny

replied, "and have a ... party."

Shouts of "Yay", "Great", "Count me in", filled the room, as bodies of varying sizes did little jigs around the lounge. Even Jessie joined in, although she was concentrating on her reading book as she did so.

"I'll be here, too," Val added, a growing smile on her face at her sister's suggestion. "It'll be fun."

"And how long is this fiasco going to last?" William grunted.

"You'll have to ask your school's union rep about that one, William," Jack cut in. "It's to be done on a school-by-school basis, so only individual schools will know."

"Damn nuisance, if you ask me – and nobody has," William muttered. "I'm off out for a walk. Coming, lads? I fancy going to see how *our* house is getting on."

"Then we'll all come," Jack butted in, turning to Val and Jenny's shaking heads. "OK, then. Jessie? Mary?"

"You children go and have a good time," Jenny said, a grin of relief appearing quickly as she nodded to Val. "We'll get some tea ready, eh, Val?"

"And have a bit of peace into the bargain," Val muttered as an aside, to the sound of the shutting front door.

"Phew," the sisters sighed loudly, as they flopped back into the soft settee, starting to giggle. "At last."

# Chapter 19

Weekend couldn't come quickly enough for Jack, as more and more he was sidelined at school. That didn't matter much because his main function was to provide the best education he could for the youngsters under his care. This he did with commensurate ease but he couldn't help it rankling.

Val and William's new house had grown rapidly over the weeks they had stayed with Jack and Jenny. That magical moment when the last slate was laid and the last strapping on the end ridge tile fixed into place was watched by the whole family. They laughed at the comical sight of a burly roofer in knee pads, shorts and laceless hefty boots, taking a bow twenty or so feet above them as they applauded when he applied his masterly finishing touch to *their* roof.

"That's what I love about *this* climate," Val said sarcastically, as they settled for mid-morning coffee and a slice of Jenny's home-made Victoria sponge. "It's mid-June – the height of an English summer – and the clouds are building, ready for the beginnings of a summer blow and splash."

As if on cue, and out of nowhere, large threatening globes of summer rain were driven into the ground by a fierce westerly, rattling the fences and almost bending the sapling trees double.

"Wow," was all William could say in amazement.

"Reminds me of a mate when I was a nipper on Scarborough Row," Jack said. "There was a huge triangle of waste scrub land between Wakefield Road, Goosehill Road and Woodhouse Mount."

"I remember that," William piped up. "There was a permanent large black circle in the middle."

"Black circle?" Val puzzled. "What was that for?"

"Bonfire Night," the brothers chorused, grins betraying their shared memory.

"October, all the lads from around would be out and about bunnywooding," William explained.

"And meck a pile on that black, burned circle, ready for Bonfire Night on the fifth of November," Jack continued. "Remember, remember the fifth of November. Gunpowder, treason and plot."

"Ee," William added dropping, unusually for him, into his native twang. "Tecks me back."

"That's the reason the black circle was … black," Jack continued. "*That* was the permanent spot for the fire."

"What's 'bunnywooding'?" Jenny asked, as puzzled as her sister.

"All the lads collected wood – cut-down trees, old fencing, broken doors, anything that would burn – from anywhere for the fire," Jack went on. "It had to be a big pile for it to burn all evening."

"Local folk would gather around," William joined in again, "putting taties in at the bottom of the fire to roast, and letting fireworks off."

"Remember how black and hot those taties got, eh, Will?" Jack reminisced, becoming almost glassy-eyed as the memories flooded back, "and raw in the middle because we couldn't wait."

"You had to drag 'em out wi' a stick, and hold 'em on

a spike or summat, to try to get inside the blackened and crozzled skin wi' out burning your lips,"William remembered, a joyful, almost child-like grin drawing him back to his almost-forgotten childhood.

"Beautiful!" they both chorused again, the remembered taste closing both sets of eyes in ecstasy.

"And the smells," Jack urged. "Do you remember the smells?"

"Burnt wood…"

"…scorched paint bits of burning door…"

"…cordite and gunpowder…"

"…from exploding fireworks…"

"…singed dog hair when Gittins' mutt Harvey got too close to the flames…"

"…sticky toffee apples mi mam used to meck…"

"…black treacle parkin…"

"…an' smoke that stayed in your nostrils for days…"

"What 'ave we let go by, eh, Our William?" Jack finished, almost in a whisper, as the wind threw sheets of rain at the windows, dispelling all memories and reminding them of the here and now.

"You were just going to tell us about your mate, Our Jack," Jenny reminded him gently, recognising the almost pained look in his eyes.

"Wind and rain?" Val chipped in.

"Oh, aye," Jack started slowly, drawing back the memory. "I knew David Free before we left Scarborough Row for Garth Avenue, when I was six. Their house, at number 29 Goosehill Road, backed on to the green triangle where David's dad, David, had built a timber garage for his beloved Austin 7. Although quite sturdy, it took a beating one very stormy night when his dad was on nights at Pope and Pearson's pit in Altofts.

"Imagine his mam's surprise to be woken up at two in

the morning by the local bobby, hammering on the back door to tell her David's dad's garage was swaying like some demented hoola-hoola girl. Because her husband's car was inside the structure, David's mam, Joyce, thought she had better phone the pit from the red call box round the corner."

"And he'd be able to get home from *down* the pit?" Jenny asked. "His car was at home, wasn't it?"

"Course he would," Jack explained. "For a start, he wasn't *down* the pit, and second, he always went to work on his bike. Imagine having to pedal back home – mid-shift – like a bat out of hell, to try to save both garage and car."

They all laughed at the picture Jack painted of David's dad pedalling for all his worth, head down and legs shooting like pistons against this demon of a storm.

"Well?" Val asked, puncturing his silence. "Did he?"

"Did he what?" Jack asked, jolting himself out of his reverie.

"Save his car," William interrupted from the edge of his chair. "Tha's got me on t'edge o' mi chair here, for god's sake, and—"

"That doesn't happen very often," Val butted in, a mischievous twinkle in her eye.

"According to David junior," Jack continued, "as he opened the garage door, he could see the wall resting on the car's precious side enough to urge him to reverse his motor out gingerly."

"And when he finally got it out," William urged, "what—?"

"The building collapsed," Jack went on, "just like the house of cards it was. It took him another month to put it back together again – more securely this time."

"And the upshot?" Jenny asked. "Make sure yon building is sturdy and safe before you entrust your treasure to its interior?"

"Well, actually, no," Jack said, smiling at David senior's perversity. "Strangely enough, he cursed that damnable bobby every time the wind blew ever after for the work *he'd* caused him. Figure that one out if you can."

–o–

"Isn't it your lad's birthday anytime soon?" William asked his brother, at tea after one particularly difficult day in mid-summer.

"When Jack was a nipper," Jenny said with a smile, "he would have corrected you on that one, William."

"Corrected? How do you mean?" William asked, puzzled and concerned he had got the date wrong. "Wrong time of year?"

"No," Jack replied, preparing to put him straight. "I would have pointed out that you only have *one* birthday – the day you are born on. All the others are celebrations of its anniversary."

"Oh," William said, to Val's grin. "I should have known. Our Mary's getting to be more like you every day."

"I've been trying to get to see him virtually since I knew he was back in this country with his witch of a mother," Jack sighed, "but with no result. There's always one excuse or another."

"Surely you have a right," Val said. "Don't you?"

"All well and good, these 'ere rights," Jack replied, with a mixture of anger and resignation. "They can also be a very expensive luxury most of us ordinary folk can't afford."

"But…?" William insisted, more forcefully than he had before.

"It's still down to his mother to allow … or not," Jack said, with a heartfelt sigh, "and I've got two *other* children who *do* want to spend time with me."

Jenny slid her arm round his shoulders, recognising one

of those rare, upsetting times her husband had given up on an issue that was close to his heart. She knew he wouldn't insist, because he felt it wasn't worth either the effort or the inevitable drain on their scant resources.

"Anyway," Jack said, a smile creeping back into his face, "I couldn't be happier with my *true* family around me. And you as well, of course, Our William."

They all smiled at Jack's funny ... except, that is, for William, over whose head it whizzed without being recognised for what it was.

"I forgot to tell you, didn't I," Jenny said, once they'd settled, "that when Flo and I went shopping to Moortown, we decided to call in for a coffee at that new caff on Street Lane."

"Oh aye?" Jack smiled. "Spending all mi brass, eh?"

"We met someone who you ought to know," Jenny went on, ignoring his comical jibe. "Somebody who's a friend with an old neighbour of yours."

"What?" he replied, an uncomprehending frown settling on his brow. "From Garth Avenue?"

"The very same," she agreed slowly, throwing in a pregnant pause while she waited for his impatient riposte.

"Come on, then," he urged, recognising her prevarication. "Do you want a special award and a round of applause before you tell me?"

"She was called Christine Smith," Jenny said slowly, again taking her time to recall.

"Christine Smith?" Jack butted in quickly. "I don't remember a neighbour called Christine—"

"No, Eager Beaver," she laughed, "*she* wasn't your neighbour but Janet was. Janet Blewitt."

"Oh my God!" Jack gasped. "Janet Blewitt. They had hordes of nippers. I think she was the eldest of six. Dennis was the youngest, and lived up to his name."

"Lived…?" Val asked, not understanding the reference.

"Dennis … the … Menace," Jack replied, slowly. "You know – stripey jersey, *Beano* comic, Abyssinian wire-haired tripe hound called Gnasher? You wouldn't believe the mischievous antics he got up to, like falling into the footings of the new concert room at Garth Working Men's Club when it was being built. He had to be carried home, battered and bruised, by a workman – and the time he pedalled hell for leather down the hill on Garth Avenue on someone else's trike, head down, without looking."

"What happened?" Val asked, surprised anticipation on her face. "The poor dear didn't hurt himself, did he?"

"He looked up only just in time to swerve around a load of coal that had been delivered that morning," Jack laughed, "losing control of the trike and ending up crashing over Middleton's garden wall at the bottom bend – trike and all."

"Oh no!" Val gasped.

"Hospital for that one," Jack finished. "Still, not long after his mam sent him to the Meadow grocery on Wakefield Road, opposite Scarborough Row, for six Penguin biscuits for tea. His mam asked why he had no biscuits when he got back, to which he replied that because *she* had said they were for after *his* tea, he thought they were all for him and he had eaten the lot. He, of course, didn't want any tea after that."

They all laughed at the typically mischievous antics only a little boy could get up to.

"Our next-door neighbours on the corner were the Hammonds," Jack went on, "and the Blewitts lived directly behind *them*. I always was envious because their gardens were twice the size of ours, and in ours there was nowhere to play when mi father had planted it wi' veg. The Hammonds' looked inviting and exciting because they grew onny weeds and head-high grasses – where you could hide. Pat and Angela and Philip were the children. The girls were older but the boy was much younger, although he *did* go to the Grammar School."

"Just two words, eh, Our Jack," Jenny observed. "Two words brought back all *those* memories. I wonder how many others are in there, ready to erupt, eh?"

"Lots," he laughed. "Janet once told me that her mam made rag rugs."

"And a rag rug is…?" Val puzzled.

"Obviously you've never had one," William slid into the conversation.

"They were rugs made out of … rags," Jack grinned, "for obvious reasons. Old worn out clothes and stuff, cut into strips and pushed through a thick hessian backing. Mi mam used to call 'em 'clip rugs'. When money was short – which was often – it was a good way of making soft furnishings to put onto a cold lino floor because the only place we had a carpet, for instance, was the front room. Everywhere else wore a hard, cold coat of linoleum, to cover uneven floorboards.

"The stairs had a carpet runner held in place by stair rods or short metal clips. I loved my rug because it had thick pieces cut from loads of different coloured materials of various thicknesses."

"How did she get the material clips through the backing?" Jenny asked, enthralled by this tale.

"Mi granddad cut a wooden clothes peg in two, lengthways," Jack explained, "and then cut a notch out near the narrow end. Once she had pushed the clip partly through, she would hook the notch round the clip from the other side and pull it through partially, so the two wings of the material would stay upright on the same side together. She'd have probably a hundred or so clips, depending on what material she had spare and how big the rug was going to be."

"If I remember right," William added," we had one each in our bedroom, and Mam and Dad had a couple in theirs.

There was one in the bathroom and one in each of the front rooms and kitchen, in front of the hearth."

"Brown and blue in the front room to match the carpet," Jack added, "and brown and dark green in the kitchen."

"Singed in one or two places in both rooms because of flying sparks and coal embers jumping out of yon fire grate," William chipped in, a grin showing excitement, for once, from the memory rush.

–o–

"Mam! Mam!" Joey shouted urgently from the back door. "Come quick and see."

"What on earth's all this hullabaloo and fuss about?" Val replied, rushing to the door, thinking one of her offspring had sprung off and hurt himself. "What am I looking at, Joey?"

"They've only gone and finished our new house, that's all," he shouted, excitement getting the better of him.

"Can't have," Val said. "They would have let us know. You sure you've got the right one?"

"The second one round the corner from the end of Sunnydale Avenue," he threw over his shoulder as he headed off on his bike. "The one with the huge window at the front."

He skidded off the end of the drive and over the long grass verge on his way out, just scraping past Jenny and shooting off as she pulled in to the drive with Flo and Jessie in the back of the car.

"But they've all got huge windows at the front," Val muttered, as Jenny snecked the front door behind her.

"What have, Sister Dear?" Jenny asked, as she flicked the kettle on.

"All the new houses hereabouts," Val replied to her sister's puzzled look, not understanding what she was on about. "Joey shot out on his bike—"

209

"I know," Jenny said. "I almost brought him back on the car bonnet."

"Because he says our house is finished, and…" Val started but was interrupted by a muffled thudding at the front door.

"Mrs Ingles?" a thick Yorkshire accent greeted Val and Jenny as they answered the caller.

"Yes," the one echoed the other.

"Well," the man said, his craggy face betraying the confusion he felt, "your house is now finished. If you would like to have a look round and make a note of any snagging you see, nip up to the estate manager's office to collect your keys."

"Does that mean we'll be able to move in, then?" Val asked, excitement getting the better of her.

"I don't think so," he went on, turning to escape, "but you'll have to ask the boss for the key soon, as he's shutting up in ten minutes."

"So, Joey was right," Jenny said with a grin, as Val grabbed her coat and boots.

"Coming to see my new home, Sister?" Val said, her infectiously excited giggle setting Jenny off.

# Chapter 20

"Joey! Edward!" Val's shrill voice pierced the stairwell. "Up in five minutes or your breakfast will be in … your Uncle Jack."

"What is it with teenage lads and their beds?" she went on, as she turned to follow Jenny into the kitchen.

The thudding of scurrying adolescent feet on the stairs warned them of the storm that was about to burst through the door. The two boys bounced into the kitchen, trying to elbow each other out of the way in their attempt to be first at the table. William and Mary were already there, along with Jessie and Jack, tucking into their first meal of the day. Porridge was already a thing of memory and most of the toast, marmalade and tea had been scoffed.

"You can have what you like, as long as it's not porridge," Val said. "If you'd been down sooner, you could have swum in it. But as it is, the ocean has been drained."

"But it's only eight o'clock, Mum," Ed complained, the sleep still lurking in his eyes.

"We all are aware of that, my lad," his mother replied sharply, "but do you see any of your family complaining? Now, be said."

Knowing that he had no chance of gainsaying his mother in this sort of a mood, Joey elbowed him in the ribs to get him to shut up and eat up.

"Why were you down *so* quickly, then?" Jenny asked, as she slid a plate of toast and scrambled egg in front of each of them.

"Because I knew that, given half a chance, Uncle Jack could – and would – eat our breakfast," Joey replied to guffaws from Jack and titters from everyone else.

"Bit of a reputation growing there, Brother," William observed, through a mouthful of toast.

"I'm glad we're off today," Ed added. "No offence and all that, Uncle Jack, 'cos we've enjoyed being here, but we'd have to be up early *every* day for breakfast and I think Joey, at least, would find that hard."

"No offence taken, old chap," Jack replied through a grin as his last morsel of toast slipped away. "Shall we see you again in the future?"

"But," Ed said, flummoxed, "we're only moving…"

"Der-er," his brother mocked, pushing his bottom lip forward with his tongue in gentle derision. "Quicken up, Brother, quicken up."

"Get a move on, now, you two," Val urged, "or I'll set your Uncle Jack on you both."

They began to shovel their food into their mouths as they noticed their uncle pull his empty dish towards him and reach for his spoon and fork while eyeing Ed's plateful, eyebrows raised in mock anticipation.

"Turnbull's Removals will be pulling up to our new house in about half an hour," Val warned them, "to unload our furniture and belongings from Birmingham. So, we need to be sharp, otherwise we'll be going back to Birmingham."

"Are you sure we can't persuade you to stay?" Jack offered again.

"No thank you, Uncle Jack," Ed replied quite firmly, to vigorous nods from his brother. "We like it here, but tonight we'll each have our own room. No more snoring and pumping in my face from my older brother—"

"And no more having to share a bathroom with either of you," Mary insisted with glee.

Joyful, excited and relieved laughter filled the hall as they all prepared to move in their different directions, according to the tasks ahead of them. Jenny and Jack stayed to see to Flo and Jessie, while the other arm of the Clan Ingles prepared to march up the road to meet their new home.

"I've loved seeing them all," Jack said, as they were clearing stuff away, "but I'll love seeing them all go, Our Jen. Won't *you?*"

"Course I will," she replied, "but I'm glad they've finally got some purpose in their lives. They are family, when all said and done."

"I just hope it lasts," Jack said, a faint light of hope waxing in his eyes. He wasn't sure about his brother's resolve but he and Jenny *would* be there in case pieces needed to be gathered.

–o–

"Only a week to go then, young Jack," Joan Cropper said, as they walked together to morning briefing. "My husband, Derek, who's a middle school head in Bradford, as you know, reckons you are very sensible."

"How's that, Joan?" Jack smiled. "Most people say I have to be crazy after such a short amount of time."

"My Derek has known *this* head for quite a long time," she replied, a serious look descending, "and *he* says he can be very vindictive and mean, especially towards talented young teachers. He likes to be top dog, apparently."

"My experience exactly," he said, a knowing nod supporting his words.

"I had a conversation the other day, by the way," she said, changing tack, "with young Robert Banks in my class. He's leaving with all the other fourth years, as you know, but he was confused."

"Robin Banks? Confused?" Jack laughed. "Never. Why?"

"That's just it," she replied, a smile sneaking through. "He said that he couldn't understand why, after the four lessons every week for as long as the school's been open, you still don't know his name. Robert Banks. Until I explained the concept 'robbing banks' – Robin Banks."

"Ha ha," Jack guffawed. "I've always called him *Robin* Banks. I thought he understood why."

"When I explained," she finished, just before the staff room door interrupted their conversation, "his face was a picture of embarrassment. The children are going to miss you, Jack. We *all* are going to miss you."

"If only that were true, Our Joan," he replied, with a polite and indulgent smile. "If only it were true."

"May I have your attention, ladies and gentlemen, please?" the head's dour voice urged its way insidiously into the room. "One or two points of note today, if…"

His monotonous drone faded away as Jack's thoughts of the six weeks he was about to spend with his family shouldered their way into his mind. Not long to go and he could reclaim his normal life, away from the boredom of this Neolithic pile he could only put down to experience. Ever the professional, he would give his whole-hearted attention to discharging his duties to the best of his not inconsiderable abilities until Friday at noon, when the school would empty of customers and the "last supper" would be laid out.

"So, the school will close at the end of morning lessons on Friday," the head's voice slowly reasserted itself, "when there will be set out a thank-you spread in here."

"Pompous, or what?" Jack thought, with a look of disdain on his face.

"Pompous, or what?" Beardy Brian whispered in Jack's

ear.

"You taken up mind reading to add to your many skills?" Jack replied quietly, as the head's entourage left the building.

"Well," Beardy Brian said firmly, "I won't be staying for any bun slinging, I can tell you. I'm away on my hols that very evening."

"I won't be staying either," Jack echoed. "I'll be off on my hols, too … in my back garden. And I've no doubt my brother and his lot will be desirous of my technical expertise in the path-laying field for their new house – just round the corner from us."

"I know which *I* prefer," Brian chuckled, as they reached his art room.

"Me, too," Jack replied, a rueful smile underlining his words.

Jack's big trouble, of course, was not being able to say no, where family and need were cemented together. He had his own gardening agenda but how far he would get with *that* was anybody's guess.

Never mind.

He had six weeks of holiday.

Pleasure and mirth washed together inside and almost bubbled over to betray his happiness at its proximity.

–o–

"Jack breaks up in two days, Joyce," Jenny said. "So how about coming to spend a few days with us next week? I'll book my two in to spend time with my mum and we can have… You'll do that, too? Excellent. We can then have a relaxing and memorable time. Let me know when… It's all the same to us. I'll have to go, Joyce, because I can hear the front door, and you know what Jack's like for his cup of tea and… You've got it. Until next week, then."

She put the phone down as Jack hobbled into the room,

pain etched across his face as he eased his hurting body into his favourite chair.

"Jack?" she gasped. "What's happened? What have you been doing?"

"This," he tried to explain, as he pulled up his trouser leg to reveal a huge, bloody lump on his shin, "is what happened this afternoon."

"My God!" she gasped, horrified by his enormous injury. "What on earth…?"

"I fell in a nole," he grimaced, recalling the time when, as a nipper, he tripped and broke his arm in a field behind his grandma's. "I often walk the length of the school front outside from my huts to the staff room in the alleyway between the playground wall and the glass façade. No problem today, as every other day. On the way back, however, some brain-dead dodo had removed a manhole cover in the alleyway – without putting up a guard rail, cone, or some sort of warning that there was a… Well, anyway, I was reading a note from the head and didn't notice that a chasm had opened up before me. As my left leg trod air, I smacked my shin into the steel frame around the hole. Fortunately, my razor-sharp reactions saved me from certain death, and I grabbed at the path as I started my descent to the Underworld."

"Was there anybody about to help?" Jenny asked, not really believing that her man could have been very seriously injured.

"Nope," he replied, as he finished his third digestive and a cup of tea to "steady" his nerves.

"It must hurt you, poor thing," she cooed. "Can I take it you won't be in school tomorrow?"

"I can't *not* be there, I'm afraid, Our Jen," he said, hutching his foot on to the stool she had brought from the dining room. "Last couple of days and all that."

"What did yon Mr Barney have to say?" she asked, sitting

gingerly next to him.

"Byrne. His name's Byrne," he corrected.

"Whatever," she said. "Well?"

"Not much he *could* say, really," Jack replied, "other than to show concern. However, he did give me an envelope as I made for the door at the end of school. It's in my jacket pocket. Not had chance to open it yet, so would you mind doing the honours?"

She drew out a windowed brown envelope with his typed name clearly visible in the window. Opening it gingerly, as if it were perhaps about to burst into flames, she was surprised to find a brief note and a … Nat West school cheque for…

"Four hundred quid!" she exclaimed. "Bloomin'eck! And a note that states a certain degree of sanctimonious regret that you've had to go through all this upset."

"Four…?" Jack gasped, a grin slowly brightening his face and taking away some of the hurt. "He's yittened I'll sue, and that's the only reason for this."

"What will you do?" Jenny asked, genuinely puzzled at what Jack's next move might be.

"Take it, cash it and say thank you very much," Jack replied with no hesitation. "Do you realise what that will pay for? A nice little holiday in Filey, and material for yon patio for you to loll and snooze on in the glorious sunshine. The onny decent thing Mr Kiss-mi-arse Byrne has ever done, and then it was out of fear. Still, small price to pay."

"One more day and a half, eh, Our Jack," Jenny giggled, rubbing her hands in glee, "then our new life begins. Six weeks, here we come."

–o–

"You always were a clumsy bugger, Our Jack," Joyce said, eyes rolling and a silent tut betraying her resignation. "And now you were bought off."

217

"Aye, I was that," Jack replied, a huge grin decorating his happy face, "and that's a first wi' yon bloke. It must have stabbed at his vitals to part wi' t'brass, particularly to me."

"So, you like our new house, then?" Jenny ventured.

"I love it," Stick replied quickly, before Joyce could jump in. "It doesn't have quite the same ring or feel as ours, but taking practicalities into consideration with my job and our growing family…"

"Growing family?" Jenny picked up on straight away. "I knew it."

"Sly or what, Our Joyce," Jack added. "Due?"

"Oh, it's only early days yet," she replied, matter of fact. "Barely more than a pin head, really, and I feel fine – although that could change overnight."

"This might be a good time to announce," Jenny began, after a moment or two's silence, "that I think – only *think*, mind you—"

"That *you* are expecting?" Jack queried quietly, to a surprised and puzzled expression on her face. "Don't forget, Jenny, that I probably know you almost as well as you know yourself."

"And that makes you a mind-reader now as well as … a … patio builder?" she asked, an impish chuckle escaping her lips. "It may be extremely early days," she assured him, "but—"

"You *know*, don't you," Jack added, nodding sagely as *she* watched his grin grow.

"We have a lot to celebrate," Stick said, "along with moving to a new house."

"You've chosen one already?" Jack queried. "But you haven't had a look around the estate yet."

"We called at the weekend," Stick replied, "when you were out."

"Wha…?" Jack blustered.

"When we were out?" Jenny said, a look of ignorance betraying her confusion.

"Doctor's," Jack added, as the realisation dawned. "Jenny took me to see young Dr Blomfield about mi lumpy leg."

"And we saw a house we liked," Stick went on, "but—"

"Not quite as good as ours," Joyce interrupted. "Still, a lovely house, and one that we could live in very comfortably and very happily."

"The profit we've made from ours will allow us to have a big corner plot and a double garage," Stick said.

"Profit you have made?" Jack puzzled. "Meaning...?"

"We've already sold ours in Altofts," Joyce grinned, chuffed that she could still spring a surprise on her long-held friend.

"Don't hang about, you two, do you?" Jenny laughed, catching Jack's look of shock.

"You always were smart, Our Joyce," he laughed. "Do you remember that time we walked into town to the Empire Matinee one Saturday? We got to the Broad Flags and you tried to skip ower some empty orange boxes outside the fruit and veg shop, misjudged your leap and got your foot stuck in one of the little ones. *That* was funny."

"Broad Flags?" Jenny said, not knowing what they were on about. "Are we talking about the same town, Our Jack? I don't recognise..."

"You of all people should know the Broad Flags, Jen," Joyce laughed. "They were on Wakefield Road, just up from the snicket into Cambridge Street where you lived."

"Just after the terraced houses, where the single-width pavement became three times as wide," Jack added, "in front of a little parade of shops."

"I bet you can't remember the shops," Stick said, throwing down a memory challenge.

"Mostly," Jack replied, screwing his brow as he tried to

bring back pictures of their shop fronts to his mind. He used stored picture images a lot to help him recall many of his sleeping memories. "I can't remember the order but I know Elsleys the butcher was one. I can remember him scrubbing down his solid wooden chopping and cutting table outside, late on Saturday."

"There was a ladies' fashion and haberdashery," Joyce added. "Miss Hilton's, I think."

"…and a fish and chip shop – Brookes's wasn't it?"

"…hairdresser's…"

"…I could have sworn there was a pram shop…"

"…Picken's shoe shop…"

"…a sweet shop I seem to remember…"

"…and a DIY place…"

"On the other side of Wakefield Road, about half way down the hill towards the Catholic Church," Jack added, "there was a little electrical shop, where mi mam bought me a portable cherry-and-grey Dansette record player, in its own carry case. She could hardly afford it but she paid four shillings a week for it. *That* machine went everywhere with me as a teenager. Any gathering, folks would ask me to nip home and fetch it. I'm sure they wanted *it* more than they wanted *me*."

"Jack?" Jenny gasped. "You – a party animal? Well, I never."

"It had an automatic record changer that took six 45s," he went on. "*That's* what folks were attracted to. I even took it to teacher training college, when I moved into halls of residence."

"What happened to it?" Jenny asked. "I've never seen it."

"Lee 'persuaded' me to get rid," he replied quietly, his words laced with disdain and sadness at losing a long-held friend. "She said it didn't fit in with our future life."

"So, when are we going to visit your new home?" Jenny

asked, once they were tucking in to roast beef and Yorkshires. "I assume you *have* chosen?"

"Course they have," Jack added, a self-satisfied grin giving him away. "It's Plot 84 on Plantation Drive."

"And how can you possibly know that, Jack Know-It-All Ingles?" Jenny mocked, confident he was making it up.

"It's the only house on the estate that fits their description," he replied, digging in to his favourite roasted new potatoes.

"Joyce?" Jenny turned to her companion, looking for support.

"True, I'm afraid," Joyce agreed. "Trust Mr Sherlock Bloomin' Holmes to work *that* one out."

"We can move in as soon as contracts have been exchanged, as well," Stick added. "No hanging about. No double moving or renting. Sorted."

# Chapter 21

Mid-summer's unrelenting heat gripped the country, prompting some water companies to impose urgent hosepipe bans, despite the wettest winter on record only a few months earlier. This was a wonderful time for nippers, rushing about semi-clad in their back gardens, shrieking as they churned through paddling pools and dodged the intermittent splash of lawn sprinklers. This was a summer to remember – or forget – depending on whether you were a child or a gardener.

Jack had always found it difficult to cope with the intense heat of even the most ordinary British summer, which didn't usually last long anyway. He'd always hated the sun, ever since that school trip to Brittany when he was twelve. His granddad had paid the twenty pounds it had cost for the week because Jack's father had refused. Jack had enjoyed his time in a different country but he had caught a terminal dose of sunburn, which had to be treated with calamine lotion that turned his angry lobster into a gentler and daintier pink.

The heat, however, didn't stop him enjoying a wonderfully exhilarating time with his daughters. He had fashioned a large patio out of concrete flags around the conservatory a local company had erected at just above cost. This was one of their obsolete range but the cane furniture had come as part of the deal, which pleased Jenny no end. Was there anything this man couldn't or wouldn't do for his family?

Now Jenny had a choice where to sit – either outside in the conservatory, or outside in the garden. Spoilt for choice or, as his mam would have said, just spoilt.

His lawn, unfortunately, was beginning to gasp in this cursed heat for want of a little more water than Jack was able to give it. Washing-up bowls after the ... washing-up, and a variety of other sources of second-hand used water, were nowhere near enough to satisfy the turf's thirst. Being a very honest man who never broke rules, he chose not to follow the herd of his neighbours who had, in many cases, hosed and sprinkled lawns close by – usually at the dead of night in secrecy, away from prying eyes.

–o–

Now a confirmed family man, Jack's only regret was that he wasn't able to spend some time at least with his son, Sam, despite court orders and calls for fairness that would allow a father to be part of his son's life.

"I divorced Sam's mother, for goodness' sake," Jack said quietly, as they sat on the beach in Filey, his sense of sorrow and injustice welling up in his throat. "I didn't divorce my son."

"I'm sorry, Our Jack," Jenny said, putting her arm around him. "This shouldn't be happening to you, but *we* love you. Isn't that enough?"

"Of course, it is," he said quickly, hugging his ladies closely. "You are all I need. It's just so ... unfair, that's all. And after all, he is my flesh and blood, too."

Jessie and Flo loved digging in the sand with Jack, making castles with turrets and battlements and moats. Unfortunately, however, the water stayed in place to repel all boarders only a very short time. Jessie's inevitable question about this problem nearly caught Jack on the hop, but fortunately he was able to pluck a plausible explanation to placate his knowledge-thirsty daughter.

"Are you sure that's right, Daddy?" she asked, looking him squarely in the eyes as he knelt by their grand edifice, whilst preventing her sister from trampling and breaching its defences.

"Of course I am, Sweetie Pie," Jack replied, trying valiantly to suppress the mirth he felt bubbling inside. "Sand is only lots of tiny bits that look solid but which let water soak through."

"Then, why doesn't the sea soak through the sand and disappear?" Jessie asked, still not releasing him from her gaze.

Jenny smiled, recognising it was time to rescue her husband from the incessant grilling their daughter was giving him. "I have some lovely sandwiches here," she interrupted. "Is there anybody here ready to eat them?"

"Yay!" Jessie shouted, breaking away from her searching, questioning glare. "Me! Me!"

"Me, too," Flo shouted, trying to mimic her sister's urgent tone.

Jack tore himself away from his building project, wiping imaginary sweat from his burdened brow as he cast a relieved grin at his psychic wife. She really *could* read minds and situations – but then, so could most other wives. Couldn't they? Men were such easy books to read and predict and their women only needed to be average readers to be able to glean the full story.

Jenny could read Jack only when he allowed her to – for her own peace of mind, so she would know at least how he felt about certain things. Usually he preferred to dwell on stuff in his own way, in his own mind. *That's* how he rationalised his thoughts and actions. *That's* how he arrived at the best outcome for everyone concerned with him. He thought that only *he* knew this, but Jenny was no one's fool.

She knew him better than he thought, allowing him to make his decisions on his own terms.

She trusted him, knowing he would draw her in – when he felt the time was right. This way, she was always involved and he kept her free of the 'difficult' stuff he needed to think through.

–o–

They had a lovely time at Filey but it was the only break away they could afford just yet, what with the expense of the improvements they had made to the house. Jenny often mooted a return to some sort of paid work, but only when they *both* considered it appropriate. Neither of them was in any hurry to embrace that step – just yet. Jack was adamant they could afford their present status quo, and they agreed Jessie and Flo needed her at home.

With the last few days of their summer holiday draining away slowly, he was determined to fit in as much with his family as possible before the trump of doom sounded once more.

The weather was still scorchingly fair, with only the occasional white smudge of a cloud wisp to haze the unusual Mediterranean sky, as they set off to visit Lotherton Hall just outside Leeds, allowing his daughters to experience open space and countryside they rarely got to see. Jack had decided they would stand a much greater chance of finding under-tree parking against the blistering sun if they set off early.

"Are we there yet, Daddy?" Jessie piped up, as they passed through Aberford on to Lotherton Lane, "I need—"

"Nearly there, my lovely," he replied, interrupting her, "and then we can find you a toilet."

"Silly Daddy Jack," Jessie said with a smile. "I don't think I can get a ice cream in the toilet."

Jenny burst out laughing at Jack's surprised face. "Got you there, Our Jack," she said through a hearty chortle.

"I need to listen more closely in future," he agreed, "and not interrupt my clever little girl. So, you'd like an ice cream, eh?"

"Yes, please," Jessie whooped, which was echoed by her little sister who was trying to join the party, not quite sure what 'a ice cream' was but, seeing as her sister had to have one, then so must she.

"A few more minutes then, my lovelies," Jenny added, "and clever Daddy will find us somewhere to stop and have a cornet."

"Have … cornet…" Flo tried to repeat, slowly.

"Why is the car bumping on one side?" Jenny asked, a concerned look jumping into her eyes as they rounded the bend into the Hall's parking grounds. "It feels like we keep hitting a lump in the road with one of the wheels."

"I need to pull over onto the grass under that huge oak tree just past the bend in the road ahead," Jack sighed. "It sounds like we've a flat tyre. If it is, I'll have to change it for the spare."

He pulled off the road into a large, shady, grassy space under the eaves of a huge, spreading, common oak tree where he hoped to park. There were few folks about, fortunately, but as he inspected the offending tyre, he found a large nail protruding from its wall, allowing the air to escape slowly. He could have limped home with it in that state but, rolling up his sleeves, he decided there was nothing for it but to break out the spare to be on the safe side.

Fortunately, the ground was baked hard, giving his jack enough of a resilient surface on which to support the car far enough from the floor to swap wheels. Sweating profusely, black-bright, and out of breath, he slumped to the floor to hoots of joy from both children and wife, when he had finished his wheel-changing trick.

"Need to find somewhere to clean up," he gasped, leaving several black warpaint-like streaks across his forehead and cheeks as he tried to wipe away the sweat.

"What's the matter? he asked slowly, as his family started to laugh. "Something I said?"

"You'll have to wait and see, if you can find a mirror," Jenny replied, tears running down her cheeks. "But Chief Sitting Bull springs to mind."

A puzzled frown flitted across his brow as he made for the washroom, betraying his ignorance of his appearance.

"You could have told me," Jack guffawed, as he sloped out of the washrooms. "Geronimo had nothing on me. It looked like I was about to fight a war with the Apache in the Canyon of Lost Faces."

"I'm glad to see you are clean again," Jessie piped up. "Did you wash behind your ears, Daddy Jack? Did you find any ice creams in the toilets?"

Jack laughed loudly at his daughter's deliberate funny, as he picked her up and threw her into the air to her hoots of delight.

"Come on then," he shouted, as he hoisted her onto his shoulders. "Ice-cream cornets all round."

–o–

"Something's been bothering me for quite some time," Jack said, once they had settled their children for the night. "Ever since mi mam died."

"Oh, aye?" Jenny replied, her concerned eyes rising over the rim of the book he had written for Jessie. "Is it something you've thought about and sorted out in your head, my lovely?"

"Not really," he replied, a troubled sigh escaping, like air from a slowly deflating balloon. "Do you remember, some time ago, my telling you about mi mam's request about her handbag, you know, the last time I saw her alive?"

"Aye?" she replied, the mystery now grabbing her too. "What about it?"

"Well," he went on, deliberately slowing the conversation, "she *had* said she wanted me to bring it to her, and I felt there was something important she wanted to tell me. She didn't, of course, get the chance."

"Jack," Jenny said softly, moving next to him on the settee, "I'm so sorry. I—"

"No," he interrupted her, "don't be. I'm sad but only because she didn't get to tell me herself. I'd retrieved the bag on the night of her wake, when all those fork-tongued harpies were gloating over her open coffin in the front room at Garth Avenue. I stuffed it in my rucksack, put it somewhere safe among my 'stuff', and had forgotten about it – that is until the other week, when I was sorting some things out."

"Did you look inside the bag?" she asked, intrigue in her face urging him to share.

"I did that," he replied, "and I found this."

He handed a sepia photograph to her, which she studied and turned over several times.

"What's so strange about a mother having a photograph of her son in her handbag?" Jenny said, the screwed-up look on her forehead betraying her puzzlement.

"Look carefully," he replied quietly, "and you'll see that it's *not* me. Notice the mole above the right eye corner? I don't have one there, do I?"

"Then who is it?" she gasped. "It's the image of you."

"This letter will reveal it all," he explained, handing over a well-thumbed brown envelope addressed to Jack's mother.

A few moments later the letter dropped into her lap, a wave of utter shock rendering her unable to speak.

"You all right, Jen?" Jack whispered, as he slid his arm

around her shoulders.

"I had no idea, Our Jack," she gasped finally.

"You can imagine *my* shock, too," he replied, tears beginning to well in his eye corners.

"Your Uncle Jack's—" Jenny said slowly.

"Son," he added. "And he's called … Jack."

# Chapter 22

Although Jack had been to visit his new school several times since his appointment, and he had had discussions with its head teacher, he was still overcome with a wave of excited anticipation.

The changes to the immediate area since his departure several years earlier were beyond recognition. The old Victorian pile that had served its neighbourhood with distinction had been razed and its footprint expunged, as if it had never been there. The new building's façade paraded slick beginnings to a brand new educational era that fitted with a regenerated and rejuvenated Broughton township.

The only bastion celebrating a bygone age was the Ship Inn, and even that had been given a newly painted facelift.

Many of the old guard of teachers from Jack's time at Broughton County Junior School had gone, unable to cope with the demands of Cecil P Barchester in his attempt to bring standards into the modern era. Sparks, Page and Awad had been replaced by more dynamic and energetic youngsters eager to etch their educational mark at the beginning of this new and exciting phase, led by a younger head who knew what he was doing and what the children needed.

"Jack," David Aston's voice spun his friend and colleague around on the first day back after the summer holidays, "it's really good to see you."

"You, too, David," he replied. "How's Irene and the…"

His voice tailed away among the hubbub of children to the known chaos that always followed first days back everywhere. There was a strange smell about the place – like a mixture of stale breath after a night on the town, and decomposing vegetable matter. But then, the building *had* been shut up and had lain dormant for six weeks or so. It had a right to smell.

"I'll speak to you later," David's voice shouldered its way back into real time as he moved between the ranks of hat and coat pegs, unfortunately sited between the kitchen and the outside doors. Overhead ducted vents from goodness knew where, set into the false ceiling, opened everywhere into this cramped space. The older children flitted in and out to class very quickly, whereas the tinies needed help and guidance.

The layout of the school was familiar to Jack but he had little idea where everything – and everyone – was, or ought to be. He knew everything *would* fall into place for him eventually, but for now the unfamiliarity tended to breed the uncertainty of it all in his mind.

"Good morning, Little People," he said to his class, as they sat chattering in their places, taking little notice.

"To ensure things run smoothly and you get the most out of your time with me," he went on affably, "you must … LISTEN TO ME!"

The last three words were delivered in a loud and commandingly urgent way that stopped them mid-sentence, and stunned them into silence.

"You are now looking at, and listening, to me – Mr Jack Ingles," he urged, a welcoming smile beginning to draw them in, "and that is the way it will always be whenever I swim into your orbit."

This message skirted the tops of the heads of many without disturbing a single hair, but there were those whose imagination and wit had been switched on by this newcomer and they liked what they heard and saw.

"Excellent," he said, beaming at his gathered throng. They were not used to being spoken to in such a friendly and *different* way, and they considered this might be worth listening to. His commanding tones were delivered in such a friendly and affably attractive way that none of them could, would, or would want to ignore. "You and I need to get to know one another quickly, face to face, and even though I know *all* your names already, I need to be able to fit faces – a bit like a jigsaw, really. Hopefully, I will have completed *my* task by the end of the day."

"Please, Sir," a tot of a redhead close by said, as she waved her hand to attract his attention.

"Yes?" he answered. "Tanya, isn't it?"

A look of stunned surprise drove her initiative out of her mind because of the speed with which he had begun to associate names with faces.

"Your question, Tanya?" Jack went on, urging her gently to light up again.

"It took Mr Awad the first half term to learn most of our names," she said, courage finally overturning her reticence.

"And I, obviously, am *not* Mr Awad," he answered, pulling a face, as titters swept around the room. They were going to enjoy spending time with *this* teacher. First impressions were so important with youngsters of this age, and straight away *they* thought *he* was ace.

The shrill and annoying sound of an alien bell cut him short, obliterating his sound and urging them all that something was amiss.

"Fire bell, Mr Ingles," a large, bluff boy with a closely cropped head pointed out. "Means we have to go … somewhere."

"Stand, class," Jack ordered.

"Fire exits on the far side of the building, if you please,"

Mr Aston's voice rang out. "Leave everything and go out in an orderly fashion with your teacher. Jack! A word."

Once his class was outside, he caught up with the head.

"No panic, Jack, but it's a real fire. Flames and smoke pouring out of the vents above the cloakroom. Looks like it might have started in the kitchen close by," David said, urging him to go to his class to register. "Fire brigade has been called."

"Cassie's not here, Mr Ingles," Tanya urged Jack, tugging at his coat sleeve.

"Then where, Tanya?" he asked, turning on his heels.

"She sneaked off to the toilet as we came out, past Mrs Jenkins' class base," Peter Smith piped up.

"Right," Jack ordered. "Stay here with Mrs Jenkins' class and I'll be back in a jiffy."

He shot off back into school, as the urgent bells of two fire engines raced down Town Street warning all vehicles to get out of their way.

By this time, thick, black, acrid smoke had filled the void left by the happy voices of two hundred or so small children, excited to be back at school for a new term as it started its skip towards Christmas.

"All present?" the head's voice cut into the terrified silence surrounding his children and staff, a hundred yards away from engines and breathing-apparatus clad firemen, who were about to enter the building.

"Mr Ingles has gone back in to find Cassie Pearson," a young teacher stammered, "who slipped away to the toilet as we were coming out."

"For goodness—" David gasped, as the front of the school, which housed the kitchen, the cloakroom bays – and the toilets – erupted in a huge ball of fire, to the shrieks and yells of fear from the children and looks of horror from the adults.

*Welcome Back Jack* is the fourth book in the series about Jack Ingles.

The other three are:

Volume One:  *Jack the Lad*
Volume Two:  *Jack*
Volume Three:  *Hit the Road Jack*

# Frank English

Born in 1946 in the West Riding of Yorkshire's coal fields around Wakefield, he attended grammar school, where he enjoyed sport rather more than academic work. After three years at teacher training college in Leeds, he became a teacher in 1967. He spent a lot of time during his teaching career entertaining children of all ages, a large part of which was through telling stories, and encouraging them to escape into a world of imagination and wonder. Some of his most disturbed youngsters he found to be very talented poets, for example. He has always had a wicked sense of humour, which has blossomed only during the time he has spent with his wife, Denise. This sense of humour also allowed many youngsters to survive often difficult and brutalising home environments.

Eleven years ago, he retired after forty years working in schools with young people who had significantly disrupted lives because of behaviour disorders and poor social adjustment, generally brought about through circumstances beyond their control. At the same time as moving from leafy lane suburban middle-class school teaching in Leeds to residential schooling for emotional and behavioural disturbance in the early 1990s, changed family circumstance provided the spur to achieve ambitions. Supported by his wife, Denise, he achieved a Master's degree in his mid-forties and a PhD at the age of fifty-six, because he had always wanted to do so.

Now enjoying glorious retirement, he spends as much time as life will allow writing, reading, and working with children in primary schools.

Lightning Source UK Ltd.
Milton Keynes UK
UKHW040659170719
346313UK00001B/4/P